P9-AQV-867

FORTUNATE
LIVES

ALSO BY ROBB FORMAN DEW

Dale Loves Sophie to Death

The Time of Her Life

FORTUNATE LIVES

Robb Forman Dew

HarperPerennial
A Division of HarperCollins*Publishers*

Grateful acknowledgment is made to the following for permission to use material in this book:

"Puff the Magic Dragon" by Peter Yarrow and Leonard Lipton. Copyright © 1963 by Pepemar Music Corp. All rights reserved. Used by permission.

The lines from *Half of Man Is Woman* by Zhang Xianliang, translated by Martha Avery, are reprinted with the permission of W. W. Norton & Company, Inc. Translation copyright © 1986 by Martha Avery.

A hardcover edition of this book was published in 1992 by William Morrow and Company. It is here reprinted by arrangement with William Morrow and Company.

FORTUNATE LIVES. Copyright © 1992 by Robb Forman Dew. All rights reserved. Printed in the United States of America. No part of this book may be used or reproduced in any manner whatsoever without written permission except in the case of brief quotations embodied in critical articles and reviews. For information address HarperCollins Publishers, Inc., 10 East 53rd Street, New York, NY 10022.

HarperCollins books may be purchased for educational, business, or sales promotional use. For information please write: Special Markets Department, HarperCollins Publishers, Inc., 10 East 53rd Street, New York, NY 10022.

First HarperPerennial edition published 1993.

Designed by J. Ponsiglione

Library of Congress Cataloging-in-Publication Data
Dew, Robb Forman.
    Fortunate lives / Robb Forman Dew. — 1st HarperPerennial ed.
      p.   cm.
   ISBN 0-06-097536-9 (paper)
   I. Title.
  [PS3554.E9288F67   1993]
  813'.54—dc20   92-53426

93 94 95 96 97 RRD 10 9 8 7 6 5 4 3 2 1

For Helen, for Dear, for Elizabeth,
and in memory of
Robert Edgar Rachal

FORTUNATE
LIVES

CHAPTER ONE

GOD'S OWN CAT

IN THE LATE AFTERNOON Dinah retreated to her bedroom in
that deadly time before the family had dinner. She had
read that this was the time of day when most people experience a drop in their blood sugar, but that notion struck her
as only a useful rationalization. She knew too well the hours
from morning to night. They bobbled by like varicolored
balloons, soft and round, like the word "hour" itself. Except
the hours between four and six of any day, before dawn or
before dusk. Those are sinister moments in which the spirit
is endangered and deflated. She imagined those two hours
drifting gray and close to the earth, flaccid and exhausted
of buoyancy.

And even though today she might reasonably allow
herself to luxuriate in melancholy while that bit of time slid
by, she knew how easily she might fall into serious despair.
She occupied herself, taking with her to the bedroom the
white wicker-and-wood lap desk that Martin had given her
for Christmas. It was stocked with cream-colored mono-

grammed stationery and embossed envelopes interlined with blue. She had requested the gift, and she thought of herself as someone who used these things, although such correspondence as she carried on was likely to be scribbled out on a sheet of typing paper at her desk, paper-clipped to a rumpled editorial cut out from the newspaper weeks before, or enclosed with a book review, or a recipe and hastily folded into the flimsy, long envelopes she bought at the grocery store and kept on hand to pay bills.

She settled on the bed, kicking off her shoes and crossing her ankles, and pulled out the packet of booklets and informational sheets that had come last week from the Freshmen Dean's Office at Harvard College. She riffled through the pages of material until she found the letter from Franklin M. Mount, Dean of Freshmen. Dinah's huge orange cat had draped himself irritatingly over her legs in the warm June weather, and she heaved him aside.

"Move, Taffy! Move over! Move over!" And the cat toppled over unresistingly onto his back right next to her, with his silky white stomach exposed. He gazed backward at Dinah and tried to purr in his snuffling way until he fell asleep. Dinah relaxed farther back into the pillows propped against the headboard and held the letter up before her at arm's length, since she didn't have her glasses.

FRESHMEN DEAN'S OFFICE
HARVARD COLLEGE
12 Truscott Street
Cambridge, Massachusetts 02138

Telephone (617) 459-1325

June 1, 1991

To the Parents of Members of the Class of 1995:

Each year, we ask parents of incoming freshmen to write us frankly and fully about their sons and daughters. Statements about our students from those who know them best help us to assign them appropriate advisers, assign resident students to compatible rooming groups, and anticipate the pleasures and the problems we will share. We would be grateful for detailed impressions about your son's or daughter's strengths, weaknesses, and interests, and also for information about any medical problems we ought to know of.

Once again she pondered the problem of the last sentence and that dangling preposition. Most likely it was unconsidered, merely an example of the new flexibility of the written as well as the spoken word, the new language that encompassed peculiar uses of such words as "impact." On the other hand, it smacked of trickery to Dinah. It might be that the staff in the Freshmen Dean's Office had conferred about this. Suppose it was a calculated effort not to seem stuffy, or an attempt to elicit informal and overly revealing replies?

She had read through all the other information sheets and pamphlets, trying to find out the intentions of the Freshmen Dean's Office, and had been truly alarmed by the cozy, conspiratorial tone of the last paragraph of a booklet called *Some Notes for Freshmen Parents:*

Don't try to hold the course you set and have been sailing together for seventeen years. It is hard to sail a ship with two pilots. You should come along, but always keep in mind that it is a new voyage, someone else's voyage. This way, college can be the shared and happy embarkation it ought to be.

Martin refused to take it seriously. "This is great! I love this," he had said when she insisted he read through the little booklet. "We buy the ticket and David takes the cruise." Of course, she understood the foolishness of all these communications, but on the other hand, suppose there was something she did or did not write—an attitude and manner she did or did not adopt—that might prejudice the Freshmen Dean's Office against her own son. Suppose she unwittingly wrote something that condemned David to a terrible roommate, or brought down upon his head the collective derision of the freshmen advisers. She had been struggling for a week to draft an adequate reply to what seemed to her a daunting request, and had finally resorted to working out the first draft on a yellow legal pad so as not to waste any more of the expensive Crane writing paper.

> 473 Slade Road
> West Bradford, MA
> June 8, 1991

Franklin M. Mount
Dean of Freshmen
Harvard College
12 Truscott Street
Cambridge, Massachusetts 02138

Dear Mr. Mount,

I can only respond to your request for my and my husband's impression of our son David Howells . . .

She turned the page back to start fresh. She couldn't use the possessive "my and my husband's," since Harvard had declined to use the prepositional construction "of which we ought to know."

Dear Mr. Mount,

Of course, we're biased, but we think Harvard is really lucky to be getting our son David Howells as a student and a member of its community . . .

She reconsidered this immediately. The tone was altogether too jaunty, even arrogant. At the very least, she decided, she would have to avoid using contractions and telling Harvard how lucky they were. Probably Mr. Mount was hoping for as succinct a reply as possible, given the gravity of the task he had set for the parents of all the freshmen entering Harvard. But his request was so provocative that Dinah closed her eyes briefly, trying to block out the images of her children that were rushing through her mind. She turned to a fresh page and decided to get right to the heart of the matter, to illuminate for Mr. Mount David's character and personality, describe to Mr. Mount David's whole life as he would live it up until the moment he entered Harvard, and she would make every effort to do this in the space of one page:

Dear Mr. Mount,

Our son David Howells has a discerning intelligence, great love for and loyalty to his friends and his family, and a generous spirit. He has always been a good student and is well liked by his peers, and we think that David will be a responsible and productive member of the Harvard College community.

Perhaps what is most remarkable about David is his capacity for empathy. It is a quality he has possessed since early childhood, but which was probably heightened by the death of his younger brother when David was thirteen years old.

13

She paused for a moment, gazing down at what she had written, and she realized that her fingers were clenched so tightly around her pen that her words were nearly illegible. This was not the right day to attempt such a letter. The white sunshine of early afternoon darkened into a thick yellow light that fell slantwise across the room, and she replaced the yellow pad, the sheets of stationery, and the envelopes with their shiny blue lining inside the wicker compartment of the lap desk. She set the desk to one side and rested her head against the pillows, letting her arms drop loosely to the quilt.

At the foot of the bed the dog had been listening anxiously to the scratching and rustling of Dinah's endeavor, but when she heard Dinah grow still, Duchess lay her head down comfortably between her paws and relaxed. Taffy didn't stir, but the gray cat, Bob, neatly perched on the wide, sunlighted windowsill, settled farther down on his turned-under paws and shifted his gaze away from Dinah to the peak of the porch roof outside, where the sweet-eyed, round-breasted doves fluttering to a perch, trekking poultry-fashion along the roof's peak, made his muscles quiver under his rough coat and brought forth tiny anticipatory chatterings of his teeth.

He was a cat who lived mostly along the perimeters of the rooms, and Dinah was sure he was only a first-generation domestic cat. He had been one of the two tiny kittens David had rescued five years ago from underneath a car in the Price Chopper parking lot. One gray-striped and the other a muddy tortoiseshell.

Neither of those two cats had ever acquired the glossy sheen, though, of Dinah's big orange cat. Taffy was sanguine in his golden glory of thick fur, and he was sweet-natured, although not especially intelligent. And unlike Bob, Taffy crossed all the rooms of the house and even the yard outside with placid assurance, and stopped to sleep wherever he might be when the urge overtook him.

Dinah and Martin had never sat down and discussed somberly whether or not to have children; they had merely stopped trying *not* to have them. It had been a decision too momentous to confront. And certainly with altogether lesser consequences, but in much the same way, they had over the years become the custodians of these various animals. Duchess was the last of a litter of long-haired German shepherd dogs—not fierce dogs under any circumstances and a strain, in fact, that breeders were trying to eliminate from the genetic pool. Dinah had adopted Duchess as a favor to the receptionist at the Vet Clinic. Melissa knew all the Howellses' animals, and over the years she had become a friendly acquaintance of Dinah's.

Dinah had arrived at the Vet Clinic one afternoon with Taffy, who needed shots, and found Melissa huddled in a chair in the waiting room weeping while the dog looked on abashed. "I don't know why her owners waited so long," Melissa said when she had composed herself a little. "Duchess is almost a year old! We've treated her at the clinic since she was a puppy. Now she's in heat, though, and they won't keep her. I have two dogs at home already, and they're both male. I'm not even supposed to have pets in the apartment." Melissa had been distraught. "I really despise those people! They just come in here and say, 'Duke needs his rabies booster and we're leaving Duchess to be destroyed.' *Destroyed!* I used to think it was awful to say you were going to put a dog to sleep when you just meant you were going to kill it. But these people . . . I think they're like Nazis!"

Dinah, of course, had taken Duchess home. But the dog seemed to have absorbed some idea of the precarious nature of her continued existence. She was a coward, racing around the rooms to find Dinah whenever the doorbell rang and forever agonizing over the possibility that the cats were more favored than she. They often appropriated her dog bed, ate chunks of her dog meal, and so subtly harassed

15

her that she would even drink every drop of water poured out for her until she was bloated with the effort as the cats sat on the windowsills watching. Dinah had learned never to fill Duchess's bowl more than half full.

Taffy padded after Dinah wherever she went in the house, and Bob, in his furtive cat life, directed his cautious gray attention toward her, too, and yet he kept his distance. He shadowed her from room to room, materializing only after she had settled somewhere, and even then he regarded her obliquely, out of range; it had been the tortoise-shell who had studied her every move, kept tabs on her, made her his business.

Dinah always had the animals in mind, one way or another—just as unconsciously she kept account of the seasons, the months, the days, and the hours—but they had come into her life spontaneously, and she had never thought of them as hers any more than it would have occurred to her to feel proprietary about all that time slipping by.

She turned her head toward the last of the sun. Beyond the tall windows of her room she could see all the way across the wide space of lawn, down the far slope of the yard behind the kitchen. She watched her children moving through the garden. David had borrowed a Rototiller and turned the soil for a garden early in the spring, and he spent hours reading gardening books and catalogues. It was his current enthusiasm.

Now he moved deliberately among the rows, turning a leaf here or there for inspection and snapping off dead blooms, and Sarah followed slowly along behind him. She dawdled among the flowers in the syrupy golden air as though she were mesmerized by the late afternoon heat, and her brother stooped to cut an armful of tall gladiolas for the hall vase and gave them over to her to hold while he moved along to the rows of vegetables. Sarah accepted the flowers and stood with her arms slightly raised and cupped around the long stems, and she suddenly seemed to Dinah to be a girl entirely unlike the everyday person Dinah thought of as her daughter. In the waning afternoon Sarah was a lovely and romantic figure, as mysterious and intriguing as a painting. As Dinah watched Sarah and David intently, she marveled that any parents were able to sum up all that they knew about one of their children in a short letter to Mr. Franklin M. Mount, Dean of Freshmen, Harvard College.

David stood up, shaking the earth from two heads of lettuce, holding them aloft to get Sarah's attention as she turned away to carry the flowers up to the house. Dinah had unconsciously leaned toward the window, and she breathed a long sigh and fell back against the pillows. If she were Sarah's age, the days would accrue slowly, each one likely to be overwhelming in its drama. Dinah let her neck go limp against the headboard, relieved that at age forty she was past the point of anticipation of a whole life to be shaped and lived, measured and judged.

She stayed exactly where she was in that moment of the late summer afternoon that is suspended on the verge of twilight. Mourning doves bobbed and fluttered on the telephone lines along the street, sobbing into the deep light; the hearty spears of brilliant gladiolas and the soft purple phlox glowed vibrantly among the thin-petaled, palely drooping day lilies, until it seemed that the taller flowers, spiking into the dimming afternoon, were themselves a source of illumination. When the view of the garden grew hazy in the fading light, she roused herself and went downstairs to organize dinner. Martin came in to put away the tools he had used to mend this and that around the house, and Sarah wandered in to set the table. David dashed up the lawn to see how much time there was before they ate and to be sure she would have the water boiling before he picked the corn.

17

"I can husk it in a second. It's better just picked," he said.

"Okay, David. Let's have it last. I'll put the water on when I take the chicken out. We can have the corn for dessert."

When they were all four seated at the table and Martin was carving the chicken, Duchess joined them for dinner. "God! That dog is disgusting," Sarah said. Duchess patiently picked up mouthfuls of dog meal from her bowl in the corner and dropped all the nuggets on the rug under their feet, where she lay down and munched along companionably. She knew Sarah was irritated, though, and her ears went flat in apology. Sarah bent over and gave her a pat.

"Sarah, don't pet the dog when you're eating your dinner," Dinah said. "It's just not clean." This was only what she said because she was Sarah's mother; there was no conviction in the words.

Sarah took little notice. "I'm going over to Elise's after dinner, Mom," she said. "Is that okay? Could you drive me?"

Dinah turned to answer her daughter, who was sitting where Toby had once sat. It *was* Sarah, fair and fine-boned as Toby had been, approximately the same age and size as Toby was six years ago when he had last sat in that very chair—restless, fidgeting with his food, anxious to be done. It was Sarah, but for a split second Dinah clearly registered the image of her second son, as though he were a visual echo. "It'll still be light, Sarah. Why don't you walk over and maybe David can pick you up later if he has the car?" And there was no dissension between them as there would have been if Toby had made the same request; Sarah was accommodating and perfectly amenable.

When Toby was alive, dinner had so often been a turbulent affair—the time of day Dinah dreaded most. Stranded between his two siblings, he had been defensive in every direction. He had believed that David got more respect and Sarah got more attention. He and Dinah had frequently been locked in a brooding combat, although away from the table they could at least retreat from one another. But they were unyielding at dinner, Dinah brisk and Toby sullen. He had been able to sense any criticism she did not speak, and even now she wondered if sometimes she had intended her expression, her tone of voice, to reveal her irritation.

Once, when he had slammed away from the table and out the back door, Dinah had leaped up and followed him. She had stood just outside the screen and shouted after him. "Goddammit! Goddammit! If you *won't* be happy, damn it, you'll ruin my life! My whole life. You don't have the right to do that, Toby! You don't have the *right* to make me so miserable!"

And she had turned back to the table to be shocked by her children's bleak faces. Sarah, only about four or five years old, had sat paralyzed on her booster seat, truly frightened by so much anger, and David wouldn't meet her eyes. But her husband's expression had been flat with grief, his fine mouth slackened in a pained grimace and his voice oddly without fervor. "Sometimes, Dinah . . ." Martin said. "Jesus Christ! Sometimes you say the most terrible things!"

It was true. She and Toby had said the worst things they could say to each other. She had believed they were equals; with Toby she had always lost her grip on the fact of her own adulthood. Nothing slipped by him, not one injustice, not the smallest inequity. There were other times when even Martin had said, "That kid's a real clubhouse lawyer! You can't win with him! There's no way to make him listen!"

But Toby *had* listened to them; he had listened all the time. He had simply never been sure of what he heard. On his fourth Thanksgiving, when Dinah was pregnant with

Sarah, they had decided to have a formal meal in the dining room. Over the course of the preceding week, Dinah had impressed on them that this was a grave event—the first year that they would not eat casually in the kitchen, or at the local Howard Johnson for the sake of quick service to small children.

As Martin carved the turkey at the table, the children grew restive, and Dinah became cross at his perfectionism as he painstakingly cut away nearly transparent slices from the breast. She urged him on. Everything else was getting cold. In exasperation he had finally severed the drumsticks, one for each child. Toby had recoiled in astonishment when his father had deposited the huge drumstick on his plate with a flourish of the silver-handled carving fork, and Martin had laughed. "That's the part I always wanted at every Thanksgiving," he said. "You get the whole thing, Toby," he said. "The best of the dark meat."

Toby sat stoically through the meal until Dinah noticed that he hadn't eaten any turkey at all. "Sweetie, don't you like that? Do you want some gravy?" He had looked up at her doubtfully for a moment, not replying.

"Can I have some turkey?"

"Well, honey, there's plenty of turkey. Don't you like what you have?"

"Daddy said he gave me the dog meat. I don't want it. I just want some turkey." He was not accusing them; he had always been generous in his forgiveness. He just wasn't sure how he stood in the family; he didn't trust his hold on them. When he was seven and went off to camp for two weeks, he signed his letters: "Your son, Toby Howells."

He had believed completely in right and wrong, and after a daylong battle with his mother, if he finally did think that her argument had merit, he would say so. He was willing to make amends, to say he was sorry. If he and she had been edgy together, their attachment was fervent. They had violently disapproved of any trait in the other that they loathed in themselves.

The summer following Toby's death, David had come across the two orphaned cats. Dinah had taken David with her when she went shopping. She had asked him to come along and help with all the grocery bags, but it was a time when she could scarcely bear to be without one of her children.

In the parking lot in the summer's heat she had thought at first that she was hearing the squeak of her grocery cart as it rocked slightly every time David hefted another sack of groceries from the basket to the back of her station wagon. But David recognized the tiny mewling sound for what it was. He had lain down flat on the graveled asphalt and maneuvered himself all the way under the bronze-flecked Trans Am, which was parked next to their own car.

Dinah had stood looking down at David's long legs emerging from beneath the car and realized with surprise that they could have been connected to an adult body. David was just thirteen, and, still, that was Dinah's most vivid memory of that day—gazing down at her son's darkly haired, muscular legs.

"I need something to bribe it with," he had called out to her from beneath the car, and she had torn open a package of raw hamburger.

A little crowd gathered, three middle-aged women and an elderly man, drawing their carts into a semicircle and watching David in silence. One of the women had moved forward abruptly when David emerged far enough to hold a kitten out to them. The woman swooped toward him and grabbed it in a peculiar, greedy lunge, and Dinah had not interfered. David had disappeared again beneath the car, and when he finally wriggled out, he held a second kitten, grease-spotted and clutching at his arm in panic.

"Twins," he announced with a real grin, unselfconscious and slightly quizzical, his dark eyebrows lifted. Dinah had been so smitten with him—momentarily at ease and handsome in the sunlight, ready for any small irony that might come his way, and with his beautiful, beautiful smile—that for a moment she had been dazzled right out of her grieving.

But none of the onlookers smiled back. They just gazed at him blankly as he sat propped up on one hand in the parking lot and extended the other kitten to them for their inspection. Dinah took the tiny cat, and David scrambled up by himself, still smiling with satisfaction at the people who stood around him.

"I don't want this cat," said the woman who had taken the first kitten from David's hand. She seemed to mean that she would have kept it if it had proved to be something else, but now she turned and deposited the kitten inside one of the grocery bags in Dinah's station wagon. The poor cat sprawled miserably over a netted bag of oranges.

And the elderly man who had been standing on the outskirts of their small assembly became quite upset. He rose up on his toes for a moment in agitation, rocking back and forth. "Those cats belong to the people who have this car. Now, that's what I think. You could go in the store, okay? They would announce it over the loudspeaker right in the store if you go to the office."

But Dinah cast her eye doubtfully over the car, obscenely canted up at the rear on a raised axle. "Would you go get a box from the manager, please?" she said to David. "One that's pretty deep." He had loped off, brushing bits of sand and gravel from his nylon running shorts.

The three women had wheeled their shopping carts away to find their own cars in the wide lot. One woman turned back for a moment. "Well, bye-bye," she said, "and good luck." The woman who had taken the first cat from David's hand moved off, though, without a word. The man stood there a little longer, still agitated, still rocking back and forth from heel to toe. But Dinah didn't feel the slightest qualm about the propriety of taking the kittens away with her. The shiny car that had produced them looked to her as if it were still at the height of its mating season. She merely nodded at the elderly little man who was filled with alarm at this unnerving turn of events in his day. But he finally calmed himself and had gone on his way before David returned.

On the drive home the two kittens had shat pitifully, terrified in the high-sided box, filling the front seat with the scent of their mother's milk, so Dinah reasoned that they hadn't been weaned. "Let's name them Bob and Ray," David said. "I'll give them a bath when we get home."

David was enamored that year of Bob Elliot and Ray Goulding—all their old records that Martin had and their program on public radio. Dinah glanced over at him as she drove and had been entirely happy at that moment that she was connected to her own son. Now and then, in that first year of paralyzing grief after Toby's death, she had been granted a few moments like that—rare occasions when she was startled out of her preoccupying sorrow by a resonating glimpse of one of her other children who was absolutely filled up with his or her own personality.

And that day David had possessed joy, too. She had been so pleased for him. Despite Toby's death, that had still been a time when Dinah believed in happy coincidence. She had thought that David's discovery of those two abandoned kittens meant that they would be a source of special solace to him and that they would be more than usually his own.

The two new cats had become hers, of course, by default. It was she who was most in the house; it was she who fed them and checked their water. One day she had taken them along to the Vet Clinic to get their shots, and Melissa had not been behind the reception desk. While she waited to get the attention of a tiny, pert girl who was busily flip-

ping through a box of file cards, Dinah had stood at the
high counter idly contemplating a display of various para-
sitic worms suspended in jars of formaldehyde and arranged along the counter next to the flea collars.

"Be with you in a sec!" the girl said over her shoulder.
At last she got up and came over to the counter, standing
on her toes to peer over it at the wire carrying cage at Dinah's feet. "Oh, you have two little kitties, don't you? Have
we seen you before?" Her name tag said *Annie*.

"Yes," Dinah said. "But I haven't brought these kittens
in before. My account is under Howells."

From the bank of filing cabinets Annie retrieved Dinah's folder, glancing through it to check the information.
"Neither one of those is Taffy, then?" she asked.

"No." Dinah agreed.

Annie stretched up on tiptoe again to look at the kittens. "Aren't they *cute*! What are their names?"

"Well," said Dinah, "the striped one's Bob and the tortoiseshell is Ray."

Annie glanced up at her intently for a moment, and
then bent over the chart to write the information down.
"What *unusual* names for little kittens," she said as she was
writing.

"Oh, well . . . you know . . . they're the comedians."

Annie didn't respond for a moment; her face went solemn while she turned the pages back to be sure the carbon
had copied. Then she smiled brightly at Dinah. "Oh, I
know! Kittens can just be so funny!"

The feline Bob and Ray weren't ever funny, though.
They were fierce in practicing their survival skills. They
tumbled and skidded across the wooden floors, but they
were so clearly purposeful, so determined, that their kit-
tenhood was never amusing. Sarah and David lost interest
when the kittens proved to be unaffectionate—not at all
mean, but diffident. Dinah, though, had been fascinated. In
that long period of time, which she still thought of as being

"after Toby's death," they distracted her, and she watched them by the hour. Bob was distrustful, and Ray was affronted by every human foible that he witnessed around him, especially hers. He glared at her if she dropped a glass or slammed a door or made any sudden noise. If she forgot to feed him, he found her wherever she was in the house and reminded her to give him dinner with a soft tap-tapping of his padded paw, claws scrupulously sheathed.

The two kittens slept curled together, but as they grew into cats they became less and less a pair. Bob went off on his own, tucking himself into a tight ball to sleep on the tops of bookcases or in the depths of a closet during the winter, and disappearing for weeks at a time during the summer. Ray took it upon himself to guard her behavior, and for a while this seemed to her miraculously coincidental. For a while it was with him, not Toby, that her daily wars were waged. If she sat down for a moment to get some of her own work done and she failed to notice Ray come into the room, he would knock some object off a table or a mantel.

"Oh, Christ!" she would shout at him, leaping up explosively, but he would only turn his back with a flick of his tail and direct all his attention to washing his leg. It was Ray who knocked the iron off the board onto the floor when she had left it turned on. She had come back into the room to discover him sleeping on its accustomed resting spot while a thin stream of smoke rose into the air from the hot iron plate lying flat on the wood floor. He curled up quietly in her chair at the kitchen table and was outraged if she didn't notice him before she sat down. She had often dropped a plate or let a fork clatter to the floor as she leaped forward after almost sitting on him. But he always slipped away just in time.

In retrospect Dinah could never pinpoint that one instant in which she stopped measuring the progression of the days from the moment of Toby's death. The end of her *active* grieving slipped up on her and caught her unawares, leaving her oddly at loose ends, uneasy and fearful. On some level was the belief that, as long as she held on to her overwhelming grief at his loss, then Toby might not really be gone.

Nevertheless, eventually and unwittingly, she loosened her grip on her fury and sorrow, and all the other elements of her life receded into their proper perspective. Over the years she stopped regarding Ray's intrusion, his persistent guardianship, as particularly coincidental or significant one way or another. She automatically made her way around him when she was working in the kitchen; it became a habit to hold any book she was reading up in the air so that he could not settle on it and prevent her from turning the pages. And despite all his apparent devotion to her he repelled any affection she extended toward him. If she put him on her lap, he would remain only so long as she held him beneath her hand.

His behavior interested David. "His choices are pretty limited. Bob's never around, and how would you like it if you had to have Taffy as your best friend?"

Dinah had laughed, but she thought David was probably right. She had become Ray's main focus of interest by a process of elimination. Once, when the cat was just a little over a year old, Dinah was working at her desk, and she had straightened up for a moment and rolled her chair backward a little to stretch her legs, Ray had let out a terrible hiss and a warning screech because he had settled on the rug just behind her, and she had unwittingly rolled onto a bit of his fur before he jumped out of the way. He was incensed, but so was she. She hadn't known he was there, and the awful sound he made had caused her skin to prickle. She swiveled all the way around in her chair and matched his furious glare.

"You stupid, stupid *beast*! What the hell do you think?" And quite unexpectedly she began to cry, a deep, alarming sobbing. "You don't *own* this place! You think you're God's own cat, don't you? You're just a pest! And I don't *care* if I roll over you and squash you flat! I can't have any peace in my own house!" And she had raised her hands to her face, trying to stop her own weeping. "You're driving me crazy! I'm *sick* of thinking about you and you're driving me crazy!" Although she yelled straight at him, crying and shouting, he didn't even flinch. She turned her chair again and bent forward, laying her face against the cool wood of her desk and weeping on and on, not thinking at all about the cat but simply given over to grief. When she finally rose from her chair the cat regarded her with disdain. You're loud and raucous, he seemed to be thinking. You are all alone in your own room yelling at a cat.

But as time passed, Ray's preoccupation with her became merely a function of the household, a part of the secret life of her days when she was home alone. If the house were otherwise inhabited, she bent the shape of her hours to encompass her husband and children and friends. And this summer the intensity of the lives lived within the rooms of her house was shifting and dissipating in a way that she could not understand.

Sarah, now twelve, was still willing to answer some of the questions Dinah asked her directly, but David, at eighteen, revealed as little as he could without being rude, as though any knowledge she might have of him bequeathed to her some sort of power over him. And while the life of the family inevitably drew in around him as they waited through the warm months before September when he would leave for college, Dinah grew increasingly desperate to be given a little access, once again, to some part of David's state of mind.

It seemed to Dinah that he was unreasonably intent on his absolute privacy. At one point, on her way out the door, Dinah had leaned back around the doorframe into the kitchen, where David was finishing his breakfast. "I'm going to the grocery," she said. "Is there anything special you need or anything particular you'd like for dinner?"

He gazed up at her in silence, with his eyebrows drawn together in pained outrage. "I don't know why," he said, "you need to know *everything* about my life!"

Dinah only sighed and pulled the door firmly closed behind her, but in the car she found that her eyes smarted with tears. What had she done to warrant such resentment?

Another day, though, when he came home from work, David sat amiably with her in the kitchen, drinking a beer while Dinah stood at the sink, sipping a glass of wine and washing lettuce for dinner.

"Oh, guess what!" he said. "I saw a girl who'll be in my class next year. We were in the same tour group after my interview."

"You did?" said Dinah, not remembering to make her voice sound less avid. "Did you speak to her? Is she a girl you might go out with?"

"Of course I spoke to her. She was having lunch with her mother at the restaurant. They were on their way to Manchester to go shopping." He had waited tables three summers in a row at The Green River Café, and just this week he had managed to be put on the shift that served lunch and afternoon tea instead of the breakfast shift, which started at 5:30 in the morning.

Dinah didn't notice David's expression tighten, and she decided that the extra sleep this week had improved David's mood. She was amazed to be getting so much information from her son, whose life she could no longer envision, who no doubt had all sorts of thoughts and did all sorts of things that she could not possibly imagine. This was not a prurient interest on her part. She would have been as intrigued to find out that he was reading Dostoevsky as she would have been to discover the nature of his love life. She only wanted to continue to know him. She dried her hands on a kitchen towel and moved a few steps toward him where he sat at the table.

"How do you know it was her mother? Did she introduce you?"

"Nope. I just leaped to that conclusion, Mom. It was just a shot in the dark." He was careful to keep humor in his voice, but Dinah was so eager for particulars, for one little way to hold on to her oldest child, that she didn't even notice.

"Well, I mean, it could have been her aunt or someone. It could even have been her sister. Her mother could have had a daughter when she was twenty and had another when she was forty. Or it could have been just a friend." She was very serious about finding out every detail of this encounter, about having it accurately filed away in her mind.

"Oh, my God! That's what the writing on the napkin meant!" David said. He looked alarmed.

"A napkin?"

"Yeah. I was just clearing the table, but I did notice that someone had written on a napkin in lipstick. It said, 'Help! I'm being kidnapped.' I should have *known*!"

Dinah laughed, and David went off to take a shower. But she was left with an abiding curiosity about the girl in the coffee shop, the girl's mother, David's conversation with them, all his movements and all the ideas he had had in his own day.

This particular evening at the dinner table, both the children were being especially forthcoming, chatting to her with a gently forced animation that she welcomed and accepted. Within their small group was the clear acknowledgment that it was she among them who was most wounded this morning when she had finally had to have the cat, Ray, put to sleep. She had taken the cat to the clinic earlier in the week because he had stopped eating and his eyes were running. A new vet had checked him over and had given

Dinah antibiotics for the cat and diagnosed him as having pneumonia. But it worried Dinah that she could coax the tablets down his throat so easily.

This morning she had awakened to a strange sound in the bedroom. She had thought Martin was snoring, but he was sleeping silently, turned on one side. Finally she looked over the side of the bed and discovered Ray, pulling himself along the rug toward her bed, too feeble to walk and gasping for air. The cat had come to get her.

She had jumped out of bed and said loudly to Martin to call the vet. He turned over slowly, coming awake, unable to make out what was going on.

"The cat is sick," she said. "I'll take him to the clinic. Call Dr. Randolph and tell her to meet me over there!" She put her raincoat on over her nightgown and took her pillow from the bed and put it down next to the gasping cat. She was very careful as she eased him onto it.

"But Dinah, it's only six-thirty. They don't even open until eight." Martin couldn't see the cat on the other side of the bed, and he wasn't fully awake. But Dinah stood up and turned to him in a barely controlled rage that startled him.

"Just call the vet. Tell her," Dinah said very slowly so as to be entirely understood, "that she killed my cat! Tell that woman that she God damned well did kill my cat!"

But at the clinic Dinah's anger ran out, leaving her limp and vulnerable in the quiet building. She was terribly sad as she sat holding Ray on her lap, stroking his ragged fur while the vet injected him with a fatal dose of the anesthetic Somlethal. His head sank forward, and his heart stopped in seconds. And Dinah had no doubt that it was better, as she sat looking down at him, than to have let him slowly suffocate. Nevertheless, she felt she had betrayed him, not by having him killed, but by witnessing him there on the floor of her room, so desperately in need, so utterly without dignity. No longer God's own cat.

Dinah had been unable to move except to shake her head at the vet to signify that she would not leave yet, and the doctor withdrew, nodding in agreement. For a long time Dinah had sat in her nightgown and raincoat in the little examination room with Ray across her lap, not thinking about the cat at all, but brought face to face once again with the terrible recognition of inevitable sadness. She had thought then that there are a few things no one ever tells women. She supposed it wasn't a conspiracy; maybe it was a kindness. When she was pregnant the first time a few people had at least suggested some of the possibilities. Martin's mother had told her that her life would never again be the same, not altogether in a congratulatory tone.

"I'll tell you," a woman in the obstetrician's office had said, "there's nothing like it in the world," also with a trace of dolefulness. But no one could have made Dinah believe in the passion of being the mother of a child. Fathers are passionate, too, but they guard their souls more carefully. They are able to experience a crisis of faith, fear of mortality—in the abstract—*apart* from the fate of their children. And while she did know women who wore their maternity indifferently, Dinah was suspicious of them even while she sometimes envied them. But she didn't really think of them as being anyone's mother. She thought that real mothers—all the mothers in the world—are simply the fools of the earth in the ways they live with hope, in the ways they must continue to believe that they can save their own children. Momentarily overwhelmed with hopelessness, she had sat leaning against the tiled wall of the Vet Clinic, abstractedly stroking the limp body of the cat.

By this evening, though, sitting at dinner with Martin and David and Sarah, Dinah was surprised to find the remembered image of her children moving through the garden in the near dusk filling her mind and pulling her to the edge of an exhausted and tentative peacefulness. She got up from the table and began clearing the plates away while David and Sarah and Martin went out to pick the corn.

"I like the really small ears," she said. "I want two of them."

A large kettle of water was boiling on the stove, and the windowpanes had misted over, so she couldn't see the three of them moving through the cornstalks, but she was suddenly pleased for the moment just to have the knowledge of their being there. She had been trying for a long time, now, to hold on to kindliness in the world, wherever she could find it, in lieu of the terrible urgency of passion.

CHAPTER TWO

AT HOME

OVER A PERIOD OF thirty years, Arlie Davidson, the How-ellses, next door neighbor, had walked a succession of dogs along a route that crossed the corner of the property on his other side to reach the meadow that sloped up into Bell's Forest. But one Saturday afternoon the new owner of that property, Raymond Brickley, who had bought the house to use as a weekend retreat, was disgruntedly inspecting the job the house painters had done in his absence when he caught sight of Mr. Davidson and his corgi. Mr. Brickley climbed down from his ladder and moved a few steps in Mr. Davidson's direction. All his mistrust of the local trades-men and his suspicion of the natives' intransigent dislike of him were suddenly brought to bear on this flagrant trans-gression of his privacy.

"Oh, you!" he had shouted across all the lovely green grass. "You! Davidson! You bring that animal on my prop-erty again and I'll call the police!" Mr. Brickley was suffused with anger, he was trembling with outrage, and Arlie Davidson was bemused. He studied his new neighbor with interest while his corgi moved busily along from one bush to another, marking his territory.

The whole idea interested Mr. Davidson, who had no great faith that the local police would show up on time even in an emergency. He smiled and lifted his arm in a dismissive gesture as he turned away again along the path. "Go right ahead," he said. "By all means . . ." Mr. Davidson's indifference, of course, only heightened Mr. Brickley's fury, and it radiated outward over his clipped lawn and carefully pruned maple trees and was ultimately absorbed by the far stand of spruces behind which Mr. Davidson and his dog had disappeared.

It was a minor incident, only the small infraction of trespassing, but Mr. Brickley's passion had momentarily been murderous. In some other place, perhaps under other circumstances, all that terrifying energy might have come to fruition; Mr. Brickley might truly have acted upon such a pure concentration of rage and frustration. As it was, though, he sat down on his terrace to await Mr. Davidson's return and dozed off while gazing out at the gentle mountains rising beyond the enormous evergreens. And in any case, Mr. Davidson came home the long way round.

The town of West Bradford has a population of eight thousand people settled into a valley in the northern reaches of the Berkshire Hills. It is the home of Bradford and Welbern College, which is the primary employer in the area. Otherwise, most of the working people in West Bradford are employed by one of the three light, clean industries that, taken together, provide jobs for a few less than three hundred.

The doctors, dentists, and veterinarians are splendidly schooled. Having trained at such places as Johns Hopkins, Harvard, Yale, Tufts, Cornell, and Penn, they have given up the competition and money of big city medicine so that they and their families can enjoy a better quality of life, although the liability insurance has gotten entirely out of hand and fewer young practitioners are moving to town.

Seven lawyers have offices in West Bradford, and they, too, have high-powered credentials, but have been drawn back to the area by nostalgia for the college where almost all of them were undergraduates. Five more have residences in West Bradford, but are associated with firms in nearby Bradford.

The town easily supports a large lumberyard and a building supplies distributor, and the masons, electricians, carpenters, and plumbers are, by and large, excellent and honest and are often poets or painters as well.

Thirty real estate agencies serve the area.

In the summer there is climbing, hiking, biking, swimming, golf, and any racquet sport. The nationally famous West Bradford Summer Theater Festival brings Broadway and movie stars right into town. There are fourteen hotels and motels, seven flourishing bed-and-breakfasts, and twenty-four restaurants, including—June through August—the nonprofit café at the Freund Museum of Art. In the early 1950s, Thomas Freund chose West Bradford as the site of his museum because of his belief that, in the event of nuclear war, his collection would be protected from the inevitable shock waves by the gentle buffer of the surrounding mountains. But he had also been much taken by the bucolic setting, with cows grazing right outside a room of Renoirs, ice skaters on the pond beyond the Monets. He and his wife are interred beneath the marble steps of the entrance.

Tanglewood, with the Boston Symphony Orchestra, is a half hour's drive away, and Saratoga, which has the oldest thoroughbred racetrack in the country and is summer host to the New York City Ballet and the Philadelphia Orchestra, is only forty-five minutes in the other direction. Any of those professionals who might have been dubious about turning their backs on life in a metropolitan area are now absolutely delighted to discover that their property values have more than quadrupled in the past ten years, although they bemoan the encroaching condominiums and developing resort complexes.

There are nine churches in West Bradford and a synagogue in nearby Bradford. Discounting church or synagogue attendance, which is large, it is hard to gauge the depth of genuine and fervent belief in God, but certainly, within the community there is a widely held belief in the need and comfort of religiousness, and the ministers and priests are generally more intellectual than passionate, espousing compassion and tolerance as opposed to the fear of damnation.

Well over 150,000 tourists visit West Bradford every year, and their influx is simultaneously welcomed and dreaded. Martin Howells's friend, Vic Hofstatter, likes to tell his story of standing in line at the local farmers' market behind a woman in a beaded sweater and with carefully arranged hair—clearly not a New Englander. He was waiting to pay for two heads of lettuce and some asparagus, and he had begun to feel sorry for the restless woman in front of him, who had a basket filled with local bread and produce in an amount that could never be prepared and consumed before they lost their freshness. Eventually she seemed to suspect she looked foolish to the girl at the counter making change from a fishing tackle box, and she turned to Vic with a hawklike glance, casting her eye over his few items.

"Are you a tourist or a native?" she asked sharply, and Vic smiled back at her indulgently.

"Oh, I live here," he said kindly. "And I have a garden of my own." He was saving her from the embarrassment of being unskilled at shopping in a strange town.

"Well, for God's sake!" she said, clearly exasperated. "I'd think you people could find somewhere else to shop during the season."

What Moira Kaplan had said at the crowded opening of the summer theater had immediately become a cliché: that the tourists should send their money and just stay home. It had even become a kind of code. Martin had been stopped in his progress along the Carriage Street sidewalk one summer morning on his way to the post office by a group of tourists who had paused to observe the buildings across the way. One of the women seemed particularly indignant, gesturing with a sweep of her arm to include the entire street and the casually dressed natives. "We have reservations for three nights," she complained. "I *did* think it would be a little more gentrified!" An acquaintance of Martin's, making his way around the group by stepping into the street, caught Martin's eye and said under his breath, "Go home now and leave a check." And he and Martin acknowledged each other with a brief nod before they passed by and went on their way.

On the other hand, it is a lucrative business, tourism, and it is sometimes quite heady to be securely established in a place where so many people want to be. Even the teenagers in town are casual and carefully unimpressed when Christopher Reeve or Paul Newman comes into the deli to pick up a sandwich.

"And what's the name on that prescription, please?" said Jennie Abrams, who works part time at the Carriage Street Pharmacy, when she looked up and was confronted with Mary Tyler Moore across the counter.

The Board of Trade had erected a modest-sized sign at the entrance to Carriage Street, the one-street shopping area, that said:

WEST BRADFORD
JEWEL OF THE BERKSHIRES

As it turned out, though, almost no one was pleased with the sign once it was up; it was so clearly ostentatious.

Whenever anything at all went wrong—when the out-lying routes became impassable in the spring thaw, when grocery shoppers faced one another over the winter pro-duce in the supermarket and inspected the trammeled-looking lettuce—the residents would look at each other and say, "Oh, well. After all, this *is* the jewel of the Berkshires," with a wry shrug. Like any other place that engenders affection, it also inspires a kind of proprietary contempt.

A certain amount of town-gown tension exists, al-though generally civility rules. West Bradford is blessed with a relative lack of cliques and no prevailing social order, partly because of the interdependency of the inhabitants. When Mike Detweiler, general groundskeeper to most of the wealthy homeowners in town, sent invitations to a slide show and narrative of his most recent trip to Malaysia, where he studied tropical plants, not one of his customers cared to offend him in order to attend the performance of the Empire Brass Quintet or to hear Richard Wilbur read his poetry—both events having been scheduled at the col-lege that same evening.

No one would deny that there is room for improve-ment in West Bradford. Because of the sudden upsurge in real estate prices and the popularity of West Bradford as a "second home" community, very few mid-to-lower income families or new faculty are able to buy houses at all. The town is primarily a community of white families, and the college and the Medical Alliance often have a hard time keeping single or minority faculty or doctors. The rate of teenaged suicide—too high at any number—is above average in West Bradford, and drug use is a prob-lem, although it is quickly being surpassed by alcohol abuse.

Certainly West Bradford has its share of poverty, and the current national recession is hitting the area hard. There were one actual and two attempted rapes on campus in the past year, and most of the townspeople believe that a disappearance and two murders of young women over the past eight years are the work of a serial murderer who has also struck in small towns nearby.

There is always a run of various and assorted small crimes—thefts and break-ins—and this past spring three men from Boston robbed the West Bradford Drive-Thru Savings Bank, but were thwarted in their escape by a combination of muddy back roads and the fact that they were spotted by the animal control officer, who was parked in his driveway eating his lunch. His suspicions of something nasty afoot were aroused when the battered van they were driving careered wildly past him up the hill, headed at fifty or sixty miles an hour toward a dead end. He called ahead on his C.B. to alert the police in Bradford as well as West Bradford, and then gave chase in his pickup. The incident was amusing in the retelling but, in fact, the three men had been panicky and well armed, and when they were finally trapped at the end of the road it was mostly just good luck that they did not kill someone.

The public schools had once been extraordinary but, as has happened all over the country since the 1970s, they have begun to decline, and a considerable number of people who ardently support public education are now sending their children away if they can possibly afford to.

Long-standing animosities and current feuds among various factions of the community endure, but when the people in West Bradford chat at the post office, or when they meet each other at the newsstand to pick up the *Times* or *The Boston Globe,* they debate the relocation of the dilapidated town garage or the desirability of putting up the town's first stoplight at a particularly bad intersection. They discuss the Red Sox, the Celtics, and even the Bruins, depending on the season. They talk about the summer theater productions, movies and also "films," the latest PBS series, or a book they've just read. But they aren't smug. They are as subject to terror, to passion, to pleasure as any people anywhere. It is only that in their circumstances they are fortunate.

Yet, in a town like West Bradford, everyone's life is fairly open to observation. For instance, no tragedies are anonymous. The survivors are identifiable right there among the citizenry: shopping at the grocery store, coaching a soccer game, teaching first grade, styling a customer's hair, practicing surgery.

Six years ago, September 20, on a lovely, crisp afternoon, Martin had picked Toby and David up early at soccer practice so the boys could shower and change before they all went out to their favorite Mexican restaurant. When Martin came to a stop on State Street, behind a car making a left turn, a young man named Owen Croft, a child of Judith and Larry Croft, a good student, a local basketball star—that boy, tired after a hard practice and preoccupied at seventeen—had cruised straight into the rear of the Howellses' small blue car at thirty-five miles an hour. The front seat, with David and Martin carefully strapped into their seat belts, was untouched, but the back seat, and Toby with it, were entirely crushed. The town was doubly wounded—anguished for the Howellses above all, but also for the Crofts. And the numerous other calamities, disasters, and tragedies that had occurred since then were, each one of them, personal to some degree to everyone in West Bradford.

His son's death would be an event that crossed Martin Howells's mind at least once every day of his life. On this mild June day, Martin walked along the crest of Bell's Hill and looked down at the village that lay across the valley and spread up the first rise of the opposing mountains, and felt a curious sense of homesickness for West Bradford, even though he was within it. He often experienced this unquenched yearning, and he had learned to hold it at bay, not to investigate it too carefully. It was a familiar state of mind that, in its vague manifestation, was really no more than a longing still to be held innocently within the years before his son died.

The day was delicate, with such a persistent but gentle breeze from the west that the full-blown summer leaves of the trees on Bell's Hill only fluttered and rustled; even the slender saplings did not bow. In the morning the temperature was seventy degrees, the humidity was low, and the cloud cover was complete but so transparent that the entire blue sky breaching the gap of the valley of West Bradford from mountain to mountain was barely glazed with pale white.

Duchess had strained at her leash all the way up the hill, but as soon as Martin released her at the height of the ridge where the trail flattened out, she had refused to move away from him at all. They continued on for a few minutes, moving along together closer than two abreast, with Duchess crossing nervously in front of him, ears flat in apprehension and hobbling him at the knees with every other step; but this was their accustomed routine, and Martin edged from side to side across the path in avoidance of her without even thinking.

He stopped and threw sticks for her and leaned against a tree where he had a view of the whole town. He could see the roof of his own house among the tops of the trees surrounding it, as well as the cars and people moving on the carefully laid pattern of streets among the bright swards of groomed green grass. The scene was comforting and familiar, yet, in the tremulous clarity of the day, the world splayed out before him seemed fragile, as if it were contained in an overturned porcelain teacup.

In the immediate aftermath of Toby's death, Dinah had not allowed anyone to visit other than Judith and Larry Croft and their son Owen, and she had not agreed to see them until several days after the private service for Toby attended only by the immediate family. She had taken calls of concern and comfort from her mother and father and brother, but she had refused to have them come to West Bradford from Ohio, and she had begged Martin to delay visits from any of his family as well.

"Dinah, people want to see us because they're so . . . *sad*. They need to grieve, too," he had said, and she had looked at him and nodded.

"I know. I know what they need. But I can't . . . I won't just . . . give him away. I can't deal with it right now. For once, Martin, for once, I'm not going to *be* polite! I don't *care* how they feel! Not any of them! Not one single one! It's not their business. I want them to leave us alone."

Initially Dinah had wept and paced the house, pressing her fists against the door of Toby's room and sliding downward in a crumpled heap as she let herself understand the fact that whenever she opened that door Toby would not ever be there again. And she had turned to Martin and embraced him, as he had bent over her there, but she had never surrendered to him any bit of her particular sorrow, nor had she accepted any of his. She had enclosed herself in a monosyllabic grief, clearly mustering great energy even to respond to their youngest child, Sarah, or to David, who was so stunned by the enormity of the catastrophe that he scarcely felt any emotion at all.

The evening they sat in the living room waiting for the Crofts, Martin looked over at Dinah and put her behavior down to anger. He envied her for it; he was filled only with a terrible lassitude and hopelessness.

Dinah sat silently on the couch with an alarmingly open expression on her face, her eyes too wide, her mouth stretched taut at the corners. Watching her, Martin felt an absurd but keen expectation that she would reveal something heretofore kept secret at the very core of herself, something that would resolve and dissipate the dreadfulness of what had happened to them.

When Judith Croft had come into the room, she had stopped short at the sight of Dinah and then stepped forward again with one hand stretching toward her. Martin had intercepted Judith with a slight hug. Martin and Dinah had known the Crofts for over fifteen years; they had served on school boards together, exchanged dinner invitations, and been dinner guests at the same houses. Martin automatically drew Judith toward him in an affirmation of their mutual sorrow and their long connection.

"I don't know . . ." Judith had begun, "I don't know how this could happen. I don't know why . . . and Owen . . . Owen doesn't know why. . . ." She was a small woman with an intense face. Her chin was slightly too square, and she had small, deep-set, but very brilliant blue eyes. Martin had always thought of her as a wiry, durable person—humorless and resilient. But that evening she had suddenly seemed gaunt and stringy and so abrupt in all her movements that it was as though she were about to fly apart. Her son loomed between his parents, taller than either of them and mute with misery. Martin found himself standing with his arm around Judith staring carefully at Owen, who waited with his father in the doorway, not meeting Martin's glance.

Owen was probably considered handsome, Martin thought, although he was awkwardly lanky, and his ears were large and stood too far away from his head. But he had beautiful, thickly lashed green eyes and blond hair, and he gave a strong impression of artlessness and even vulnerability. Martin was confused as he studied him. He had been thinking of Owen as the boy who had so carelessly, so recklessly, driven his car straight ahead into traffic that had stopped inconveniently, instantly killing Toby. And although he had seen Owen Croft around town over all the years since Owen was first able to ride his bike at about age six, Martin had imagined him as dark and sullen and sulky.

Surly and spoiled, a doctor's son with too much money, too little caution.

"Could we sit down, Martin?" Larry finally said, still stranded at the door with Owen. And they had come into the room and settled on the chairs, but no one spoke until Owen turned to Dinah. His voice was strained and husky.

"I know there's nothing I can say that will change anything," he said, and he looked to Dinah for a signal, but she had her attention fixed on him only marginally, which made Martin cringe for him in spite of himself. Owen bent forward in his chair with the urgency of what he needed to say. "I was just driving *home*. . . ." It was an appeal. He was only going home; he was not rushing to any place particularly desirable. "I'd just gotten off from practice, and I was late. . . . The sun was in my eyes and I didn't *see*. . . ." His face suddenly tensed in an effort to fight tears, his mouth crumpled inward at the corners, and still Dinah simply gazed back at him, abstracted. "I didn't *see*. . . ." He couldn't go on with what he was saying until he looked down at his hands and took a long breath. "I don't even remember thinking about it. . . ." Finally he couldn't go on at all, but just bent his head to his hands. The adults were frozen where they sat, with Owen's words hanging over them.

Judith had begun to cry then, and she reached out her open hands in an appeal to Dinah. "Oh, *Dinah*! What do we do now? What do you want us to do? What can we do?"

For the first time since the accident, Dinah's attention seemed to become engaged. She blinked at Judith and her mouth quivered. "What can we do?" She spoke as though she were repeating a phrase in a foreign language whose meaning wasn't entirely clear to her. "Well . . . I don't know." She sat back in her chair, giving way to exhaustion all at once, her face becoming less taut, her eyelids drooping. "Well . . ."—and she gestured outward with one hand— "we just go on, I guess." And Judith leaned her head against the back of her own chair and closed her eyes while tears ran down her face.

Larry Croft looked from Dinah to Martin, but he didn't speak for a moment. "Owen's talked to the police, of course. We don't know what charges . . ."

But Dinah held her hand up to negate what he was saying, what she was hearing. She rose from her chair in oddly uncoordinated slow motion and turned away from all of them, making her way slowly off down the hall, her arms extended slightly, palms outward as though she were moving in the dark.

Larry got up, and Martin rose with him, although Judith continued to sit with her eyes closed in silent weeping. Owen had straightened up, but he was teary and he didn't look at anyone. They were all helpless in the silent room, and Martin realized that that was what Dinah had understood almost at once when she had heard about Toby's death—the pointlessness of all their overwhelming sorrow.

"Maybe this was the wrong time to come," Larry said. "What we wanted you and Dinah to know is how sorry we are." He paused again and ran his hand over his head where his hair had receded. "Oh, God . . . I don't know any way for you to know how sorry we are." He leaned toward Martin and grasped his upper arm in an attempt to draw forth Martin's comprehension of what he was saying. His tone was confiding. "I mean, here we are with our own son standing right here. But we aren't making any excuses, Martin. Owen's not either. He never did. He never did to us or the police. . . ."

Martin found himself overtaken with an unspecified sensation of pity so powerful that he felt light—unfettered by his own body. A sweet, metallic taste rose in the back of his throat, and he shook his head to stop Larry from continuing. "We just go on, Larry. We just go on. Dinah's right. We'll just have to go ahead." He looked over inclusively at

Owen and Judith, who was drying her eyes and rising from her chair.

And Martin, remembering all this, saw now that after that meeting they all had gone ahead—what alternative had there been?—but they had only progressed in fits and starts, and the amorphous sorrow and shock in the town concerning Toby's death had been left unresolved, glimmering through the air over West Bradford and in the atmosphere of all those other places where Toby had been known: his aunts' and uncle's, his grandmothers' and grandfather's, and within his own house where it suffused all the rooms.

Several weeks after Toby's death, Martin had put Duchess on her lead, intending to follow this very same route up Bell's Hill. He had started out in a mild October drizzle, but as the rain increased he had changed his course and made his way along the village streets, tramping stolidly through the puddles.

He rounded the baseball field of the high school as the rain grew stronger, the drops full and hard and gusting over him in sheets when the wind picked up. He crossed the sidewalk to the gym and pushed open the wide door that led into the rear of the building. As soon as she realized that she was out of the rain, Duchess shook herself vigorously, spattering him with water, and he looped her leash around the metal stanchion supporting the bleachers.

Martin would have liked to join the small group of parents in the center of the bleachers who had arrived early to watch the basketball practice before driving their children home in the heavy rain. They had discarded their dripping jackets in a pile and were talking among themselves in a comradely murmur. With Duchess in tow, however, he had no choice but to sit unobtrusively at the foot of the far end of the bleachers near two women who had climbed higher up in the stands and were chatting softly while glancing at the cheerleaders practicing farther down on the sidelines.

The basketball team was almost languorous in their warm-up drills, waiting for the coaches to organize them. A dark-haired boy passed the ball off to his teammate and moved over to the bleachers where the cheerleaders sat. He approached a small girl, sitting about four seats up, who wouldn't glance his way. Finally he fell forward slightly from the hip, resting his forearms widely on either side of her, and she made a great point of straightening up to peer over his shoulder, refusing to look at him.

The boy bent farther over the girl, and she finally looked right back at him and smiled, raising her hand to brush his hair back from where it had fallen over his forehead. The two of them said something to each other before the boy stood back and moved away. Watching them, Martin was suddenly surprised by a memory of uncomplicated adolescent lust, and his attention was caught with an odd alertness, as though he remembered this very building, the high struts of the roof, the echoing thunk of the ball, the diminished, hollow murmuring of a few people in an empty gym.

Most of the girls sat scattered over a small section of the far bleachers while two of them demonstrated a series of leaps and turns again and again. Now and then one of the seated girls would rise and step down the bleachers to join them until she, too, mastered the sequence. They were not shouting their cheers; they were concentrating on the choreography and only talking quietly among themselves.

When Owen Croft came out of the dressing room behind the two coaches, the atmosphere became subdued. Martin had not realized until that moment that he had been expecting to see Owen, but now he watched him carefully. Owen didn't see him at all. In fact, Owen kept his head down, his eyes averted, and he didn't turn to talk to anyone; he simply moved into a loosely organized rotation beneath the basket, turned, put the ball up, and moved off.

Both the women sitting above Martin, and the larger group of people farther down the stands, were quiet while Owen pivoted, ran, shot, moved. A kind of sympathetic solemnity was heavy in the atmosphere as Owen continued to radiate his own isolation within that group of lanky boys. And Martin felt it, too—an aching suspense, a communal need for resolution, absolution.

There was a dramatic hesitancy in the movements of the cheerleaders whenever they passed by Owen if he was sitting on the bleachers watching a play. They would offer a solemn tilt of their heads, or touch his arm, or briefly brush his shoulder without engaging his eye. In his presence that afternoon, they perceived themselves as fragile and tentative. When one or another of them spoke some word to him, he didn't answer or turn his head; he remained overwhelmed and unreachable, and therefore he was suddenly the heroic center of all the sweet radiation of their grave concern.

The pale light that fell from the high windows of the building illuminated the shifting bodies without variation or shadow. Every aspect of the scene had an equal vibrancy of color, like the landscape of a dream. Slowly the players moved into separate teams. Five boys loped into the near court, but the only one Martin knew was Winston Grimes, the starting center.

The drills became smoother, the pace quicker and purposeful. In the far court Owen came in under the basket for a lay-up, and then the team moved into another pattern, an elaborate series of passes, while the defensive players flung themselves violently in the paths of their opponents, lunging and waving their arms while the offensive players pivoted and searched for an opening. The two practice teams were serious now, and the increased adrenaline was tangible under the lofty roof. The calling back and forth of the players echoed harshly, and the damp air was filled with a pervasive, tangy scent like wet hay.

Martin sat perfectly still, but he was infected with that same surge of adrenaline. His whole body was tense, his senses heightened. A remembered knowledge of communal masculinity under the attention of pretty girls along the sidelines swept over him, and he knew again, just for a moment, that simultaneous male arrogance that had rendered him and his teammates haughty and indifferent—even contemptuous—of those very girls whose presence spurred them on.

All at once Martin had become lost to his thirty-eight-year-old self and was affected with an absolute loss of self-consciousness or restraint. Without a pause, without any consideration, he was up and off the bleachers, trotting diagonally across the court. He too, just like those lovely young women and the leanly muscled boys, was drawn toward Owen Croft. Jogging slowly across the floor, his treaded boots thumping against the parquet, he didn't notice the surprised faces of the players under the basket as he approached.

Owen was under the basket holding the ball in midair, cocked over his head. Martin took two long strides and launched himself forward, landing his head solidly under Owen's breastbone—a football tackle—and clasping him around the waist. Owen was slammed backward, his long legs bent under him, his head bouncing up after thudding against the floor. There, lying on the floor of the gymnasium, clasping Owen Croft tightly, and short of breath, Martin was finally trapped in a long moment of realization. He came back to himself the instant Owen's head had hit the floor, and it was as if those following seconds became elastic, stretching out too far for him ever to escape them. Finally he pushed himself up and away from Owen, getting to his feet and brushing himself off without looking up at all the faces turned toward him.

And Owen was pushing himself to his feet, too, where he stood for a moment before turning and moving slowly off toward the dressing room. One of the coaches left midcourt to follow him, but no one else moved. Once the onlookers had recognized Martin, they were horrified. Several people in the stands had risen to their feet, but most had stayed exactly where they were, stunned. The teenagers were awed by these consequences more profoundly than they had understood the fact of Toby's death, and the adults were filled with dismay and pity and relief.

One of the coaches caught Martin roughly by the elbow as he turned to leave, but Martin swung around so furiously, in a slight, aggressive crouch, that the coach drew back. The two men spoke briefly, and Martin moved away, stopping to collect Duchess at the far end of the room. The spectators relaxed a little and sat back down or rearranged themselves in the bleachers. No one had been seriously hurt. In fact, there was an unspoken feeling that something had been brought to a conclusion.

Martin paused once more on the ridge of Bell's Hill, before following Duchess down the steep incline that would lead him into the parking lot of the Freund Museum. Only now, six years later, did it occur to him exactly what had propelled him across that basketball court. It was simply that he had not been able to bear the innocent self-centeredness of Owen's own suffering.

He clipped Duchess back onto her leash. His thoughts turned to the soft day ahead. He had awakened this morning already making a mental list of chores to be done. When he had been on the roof some weeks earlier to unclog a gutter, he had noticed that several slates needed replacing. Water had seeped beneath them and then had frozen and dislodged them sometime over the winter, and he had made a quick inspection of his household to discover any other ravages of the past unusually brutal February.

But surely at seventeen Martin had not really believed in weather, had not really known about gravity, had given no thought to the seasons as they happened around him. When he was the age Owen had been when Toby was killed, Martin had taken the natural world for granted. Living on the earth had not impressed him with the slightest degree of humility.

No doubt he had understood that dramatic weather has dramatic consequences, but he had not known that just a little bit of weather can weigh down the soul—the prevailing wind that moves west to east, the cold that sweeps in from the north, the stifling heat that might settle over the village of West Bradford in long days of damp haze. Not until he had become a householder and begun his yearly battle with the storm windows, the peeling paint on the west wall, the sump pump in the spring, the winter-killed evergreen branches to be trimmed back, had he sometimes succumbed to the melancholy that accompanies the recognition of inevitability.

In the saturated air that long-ago afternoon in the gymnasium, it had maddened Martin that Owen's very sadness had been perceived by those around him as a virtue. But what could someone Owen's age have known about anything, and what difference would it have made how Owen felt?

As he made his way home, Martin battled a feeling of chagrin. In that gymnasium so long ago he had behaved like a person who had not understood the absurdity of indignation. That one moment of futile aggression had been induced by his realization that Owen's agony was inevitably self-centered and peripheral to the real tragedy of the loss of Toby. But of course, so had been his own grief. As inevitable as it is, there is no *use* in grief, that's what he had not understood. It only battens down one's sensibilities a little more, further delineates that little core of "self," and makes it even more necessary to repress one's own knowledge in order to get on with the days.

CHAPTER THREE

A PERFECT THING

EARLY ON THE MORNING of the Howellses' annual Fourth of July party, David came down so early to work in the garden that ground fog still pooled and swirled at the foot of the yard. Even parts of his own small garden were obscured from him. He had not slept at all after taking Christie home from a late party. Near dawn he had pulled on jeans and an old blue shirt, and carried his shoes through the barely lightening rooms and crept out the back door before sitting down on the steps to put on his old L. L. Bean bluchers.

He and Christie had gone to a party on Squire's Hill where there was a fluctuating group of twenty to thirty. They had sat around with Ethan and Sam, who was with Meg Cramer most of the night. By the time David got Christie away, Meg had wandered off, and Sam was stretched out on the low stone wall next to the Park Service built-in barbecue pit. Ethan was mixing drinks of vodka and cranberry juice for everyone, but David had brought a six-pack and sipped a beer.

Sitting there on the grass, watching the four of them get drunk, David had suddenly been as bored as he had ever remembered being in his life. The sensation had frightened him because it was a feeling he had fought this whole last year of high school. He had turned all at once, just at the moment Sam was taking a last drag on a cigarette, holding it between his thumb and index finger, in a manner that for the first time filled David with scorn because it seemed so affected. He had been overwhelmed by the idea that all he had thought about Sam, who had been his best friend since third grade—all he had thought about him or any way in which he had ever valued him—was false. Simultaneously, however, he had been filled with a longing for Sam's easy friendship.

Sometime after midnight he and Christie had broken away from the group; but when they approached her house, the patio lights were on, and they could see Mrs. Douglas sitting out in a lawn chair by the pool, her cigarette making a bright arc every few moments, up and back. Through the filmy curtains the shadow of Christie's father could be seen moving through the house, past the lighted windows.

"Oh, God, David. Don't take me home."

"Are they waiting up for you?"

"No. They went out before I left. They probably just got home. I just don't want to have to talk to them right now." So he had pulled the car over to the curb two houses down the street. He had been unaccountably impatient. He didn't even want to touch Christie, but he had reached over and put his hand on her neck under her soft hair in a pretense of comfort. She sat still for a moment, her head bowed under his hand, and then with a sudden spasm of rage she had straightened, rigid against the door, and thrown his hand off.

"I really wish you just wouldn't touch me when you're in a mood like this!"

He hadn't said anything, but he put his hand on the steering wheel and leaned his head against the headrest.

"You're getting ready, aren't you, not to care at all about anybody? Won't that make your life easy? Won't you be *free*? You can just go away with your great, fucking *brilliance,* and your . . . *superiority,* and when you think about me you can just say, 'Oh, well, Christie was so intense. Christie had so many *problems*! Christie's so young!'" Her face was splotchy and glaring, and he looked away from her, out the window.

She rose to her knees and swung her hand at him ineffectually, just grazing the side of his head. "Don't you dare look away from me! Don't you dare . . . don't you dare! Even Ethan and Sam! You're not even honest with Ethan and Sam anymore. You're like, 'Oh, it's so awful for me to have to be around all the barbarians!'" She made her voice light and feminine, implying an unsavory kind of fastidiousness.

David had been quiet and hurt, at first, because he had never thought he felt superior to, and certainly not any smarter than, Ethan or Sam or Christie herself. But even as he was offended he was bored, and the boredom was quickly translated into anger. He didn't have any way of knowing that what Christie perceived as his sense of superiority was really a kind of emotional stinginess, a protective reserve peculiar in someone his age. Usually when David was angry he kept it to himself; he merely left the room. And last night he had not yelled back at Christie, but his voice had somehow expanded in volume so that it had a hollow, desperate sound even to his own ears, and he had slammed his fist against the dashboard. "I can't *do* all this at once, Christie! I can't be *nice* to everyone all the time anymore!"

She had sat back and simply studied him for a moment while she wiped her eyes with the backs of her hands. Then she had smiled weakly. "God, David!" And at last she had laughed a little. "You're not as nice as you think you are, anyway."

"Okay," he said.

"Okay," she answered.

"Are you coming over tomorrow night? For the party?"

She didn't say anything for a moment, but then her words became exact, as though they occurred to her for the first time as she spoke. "Your house is probably my favorite place to be in the world," she said with no hint of sarcasm, and he turned then to look at her face, which was composed. "It's like a visit with the world's last happy family," she added, while she took her brush out of her purse and began pulling it through her curly hair, smoothing it as best she could away from her face. But that last remark had irritated him more than anything else she had said the whole night.

In the early gray of the morning damp, as David carefully weeded between the rows, it made her seem stupid to have said such a thing. In his remembrance of that one sentence he thought he heard a false note, a way Christie thought she should sound. What could be happening to him that lately he scarcely liked any of the people he loved? Why was it that no one he knew possessed any quirk of personality, any point of view about which he was the least bit curious? It frightened him that the world to which he was so accustomed had taken on the flattened aspect of a badly animated cartoon.

And, as he worked painstakingly down one row and into the next under the rising sun, he became more and more agitated, more irritated, although now his disgruntlement was amorphous, as though it shrouded him from without rather than springing from within. Nothing except this little plot of ground seemed to be right in the world just at the moment.

Dinah was able to walk up and down the stairs of her house, and in and out of the rooms, and think of it as a spare, clean, crisp apple of a place—a perfect thing. The building was a simple one, an old gray farmhouse with good bones and a plain face, and the interior was not *decorated,* but she had thought about the color of the paint, the fabric of the curtains, the arrangement of the chairs and sofas and lamps and rugs very carefully. It seemed to her legitimately beautiful, like an original Shaker box, austere but not contrived. But, in fact, this view of her house was a product of her own selective vision; her household burgeoned with the collected detritus of the lives of the people who lived in it.

The mantelpieces in the dining room and living room were crowded with a variety of things the children had brought home from school over the years—a lumpish blue candlestick Sarah had made in fifth grade, a varnished wooden plaque with "Howells" etched into it by Toby with the woodburning kit he had gotten for his eighth birthday, an overlarge white mug emblazoned in gilt script **"Mother . . . A Mother Is Love,"** which David had given to her one Christmas as a joke because of its inherent ugliness and its silly sentimentality. After unwrapping it, though, she had put it on the mantel to get it out of the way, and it had been there ever since, a receptacle for pencils, felt-tipped pens, paper clips, rubber bands, Chap Sticks, and safety pins.

The handsome glass coffee table in the living room, the little desk in the hall, the sideboard in the dining room, even the wide sills of the old windows were crowded, if not actually cluttered, with oddments—old *National Geographic*s; empty eyeglass cases; dried, shedding flower arrangements that Sarah had made in a summer crafts class; scraggly plants potted from cuttings. The windowsills were liberally scattered with deep baskets because whenever Dinah perceived that here was a place in which objects were inevitably bound to collect, she stopped at Farrell's Store and bought a nice, roomy basket and merely swept everything into it. Tiny, smudged price tags were still suspended from the handles of several of those baskets by little interlooped white strings.

Her house did not encompass the crisp asceticism she believed it did—it had the rich fullness of a ripe plum—but she was happy with her notion of the pleasant austerity of her surroundings. Although Dinah loathed the idea of materialism, she had an almost visceral connection to the place in which she lived. For her it represented a victory over chaos, over despair and disorder. She both enjoyed having guests and begrudged their sharing any part of her hard-earned grace.

In any case, she always thought of their annual Fourth of July party with a shadowy sense of martyrdom, a vague feeling of self-sacrifice that had in the past always proven to be worth the end result. When twilight came, she would create a bit of fantasy for all the smaller children, bringing the magical fairy Moonflower to earth, provided Martin took care to check the pulley mechanism he and Vic Hofstatter had rigged over the porch roof almost fifteen years ago.

Martin and Vic had founded a small literary magazine, *The Review*, soon after the Howellses moved to West Bradford. As a result, the Hofstatters and the Howellses spent so much time at each other's houses, while Martin and Vic argued over solicited manuscripts and sorted through unsolicited ones, that Ellen and Dinah had fallen into a necessarily informal relationship. Dinah would see to the children, while Ellen might take it upon herself to peruse the refrigerator and start dinner for them all.

The Hofstatters lived almost twenty miles out of town, and in the first few years of the venture, *The Review*'s offices had taken over the Howellses' living room during the school year. Dinah was running the local Artists' Guild then, and Ellen would often arrive early in the day with wine or groceries for the evening's meal and work at her own writing in an unused bedroom while the children kept out of her way unless there was an emergency. It saved the cost of a baby-sitter, and in those days all four adults got involved with the makeup of the quarterly magazine, sitting at the kitchen table long into the night. By now, *The Review* had become respectable and mainstream, and some years ago the college had allotted office space and even the salary for part-time help in sorting through the three thousand or so submissions and dealing with the heavy correspondence.

The advent of Moonflower had begun as a diversion for the children when they were small, conceived one evening when Dinah and Martin and Vic and Ellen had grown tired of debating the merits or lack of them of an essay that Martin wanted to publish in the magazine. They had fallen into reminiscences, and Martin had described his great-aunt's wonderful invention and customary presentation of the magical fairy that he had marveled at each year when he was very young in Sheridan, Mississippi.

The Hofstatters had become contagiously enthused about re-creating the whole experience for the Howellses' own children, and they had stayed on later than usual, elaborating on the idea and planning how to carry it out. When David and Toby, and eventually Sarah, had become too old for such make-believe, Dinah and Martin had integrated it into what had become an annual party, and they had invited younger faculty and friends to join them and bring along their small children. The occasion had grown into a buffet supper for about forty-five adults and, sometimes, as many as fifteen children aged six and under. This year only nine young children were expected, and Dinah had prepared for them with care.

On the night of the third, she had eventually realized that she wouldn't sleep as she lay in bed anticipating the pleasure of the smaller children and her own corresponding satisfaction and Martin's and Sarah's and David's.

After all, this was David's last Moonflower summer before he left for school. And Sarah had asked if she could have two friends join them, which was proof that the party remained special to her, a celebration that had been shaped over the years into a unique festivity of her own family.

Dinah counted on rituals, the reassurance of them, and she believed it was especially important for David, in this last official summer of his youth, that the party go off well. She had a hazy idea of how she wanted David to think about his family—literally, how he would imagine them when he might be walking across campus or sitting in his dorm room reading, with his feet propped on the window-sill. If he was pushing his tray through the cafeteria line and happened to let his mind drift and began to wonder what his family was doing, she wanted him to picture them on the wide screened porch among so many friends and excited small children.

To Dinah, the appearance of Moonflower—having become a conspiracy among them—was part and parcel of their undeclared conspiracy to live together as a family, to continue to love each other in spite of anything at all, to be bound, as families are, by an absolute and unbreachable loyalty. Before Toby's death, their association had merely been a condition of each one's life; now it was an unacknowledged decision. Sometimes it seemed to Dinah that her family was becoming a unit too fragilely joined, and she was overwhelmed with anxiety these days that they were about to break apart like Humpty Dumpty—never to be put together again.

These past few months had baffled and troubled her. Although she didn't expect the anguish of the loss of Toby ever to leave her, she had recovered from the initial preoccupation with the pure, terrible grief of it. These days, though, she often found herself flooded with shockingly intense sorrow and an unwarranted feeling of desolation and loneliness. Every aspect of life had become perilous to Dinah, and all she knew how to do was to hang on to her life exactly as it was, to let routine and necessity direct her days. And now she was especially anxious to give David a gift of this final ritual, to give him a perfect picture of his family that would be his defense against any feeling of isolation that might overcome him once he had departed a safe harbor.

The night before the party her restlessness had propelled her through the rooms of the house, as it often did, and finally outside, since it was warm, with the cats following her at a distance. The long yard was enclosed by tall cedar hedges, and Dinah often strolled across the grass in her nightgown, trailing silently along the narrow white ribbons of cat-worn paths crisscrossing the lawn or following the slate steps down to the garden.

She had passed at least two hours roving about the yard, pausing and musing, infused with and overstimulated by anticipation of the next day. She no longer battled the images that kept her awake—the detailing of party plans, mental lists of things to be done and the sequence in which she would do them. On any sleepless night she had learned that she had to wear out her own sensibilities; she had never managed to medicate or meditate them into submission. But last night at least she had managed, as she sometimes did, to trick herself by settling in an odd corner, where sleep had overtaken her absolutely. She had awakened abruptly at dawn, huddled into the wicker swing on the screened porch, cramped and chilled but pleased to have weaseled a bit of sleep out of the dark.

By ten-thirty in the morning Dinah had nearly finished preparing the garnishes for the cold supper she would serve buffet style that evening. While Sarah joined her in the kitchen to assemble the children's prizes, Dinah had frosted several branches of lemon leaves with egg white and kosher salt and left them to dry beside the frosted cherry tomatoes. She stuffed the hard-boiled eggs and refrigerated them under dampened paper towels and plastic wrap, and she did the same with the freshly sliced breads, alternating dark and light slices in shallow wicker baskets. The day before, she had spent almost eight hours cooking, which had made her sweaty and cross even in the mild heat, but now she was enjoying herself.

She stood at the sink looking out the window as she washed her hands and rinsed and dried the knives. David was in his garden, and she thought she would take a break and go chat with him for a few minutes. She could find out if he wanted to entertain the smaller children while the festivity was being arranged. She could simply join him in the beautiful day and gather the lettuces and basil and dill flowers and parsley she needed for the last-minute embellishment of the various platters filled with food.

She was delighted this morning at the sight of him glazed with pale sunlight that lit his blue shirt and his fair hair under the fragile-looking sky. She often joined David in the garden on summer afternoons when he got home from work; it seemed to her a sociable time without any need to make small talk. Usually she busied herself with weeding and didn't interfere with the design of the garden, although she was uneasy with the order her son had imposed on the little plot of land. He had planted not only the vegetables but the flowers, too, in militant rows according to species.

She put her basket down and smiled over at him. "Isn't it lucky that we've gotten such beautiful weather for tonight?" she said idly, but he didn't look up from his careful job of transplanting seedlings. "I don't know if you want to distract the children—you could play the guitar. You could do the songs. That always mesmerizes them. Especially if you let them try playing the guitar themselves. Or maybe you want to set up the prizes?"

David hated to have company when he was working in his garden, although he had never said so. He still didn't understand why anyone else's presence seemed to him such a profound intrusion. He knew his irritation was both unreasonable and ungenerous, but it didn't abate.

Dinah stooped and began to collect the various lettuces she would use for the salad. She looked over at him once more. "Is Christie coming tonight? She isn't working over the Fourth, is she?" Dinah considered Christie for a moment: she was a small, shy girl with whom Dinah found it difficult to have a conversation.

"Christie!" Dinah would say. "It's so nice of you to drop by. How are you?"

Christie would smile and duck her head of curly brown hair. "Fine," she would say, not meeting Dinah's eyes.

"Well, it's so cold out. Come on in!" And Christie would come in without a word.

"I'll see if David's upstairs. Did you want to see him?" And Christie would just smile and look at Dinah, with her soft brown eyes glancing up from beneath her bangs. She reminded Dinah of a cocker spaniel her family had inherited from neighbors who moved to England when she was a little girl. The dog had been sweet but disappointingly retiring, and Dinah's mother always suspected the poor animal had been traumatized by the two little boys of its former household. Perhaps Christie, too, had been somehow disturbed and wounded. It was impossible to dislike her, but privately Dinah found her tiresome.

"You'd think that simple curiosity would prompt her to ask just *one* question," she had said once to Martin as she sat drinking coffee after a dinner at which Christie had been a guest. "It seems to me that—at least after a while—any sort of intelligent person would be *interested* in other people. You know what I mean? I mean, it could be pretty basic stuff. 'How are you, Mrs. Howells? What do you think about the Brazilian rain forest? Eastern Europe? The depletion of the ozone layer? The stoplight they might put up on State Street?' You begin to wonder if she ever has a single thought! A pinpoint of curiosity! When I try to talk to her I feel as if I'm conducting an interrogation!" She was staring down at her coffee as she stirred it absently, but she had looked up to see David standing behind Martin in the kitchen doorway.

He had been so angry at his parents at that moment that it was reflected even in his stance, his shoulders tensed, his whole upper body seeming knotted, exactly as he had stood at age two before losing control and falling into an incoherent tantrum at being misunderstood or thwarted. But that night he had been alarmingly icy with unforgiveness. He had very calmly accused his parents of being nothing more than academic snobs, of knowing nothing of any real importance, of being incapable of understanding anything at all.

Dinah had apologized profusely, but ever since she had been so uneasy around Christie in David's presence, and so intent upon being fair and friendly, that her behavior had escalated into a kind of hysterical animation. Now she not only determinedly asked Christie all sorts of two- and three-part questions, but she answered them for her as well.

"Are you enjoying your part in the musical, Christie? Or do you find that it just takes up so much more time than you ever imagined? Is Mrs. Hartwick able to direct with the same *real* authority as Mr. Walters, or is it actually better to have someone a little less arrogant? Sometimes, he was really insufferable." Dinah's questions were always multiple choice, and her answers were equally frantic and complex.

"Of course," she would continue, after increasingly minimal pauses during which Christie would smile at her blankly, "anyone would enjoy performing if they had a voice like yours even if it does eat into your life. Not your *voice*! I mean, so much rehearsing leaves you almost no time for yourself. David says you've had to give up Saturday mornings and even the evenings. There's always *some* moment to be squeezed out of the day though, I suppose, to fit in what you absolutely have to get done. They say that it's the busiest people who always have a moment to spare. You're very organized, I imagine. I had forgotten that Mrs. Hartwick assisted in last year's production. She'll probably be fine!"

Whenever Dinah came to a full stop, Christie would sometimes smile and mutter an agreement, sometimes not. "Well!" Dinah would exclaim, with the air of a person who can scarcely bear to pull herself away, "I'd better get busy! I have a million things to do." And she would exit the room, exhausted.

In fact, she was rather hoping that Christie wouldn't be able to get off work for the evening. To Dinah's astonishment, Christie had gotten a much-coveted part-time job at the tourist information desk of the Freund Museum, a job usually staffed by teenagers, but one that was always advertised as requiring "interpersonal skills."

"Frankly," David said, while still transferring plants from small green containers to the darkly troweled earth, "I've always thought this whole party is a lot more trouble than it's worth. Christie said she would do the songs. I'm not crazy about having those kids fool with my guitar."

Dinah was surprised by David's bad mood; he had been so cheerful yesterday. "Well, sweetie, you could use your old one. Of course, I didn't mean you should let them handle the one you play." She heard her own voice wheedling in revolting supplication over the space between them. When he didn't respond, she was quiet. *She* had bought both guitars, the first one expensive, the price of the second one horrifying to think about even now. But they were gifts to him, she counseled herself; they were his own. "Anyway, I may need you to operate Moonflower's pulley," she said with an old note of authority. "Ellen called this morning with a terrible cold. I don't know if she and Vic are coming."

"Okay . . . Well . . . you takes what you can, and you deals with what you gets," he said, clearly mimicking someone clever, someone black, someone he admired, and someone she had never heard of.

She cast her eye over the rigorously organized rows of vegetables and flowers that defied inherent grace. She viewed it as a slight to any natural aesthetic sense. She didn't really like to give parties, she thought, and she only repeated this one summer after summer because she knew, even if they didn't, that it was a custom her children would miss. But she put the thought aside and tried to calculate how many heads of lettuce she would need, how much parsley; would there be enough dill flowers for decoration or should she not bother with them?

"You know," she said mildly, while she bent to unearth another head of curly Winter Density lettuce, "you didn't have to plant these flowers in *rows* like this, sweetie." It seemed to her a waste that David took such care with a garden that was not in itself very pretty at all. "But these carnations are lovely, aren't they?" He didn't answer because she wasn't asking a question as much as commenting to herself. "For years I wondered what the British meant—in all those books—always talking about 'pinks,' and I finally found out that they were just carnations. If I had only known sooner I would have called them pinks myself, and I would have liked them better. Like all those lime trees in Chekhov. Well, one of the Russians, anyway. Whenever I thought about limes I felt languorous . . . it probably isn't Chekhov. . . . But it was years before I ever saw any carnations *growing*! When they come from the florist they look as if someone has made them out of crepe paper. Really, I still hate them in arrangements. But big masses of them together . . . You've had good luck," she went on. "I'm awfully glad you're so interested in gardening."

She spoke to her son with such hearty encouragement that he was suddenly alert. He heard the false cheer that often obscured a dangerous edge, and he paused to glance at her where she bent to her chore with efficiency and a determined smile which she turned toward him. "This is so good for you, I think. Most people start a garden when they're already too old. It's always seemed to me that gardening is a hobby that should be for the young. It's such a good way to learn about life!" She was emphatic, her words tumbling into the day with blocklike certainty.

Dinah had no idea how she looked squatting on her haunches in the flowerbeds, with her hands slightly chapped and her clothes and hair in early-morning disarray. She used a trowel to dislodge a clump of bishop's-weed, and she tightened her lips in a little moue of concentration. She was pleased that she had managed not to betray her irritation at David, and she attacked the weeds with vigor, but David had stopped his work and turned to look at her when she spoke.

All at once she seemed monstrous to him. He was almost light-headed with sudden loathing as he watched her bend her head with the effort of prying loose the root system. She stood up slowly to stretch, grasping herself at the waist, elbows cocked at an angle to lean backward. Her mouth went round in an exaggerated exhalation, and she smiled toward him as though she were innocent. He could scarcely bear to continue looking at her.

In one moment she had destroyed the pleasure of his garden. He had planned it all so carefully during the last long months of high school, and over the past month it had begun to seem to him that the balance between the effort he made and the actual result was a perfect thing. Just as she was forming the words she had tossed out into the air, he had been wrestling with the notion—as he transplanted the stringy little seedlings—that he was at last getting a grip on something so much larger than his limited experience. Now he was abashed and infuriated. With one casual sentence his mother had made the need for *meaning* into a trivial thing that one merely cultivated on a sunny day.

He had pinned his hopes on the belief that, if he was careful with his garden, the nature of things would be made perfectly clear to him. He had his own idea of how to go about discovering how things really were. He was looking for the plan of things to become apparent. It was unbearable to him to think that his desire for understanding was commonplace, and that his mother—in all about her that suddenly struck him as simplistic—was an insensitive fool.

He was bereft as he looked at her with her sturdy smile and her graying-blond hair wisping free of the pins that held it back. How was it that he had never realized how oblivious she was to the consequences of what she said and did in the world? He turned his back on her and bent again to the tray of seedlings. He didn't trust himself to say another word; in fact, he felt alarmingly suspended between sorrow and rage.

For her part, as she made her way up the steps with her laden basket, Dinah was thinking how uncommunicative, how . . . cruel! . . . David was on this particular morning when she was going to so much trouble on his behalf and on Sarah's, too. It shocked her when one of her children was unkind. And she was frightened that over the past year David's newfound glibness and cynical humor—often amusing only by her sufferance, only if she agreed to be laughed *at* and not *with*—might be merely a veneer that covered some real dislike of her that she could not get at, that she could not fathom.

Franklin M. Mount
Dean of Freshmen
Harvard College
12 Truscott Street
Cambridge, Massachusetts 02138

Dear Mr. Mount,

Of course, I don't know how old you are, or whether or not you have children yourself. If you do then you'll understand that if you have a child of four who suddenly learns how to tie his or her shoelaces after weeks of frustrated attempts, then that child will be happy. (Although I do know that if you have a child of four, he or she probably has shoes with Velcro straps, but those were invented too late for my children. I'm simply trying to give you an example.) When your child is sick and running a fever you can give her Tylenol and spend time helping her connect a dot-to-dot picture, and she'll be pleased and comforted.

Well, I'm trying to explain that when I was the room mother for David's first grade class, and the door decoration I made won the West Bradford Public School's "Best Halloween Door Decoration Contest," it seemed to me that I had done all I could do to be sure David was content with his life. And after each birthday party, and every Christmas morning, every time he made up with a friend or had some small triumph of one kind or another—after every one of those instances and many others, David was happy. And I also knew, just in general, that he loved all the people in his life—his brother, his sister, his father, and me. But I may well have failed him, because it never crossed my mind, you see, to teach myself or to warn him that it might not always be so.

CHAPTER FOUR

MOONFLOWER

SHE WAS TOO DISTRACTED by the problem of David's strange mood to take much notice of the children's prizes Sarah had left spread over newspapers on the table to dry. Dinah made an effort to turn her mind to lists, to chores ahead of her in the day, and she filled the sink with tepid water and added a handful of salt, swirling it until all the crystals dissolved. The loose-leaved lettuces—Winter Density, Boston, romaine, and escarole—fanned out gently when she immersed them, heads down, sloshing them plungerlike so the water reached up into the curly, innermost leaves where the slugs recluded. She wished her thoughts would run through her mind in the same manner that a child runs a thumbnail along the keys of a piano so that each note sounds with equal resonance. She was weary of considering, weary of measuring all the tremors of her life in order to keep herself balanced in the aftershocks. Without thinking, Dinah brought one dripping hand from the water and brushed it across her cheekbone and through her hair, resting her temple in her palm for just a moment.

She stood splashing the greens about absentmindedly, gazing once again out the window at David, who was standing among his plants, his thumbs looped in the waistband of his jeans, his feet apart, almost in a caricature, Dinah thought, of the stance of a man who is master of all he surveys. She had a flash of memory of some movie from her youth—starring Troy Donahue or Gardner McCay—set in Hawaii. The hero standing just so, while behind him his whole sugar plantation is going up in flames, improbably unbeknownst to him. But the memory gave Dinah a little frisson of satisfaction.

She dried her hands and moved over to inspect all the trinkets and surprises that Sarah had so carefully embellished and spread out on the table to dry. But Dinah simply could not fend off a melancholy which was very much like the inevitable dolefulness that always accompanies a celebration of New Year's Eve. She had fallen absurdly into a mild state of mourning for this whole occasion that was yet to happen. She browsed over the table, picking up this item or that to inspect and admire, turning it to see how it refracted the light; but this morning the prizes no longer seemed inherently magical as they had in previous years.

This past Halloween Dinah had bought nine elaborate, shiny gold, sequined cardboard crowns at the drugstore. Sarah had used Elmer's Glue All to write each child's name on one of the crowns and then sprinkled red glitter over the tracery, carefully shaking off the excess into a paper bag. Now Dinah lifted each sequined, glittery crown to test it for dryness before she cautiously placed it in a carton along with the dozen artificial white doves that she had bought at the florist and that Sarah had also gilded with glitter so that they shimmered with gold. The tips of their fanned wings were burnished with metallic gold paint from a kit of children's art supplies that Sarah had unearthed in her closet. She had used a nearly exhausted set of acrylic paints and a tiny eyeliner brush to decorate matchbox cars from the supermarket with elaborate little scrolls and flourishes after she had sprayed them gold and let them dry overnight, and there was a tangle of gaudy but impressive dime store jewelry that Dinah had bought over the past year whenever she noticed a particularly remarkable piece at Newberry or Kmart.

Dinah sorted through the garish medallions, the brilliant beads, the rings and bracelets, and saw them as they really were. She could not remember now how those small children would perceive them—she had lost the feeling of fluttery anticipation that had kept her awake the night before. She knew she was reacting to David as if he had been the one to tell *her* that there was no Santa Claus, no Easter Bunny, no tooth fairy. She set the carton containing all the trinkets and decorations out in the garage where no wandering child would discover it by mistake, and she wondered if, indeed, she had become foolish even in the eyes of her guests. She wondered if David was right, if the whole party was viewed as too much bother and was tolerated only on her behalf.

But she continued to rehearse the rest of the day in her mind while she took a tomato from the basket she had brought up from the garden and rinsed it off under the tap. She was hungry, and she merely bent over the kitchen sink, where the lettuces still soaked, salting and eating the tomato out of hand. For a moment she gave up thinking about David; she gave up wondering what she had done that was not to be forgiven and gave herself over to sating her appetite. She was so involved in the pleasure of her lunch of that sun-warmed tomato that she didn't notice anyone at the door. When she looked up, a wistful-looking young woman was observing her carefully through the screen.

Tomato juice dripped down Dinah's chin and ran down her wrist beneath her watchband as she straightened from the sink in surprise, and she was at once embarrassed and irritated. A little girl who couldn't have been more than four sagged into the woman's side as though the two of them had been standing there for some time, and it occurred to Dinah with dread that they were probably Seventh-day Adventists. Weren't they always the ones who brought some child along with them? She thought so. She took her time rinsing her hands under the tap and drying them on a paper towel. She had given up random kindness over the past few years, and she frowned slightly as she went to the door.

"I'm sorry," she said, "but I have guests arriving this afternoon, and I really don't have time to talk with you now. Why don't you leave some literature for me? If I'm interested I'll send a donation."

The little girl didn't look at Dinah, but the woman smiled gently at her. Dinah was sure that smile bespoke persistence. "I ought to tell you," she continued more firmly, "that I'm really not interested in discussing my religious beliefs with you. To tell you the truth, I think any sort of proselytizing is a real intrusion on my privacy."

Dinah was becoming quite passionate, and she hadn't meant to give even that much emotion away to this woman. She was disappointed in herself; it was pointless ever to explain anything to these people. In one more minute, this woman would launch into her spiel, and Dinah would be forced either to stand there and hear her out or to shut the kitchen door in her face. That must be why they brought children with them, Dinah thought. It's hard to shut the door in a child's face, although not this particular child, perhaps, whose face was still half buried in her mother's skirt, but whose expression at the moment was unusually truculent.

"Dinah," the young woman said a little breathlessly,

"I'm Netta Breckenridge and this is my daughter, Anna Tyson."

"Oh . . . Of course!" Dinah said, realizing that she was supposed to know who these people were but having no memory of anyone having mentioned them to her. And she still wondered what they were doing at the door in the middle of this of all days. "I'm so sorry," she said as she unlatched and held open the screen. "We get all sorts of people . . . I thought that . . ."

"I guess we must be early," Netta said. She was a small woman, but she moved into the room with the kind of languid drift of someone much taller and longer-limbed. Her ankle-length skirt rippled with each step, her sleeves fluttered gently, and her daughter dragged like an anchor in her mother's wake as Netta crossed to the table and sat down. She settled slowly while all her clothes seemed to billow around her and finally come to rest. "Oh, I hope we're not the first to get here. Martin said the party started in the afternoon." While Anna Tyson tugged at her arm, Netta sighed and arranged her skirt around herself until at last she was comfortable. She leaned her elbow on the table and rested her chin in her hand while Anna Tyson sprawled halfway across her lap. Netta seemed perfectly at ease.

"Well . . . but it isn't even *noon*," Dinah said before she could stop herself, but she hadn't offended Netta, who turned a sweet smile on Dinah once again.

"Oh, yes. I understand," she said kindly, as if Dinah had confessed some failing of her own and was being pardoned for it. Netta's voice was dreamy and whispery, like a sleepy child's.

Dinah stood there stranded in the kitchen and studied Netta. She was one of those women who were considered attractive in academic circles. She had a thin, distracted look of disorganization, as though she had too many things on her mind. Her hair was light brown and cut short and had once been permed, but today it straggled around her face in a limp frizz, giving her a woebegone look. And just as Dinah had this uncharitable thought, Netta swept her hand through her hair, as though it were shoulder length, and shook her head backward in that characteristic gesture of women with very long hair who are settling it behind their shoulders.

"Do you have some chocolate milk by any chance?" Netta asked, with a glance down at her daughter. "There's so little she likes to eat, and I know chocolate milk isn't good for her. I mean, it's like a bribe. But she'll be so tired later if she doesn't have something now. I *do* make it with whole milk, though. I don't really believe it could possibly be healthy to deprive children of *every* sort of animal fat." And she shrugged elaborately in a conscious gesture of bewilderment. "But none of them agree. All those experts. I've learned to trust my own judgment, pretty much."

Dinah looked at Netta more closely. With her down-slanted pale eyes and too long, pointed face, she was almost elfin. We don't have chocolate milk," Dinah said apologetically in spite of herself, "but we have just plain milk." She paused for a moment. "Oh, but it's low-fat, I'm afraid."

"Well . . ." Netta drew this word out a bit so that it encompassed a tiny sigh of disappointment, "if you have cocoa powder or baking chocolate and sugar I can make her some chocolate milk. It's the only thing she'll accept in the middle of the day."

"I'm not sure. . . ." Dinah was nonplussed, and she turned to the sink and began lifting the lettuce, head by head, and setting it to drain in a huge colander, leaving behind brackish, gritty water floating with tiny insects and several curled slugs. She opened the drain and made sure that the water was emptying before she looked back at Netta.

"I don't know. I'll have to look." As she began searching the cupboards, Duchess came rushing up the back steps, back from her walk, whimpering gutturally and wagging all over, as though she had been abandoned for days and had finally found her home again. Martin always let her off her leash when he reached the corner of the yard, and she made a dash for the door while he followed more sedately. Dinah was relieved. Martin would know how to dislodge this woman from the kitchen table and get her to go home.

By now, Netta and Anna Tyson had established a kind of determinedly huddled, martyred presence at the corner of the table—like refugees—and Duchess was busily greeting them with enthusiasm. Martin didn't even notice them right away, though, when he came into the room.

"I'll go on and get the ice," he said, "and if there's anything else we need just write it down." He coiled Duchess's leash and dropped it into the basket on the windowsill, and then he saw Netta, still resting her chin dreamily in the palm of her hand while Anna Tyson moved in even closer to avoid Duchess.

"Oh, Netta! You didn't have any trouble finding the house?" As he moved toward the table, she straightened up and smiled and extended her hand. Martin was oddly awkward all at once, Dinah thought. He took Netta's hand in a regular handshake and then covered it with his other hand in a sort of avuncular pat. His shoulders hunched forward in a protective manner that Dinah had never seen before, although Netta was so small that Dinah imagined Martin felt as outsized as she did. Netta's minimal presence made one want to take up less space in the room.

He turned to Dinah. "So you've met Netta? And Anna Tyson? Anna Tyson is four years old, and I've told her all about Moonflower. Netta's a visitor this year in the Philosophy Department. She's a Fennel Doyle Scholar. We're publishing one of her articles in *The Review*."

"Oh ... that's wonderful!" Dinah said. "Yes, we've met." She smiled fiercely at Martin, who looked pleased with himself. "And they can stay for the party this evening?" Dinah asked in as neutral a voice as she could muster.

"Absolutely!" Martin said. "Everyone should have one visit with Moonflower." Meanwhile, Anna Tyson had flipped over against her mother's knees and was arching backward across Netta's lap, staring blankly back at Martin.

"Well, I'm not sure how late we can stay," Netta said, lifting her hand in a slight gesture of demurral, but Dinah interrupted her.

"It'll be just wonderful for Anna Tyson," Dinah said with the same note of cheer that had alerted David earlier in the morning to his mother's mood. "In fact, Martin, Anna Tyson needs some chocolate milk. It's the only thing she'll have for lunch, but we don't have any. Netta offered to make it out of baking chocolate. I'm in such a rush, why don't I let you help her. There's bound to be some somewhere in the cupboards."

Dinah dropped the uneaten half of her tomato into the garbage disposal and turned it on under rushing water and said loudly over the noise it made, "You'll need sugar and vanilla. We probably have some vanilla, but I don't have any idea where. I *never* bake," she confessed to Netta, with dissembling warmth. "It might be with the spices. And you'll need the double boiler. It's behind the big skillets in the corner cupboard next to the stove. I think I'll go up and shower and get dressed, since I don't know if Ellen is going to get here or not, and I may have a lot to do. But before you go out for ice, please check with me in case I remember anything else I forgot to buy. We might need more white wine. It's on the counter. See what you think!" And with a brilliant smile at them all, she walked out of the room through the swinging door, while the disposal still churned loudly under the running faucet.

Upstairs Dinah waited tactfully outside Sarah's door while her daughter ended a somber and murmured conversation on the phone. After she had hung up, Dinah entreated her to make some sort of crown for Anna Tyson.

"Oh, great!" Sarah said. "With what?"

"Just use poster board and aluminum foil. Anything. Lots of glitter. The prizes are wonderful, Sarah. They're so *intricate*! You're really gifted at that sort of thing, sweetie. . . ," but Sarah shot her a baleful look, and Dinah let the enthusiasm drop out of her voice. "Sarah. Just get it done! *Before* your friends come over! This whole fucking day is falling apart," she said in an exasperated undertone, feeling her control begin to unravel as she turned away from her daughter. "And be *sure* to put her name on it!" She was halfway down the hall toward the bathroom before Sarah said a word.

"God, Mom! She can't *read*!" But Sarah only muttered her reply, and Dinah felt a momentary relief at her own tiny rebellion. The use of the brutal, short, now meaningless obscenities or vulgarities that her younger friends or her East or West Coast friends and her own children tossed into the air without a thought gave her enormous satisfaction. Dinah had absorbed bits and pieces of her mother's upper-middle-class Southern upbringing and her father's snobbish aversion even to slang, so when she spoke any of those words—fuck, shit, crap—they made a surprising chunk in the rhythm of her sentence. She flung them out into a room with relish—she enjoyed the explosion, the furious crunch and hiss of their sound, the surprising release of tension to be had from their utterance.

And anyone listening paid attention and was distressed, even her own children, and especially Martin. "That sounds so ugly when you say it," he had said to her once in the midst of some outburst of hers.

"Oh, *please*! Men use language like that all the time. For God's sake, most of our friends use much more graphic language than I ever do. Why doesn't that bother you?" she asked.

"They don't. Not when they're mad. I don't know why it bothers me, but it just does. It bothers me when anyone loses control like that. It's really unpleasant. The children hate it. They leave the room. I don't think you have any idea how you sound."

She had silently granted him that—it was language she, too, was unnerved to hear when it was used in anger. She had been slightly abashed; she was sorry to some degree, but not entirely. "Well," she said, before realizing that what she was about to tell him was something she had thought for quite a while. She turned slightly away from him so that he wouldn't see the censure on her face. "The thing is, Martin, that you don't *need* it! You've never had a proper sense of outrage."

Gradually, of course, Martin had picked it up, too. If he stubbed his toe, or the hot water ran out in the middle of a shower, or Duchess slipped her collar and went streaking off across the fields. "God-damned-mother-fucking-son-of-a-bitch!" he would mutter to himself, but within earshot. And when Dinah heard him, or on that rare occasion when she was struck by her own words, she did recognize that in theory they had slipped just a notch lower in her private measure of their effort to hang on to all that was civilized. In the abstract she was disappointed in herself, but in practice she never regretted her words for a moment.

She left Sarah to deal with the extra crown, and she spent far more time than usual soaking in the bathtub before carefully putting on eyeshadow and mascara and polishing her fingernails and toenails with some of Sarah's nail polish, which she had always considered a bit tacky in any shade. This color was brilliant; it was labeled British Red.

When Martin rapped lightly to ask what else he should get besides ice, she kept her voice neutral and was glad to have the door between them. She knew the puzzled look of apology that would cross his face if she confronted him with his unmentioned invitation to an extra child to this carefully planned party.

She put on low-heeled sandals and a deep blue muslin sundress that Vic and Ellen had brought her from Mexico. It had a scooped neck, short, pleated sleeves, and the bodice was fitted just below her breasts. The skirt, cut on the bias, fell narrowly past her waist to flare extravagantly around her calves, and the hem and bodice and sleeves were embroidered elaborately with intricate pale blue, coral, and metallic gold and silver flowers and birds. Dinah rarely wore the dress because she didn't trust the dry cleaner not to destroy it. But today she hoped it would make her feel festive.

She walked through the rooms, seeing to one thing and another. Vic and Ellen had arrived after all; and while Ellen had disappeared upstairs to arrange Moonflower, everyone else had congregated on the screened porch off the kitchen. Christie and David were doing a rough run-through of some of the children's songs, and Anna Tyson was stretched out asleep in the wicker swing with her head in Netta's lap. Netta, so small, gently swayed back and forth, the very tips of her toes barely brushing the floor. As the swing moved backward, she swung her feet beneath it just as a child would do. While Vic and Martin were sitting and chatting with her, Dinah found the chocolate-streaked double boiler pan and a smaller pan scummed with scalded milk left to soak in the kitchen sink.

As she scrubbed at the milk with steel wool, she realized that she could hear David and Christie quite clearly through some trick of acoustics—they were all the way across the long kitchen and outside the window, but their voices were low and tense and embarrassingly audible. "Oh, Jesus, Christie! It's impossible . . . I'm *not* mad, but I'm *sick* of you asking me about it. . . ."

Dinah flinched at the lack of charity in David's voice, but she was curious in spite of herself and froze there at the sink to find out whatever it was that Christie could be asking him. She felt mildly relieved that she was not the only one from whom David withheld information. But before anything else was said, David got up and moved away to sit with the group at the far end of the porch, and Christie stayed where she was, trying out chords on the guitar. Dinah began to take things out of the refrigerator to let them come to room temperature.

She had made potato salad the way it used to be made before potatoes became chic—with sweet pickle and onion and green olives; and she had blanched and marinated an assortment of vegetables—green beans, carrots, cauliflower, mushrooms, zucchini, broccoli. She had roasted a turkey and glazed a ham the day before, and Martin had grilled a beautiful London broil. The menu for this party never varied, and Dinah had the timing down to a science. It was plain fare that children would eat without being squeamish and that adults would enjoy. The meats were sliced, the eggs boiled and stuffed, the garnishes assembled, and she was arranging trays of vegetables when she realized that Christie had moved down to the other end of the porch, too, and now Dinah could hear the general conversation, with Netta's soft voice rising and falling as the primary note in the flow of sound.

Ellen joined Dinah just then in the kitchen. "I've got the pulley working fine, I think, although Moonflower's a little the worse for wear." She washed her hands at the sink.

"I don't suppose anyone will notice, though, but I think we'd better use the spider tonight. I restrung the wire with a nylon fishing line, and it should show *less*, but it could be that light will reflect off it, or something." When Dinah didn't make a sound, Ellen realized that she hadn't heard anything she had said.

Even though it was soft, Netta's voice had the quality of carrying, with a syllable here or there flashing out in absolute clarity as though her confidences were like the metallic threads in Dinah's skirt, illuminated randomly by any light. "Oh, I haven't really minded. I know how *threatening* stray people can be. But I guess I was surprised. Oh, yes . . ." The pattern of her speech was compelling in its lilt and in its gentle, prolonged sibilances, almost a lisp. "I really was." Her words were followed by a long silence that had the quality of a breath caught, a hint of suspense in the air. "I don't suppose I really did expect . . ." Netta's voice trailed off into a pale note of wonder. ". . . well, you don't expect jealousy these days . . . you really don't. What I'd gotten used to at Harvard was a kind of cooperative misery." She gave a pensive, deprecating little laugh. "Or elation. Oh, but never the sort of . . . well . . . *envy*. From other women. It gets very lonely, you know." Her tone was that of resignation, not anger. Resignation with a trace of perplexity. Once more there was a hush in the conversation. Dinah and Ellen exchanged a glance, and Ellen headed for the porch, rubbing her still damp hands together.

In spite of the lurking cat, Taffy, who never hesitated to investigate the counters, Dinah left the tray she was arranging uncovered and escaped into the living room, from which she removed any fragile objects that might be in reach of small children. But everywhere Dinah went in her own house, as she arranged flowers in a vase or moved through a room to put out bowls of nuts and olives, straightening this or that, she felt she was intruding. Sarah's friends had arrived and the three girls had taken over the dining room. Although they were friendly and offered help, their conversation came to a stop whenever Dinah passed through. The house was blossoming with intimate conversations, furtive discussions, muted confessions.

Just before four o'clock, when people would begin to arrive, Dinah returned to the kitchen to make the final preparations and discovered Netta there once again. She had hoisted Anna Tyson up on the countertop next to the sink and was gently swabbing her daughter's sleep-swollen face with a dampened towel. As Dinah leaned against the counter and watched Netta and her daughter, she felt a lessening of the tension she had experienced all day.

She could hear Vic and Martin still chatting on the porch. ". . . a *luminosity* to her intelligence. Don't you think so?" Vic was saying. Dinah could hear Christie in the living room trying to persuade David to do the spider song. ". . . but you know they'll all get silly if I do it. Especially the little boys. It won't kill you, David." And she could hear Sarah's stereo from upstairs, where she and her friends had retreated. This one moment of peace in the kitchen was soothing.

Anna Tyson turned her head away from her mother's hand and stared at Dinah in that belligerent state of sudden wakefulness that small children sometimes experience. "Why are you wearing those shoes with your toes showing?" she asked sulkily in Dinah's direction, and Dinah just smiled back at her, not answering, but reminded of how cranky her own children had always been—and sometimes still were—in the moments before they had to give up wakefulness or just after they had come out of sleep. She felt indulgent and fond of Anna Tyson, whose face was still flushed and blotchy from her nap, and who resisted her mother's ministrations so vigorously that

Netta finally lifted her down to the floor. Netta leaned over the sink and cupped water in her palms and splashed her own face while Anna Tyson approached Dinah.

Anna Tyson stood with her hands at her sides, her mouth a disapproving line tucked in at the corners. "My mother says I can't wear anything shiny." She was looking at Dinah's dress.

"My mother says the same thing," Dinah said lightly, with a little laugh so that Netta would realize that she wasn't insulted by Anna Tyson's rudeness. But Netta didn't appear to notice. Anna Tyson silently studied Dinah, as though she had encountered another species.

"You painted your toenails red, didn't you? Why did you do that?"

Dinah was feeling far less fond of Anna Tyson by now, and she was at a loss to find a diplomatic way to respond. She looked to Netta for assistance, for a word to ward off her own daughter, but Netta was merely watching them while she gently patted her own face dry with a dish towel. Finally, though, she dampened the towel again under the faucet and stooped down to Anna Tyson's level, and Dinah didn't want to hear the little girl chastised; Dinah was anxious to deflect Netta's attention from anything Anna Tyson had said.

"You know," Dinah said conversationally, as though she hadn't paid any attention to Anna Tyson's behavior, "Anna Tyson's really a lovely-looking little girl." Dinah said this in a manner of reassurance, because she really thought that Anna Tyson was one of those children who just look like anyone; there was nothing arresting about her, she wasn't lovely or unlovely. But Netta's face registered a discernible reaction for the first time, and it was disapproval.

She rose, carefully refolding the damp towel and aligning it neatly along the edge of the sink. No one spoke

at all while Netta observed the precision of her own movements. With apparent reluctance she faced Dinah, speaking
slowly and with great patience. "You know, I'm sure you
would never have made that remark if Anna Tyson were a
boy. I know you meant it as a compliment. People always
do. But don't you see how it focuses Anna Tyson's attention
on all the wrong assets? I'm sorry, but I really find unconsciously sexist remarks more and more intolerable. I know
you meant it kindly, but I don't want Anna Tyson to define
herself by how she looks."

Dinah was so astounded she couldn't speak. As she
stood in the kitchen reviewing exactly what Netta had just
said in her careful and deliberate speech, it crossed Dinah's
mind that Netta had the same personality as the spell-
checker on Martin's computer. The spell-checker made no
allowances, had no sense of humor, no knowledge of context, no social radar. Dinah found that her usual impulse to
save people from themselves—to save them from knowing
what fools they have made of themselves—had entirely de-
serted her. She didn't feign agreement, she didn't gently
reinterpret Netta's words for her so that later Netta would
believe that she had made her point tactfully or even politely. Dinah simply turned away and went out to the porch
to wait for the guests to arrive.

David watched as Dinah drifted through the rooms,
collecting the children while the party went on around her.
She stopped and smiled and greeted people here and there.
And David had no memory of ever perceiving her as foolish
or threatening. He admired the way she bent down to this
child or that, never altering her voice the way many adults
do when they speak to children.

"You'd better come with me out to the porch so you
can practice the Moonflower song. You know about Moonflower, don't you?" And the child would shake his or her
head solemnly—even suspiciously, the older ones.

86

"Ah, well . . ." and she would take the child's hand and explain as she led the little girl or boy out to the porch, where Christie was already going over and over the songs with the other children assembled there.

"I haven't seen Moonflower in . . . oh, an awfully long time," David heard Dinah confess wistfully to a little boy who was trailing along beside her with some reluctance, "because she's not a bit interested in grown-ups. She thinks they're too judgmental, you know," she added conversationally. Although the little boy, who was probably no more than four years old, had no idea what that could mean, he nodded in agreement.

"She might not come, of course," Dinah added matter-of-factly. "She's very moody. I just hope that no one hurts her feelings. But *sometimes*! Well, sometimes she does appear at this time of year, just when the light is fading. We can hope. . . . She's very shy, though, you know." And she looked down at the child to whom she was talking, and he nodded mutely, understanding Moonflower's reluctance perfectly as he was being led through this house that was not his own by this tall woman. But slowly he gave up his disbelief in the face of Dinah's skepticism.

"The thing is, it's so frustrating!" Dinah said a trifle petulantly. "Sometimes she just sulks and *won't* show up and do her beautiful dance. She's *so* vain!" Dinah was clearly scornful, and she added softly, "I really don't approve of her very much, because it's not as if she *does* anything helpful. She's a . . . oh . . . a *common* sort of fairy. Except, of course, that she's so beautiful, and her dance is so pretty. We can try to flatter her enough to bring her out of the trees, but I just don't know if she'll show up."

"I know she'll come!" the little boy said suddenly, practically shouting at Dinah with conviction.

David was talking with Netta and Anna Tyson when Dinah approached, and Anna Tyson eyed her doubtfully. Dinah bore her no goodwill at all, and she only asked if she wanted to join the other children out on the porch, and Anna Tyson shook her head. "Okay. That's fine, but you're welcome to change your mind," Dinah said and moved past her to speak to a little girl nearby.

David gave his mother an odd look, but she was so irritated at him for standing there drinking wine and talking to Netta while Christie dealt with all those children by herself, that she simply looked back at him blankly. Besides, she had caught snatches of David and Netta's conversation as she passed by them to greet other guests, and she didn't want to stay in the vicinity. ". . . because our sex life was fine until I got pregnant. I mean, we had Anna Tyson . . ." and Netta gestured slightly to indicate her daughter, stolidly present beside her and listening carefully to every word.

". . . and he could only have sex with my closest friend. She lived with us to take care of Anna Tyson, and . . ." Dinah glanced at David's face and saw that his expression was exactly like that of the small children to whom she spoke of Moonflower. ". . . you know, when I first met him I was repulsed and attracted—all at once, all at the same time—by his . . . oh . . . almost a feminine sensibility. So, of course, until I *realized* I just thought he might be bisexual, but it was just that Celia was right there. . . ." The children always pretended that they already knew all about Moonflower; they pretended that it was nothing out of the ordinary, their faces carefully unperturbed, just like David's as Netta leaned toward him. "I think that in his mind she became me, you see. It was just that *responsibility* made him impotent." Netta was speaking earnestly, and with that repeated gesture of flicking her hair back and shaking it to settle behind her shoulders, although her hair only reached the nape of her neck. Oddly enough, that gesture, more than Netta's words, grated on Dinah's nerves, and she led the last stray child away to the porch, leaving Anna Tyson behind.

The light had faded beyond the softly lit rooms, and the adults refilled their drinks and began to make their way to the porch as well. David joined Christie and took up his guitar. The children quieted down at once, and after a few trial runs, and under the weight of his stern expectation, they sang along with him:

> The itsy bitsy spider
> Climbed up the water spout.
> Down came the rain
> And washed the spider out.

> Out came the sun
> And dried up all the rain.
> The itsy bitsy spider
> Climbed up the pipe again.

When the luminous blue spider dropped down over the roof of the porch, floating and bobbing in midair, the children shrieked with combined excitement and terror. Dinah gave Vic an imperceptible nod, and he disappeared from his post at the door to tell Ellen that none of the spider's wires could be discerned in the dusk.

"No, no," Dinah said, and she moved among the excited children, bending down to explain. "*That's* not Moonflower! She's just waiting to see if it's safe. And, of course, I've told you how vain she is. She wants to hear you sing a song. She thinks she's much better than that spider. He has to spin a web to come to earth, you see. Why, Moonflower . . . well, she can *fly*. You've got to sing another song for her, though! Whenever she's not sure if she'll come or not, she sends down her friend the spider. He checks to see that everything's safe. But, really! You've all got to sing!"

Long ago, in Sheridan, Mississippi, when Martin's great-aunt had brought the magical apparition to earth on one of the evenings of summer when the moonflower vine bloomed on her veranda, he remembered that he and his cousins had been instructed to sing "Jesus Wants Me for a Sunbeam." But Dinah and Ellen had secularized it, substituting a Peter, Paul, and Mary song that both the children and the adults would know.

David changed chords and began singing harmony to Christie's purer contralto.

> Puff the magic dragon
> Lived by the sea
> And frolicked in the autumn mist
> In a land called Honah Lee.

The children were hesitant to join in, and David, with feigned exasperation, exhorted them to sing. "Okay. Okay, you guys! Mark, I can see you're not singing, and I'll tell you . . . Moonflower's not coming if she doesn't think everybody *wants* her." And the children did finally begin to sing the refrain. They were familiar with the song from kindergarten and day care and tapes and videos their parents bought for them, although only the older ones knew the verses.

At last a shimmering golden shape, doll-sized and lighted from within, and with clearly discernible, pale, moving wings, made its appearance just over the edge of the porch roof. The children rushed forward and pressed themselves against the screen in an effort to see better. David and Christie continued to sing.

> Oh!
> Puff the magic dragon
> Lived by the sea
> And frolicked in the autumn mist
> In a land called Honah Lee.

Little Jackie Paper
Loved that rascal Puff
And brought him string and sealing wax
And other fancy stuff.

"You've got to keep singing," Dinah said softly, ush-
ering the children back from the edge of the porch, back
into their little cluster around David and Christie. "I think
she's going to dance for you," Dinah whispered urgently,
"as long as you keep singing for her. Isn't she beautiful?
She's so beautiful! Please sing for her!" And she turned to
the parents, who were standing back against the wall, looking on indulgently. "Everyone has to sing, now! All of you
sing along!" And each year the parents did sing along, and
each year they were momentarily taken aback by the pure
delight on Dinah's face.

Oh!
Puff the magic dragon
Lived by the sea
And frolicked in the autumn mist
In a land called Honah Lee.

Together they would travel
On a boat with billowed sail
Jackie kept a lookout perched
On Puff's gigantic tail

Moonflower spun and twirled up and down the length
of the porch, halting hummingbird-like with her translu-
cent wings beating, and then darting away while the group
on the porch repeated the refrain over and over. One little
boy could not contain himself, and he rushed to press his
face against the screened wall. His father came forward and
picked him up and let him straddle his shoulders, while

they all sang on. For a moment there were only David's and Christie's voices in fairly complicated harmony through one more stanza.

> Noble kings and princes
> Would bow when e'er they came
> Pirate ships would lower their flags
> When Puff roared out his name.

> Oh!
> Puff the magic dragon
> Lived by the sea
> And frolicked in the autumn mist
> In a land called Honah Lee.

Christie and David leaned together, their voices intensifying. Attractive and self-absorbed, they sat at the center of things, observed by everyone, emanating a kind of oblivious, youthful sexuality the parents had long ago passed through and the children, of course, had not yet reached. The two of them had become so involved in singing the song, involved in the satisfying combination of their voices, that the music reverberated in the soft air. The whole assembly felt a need to join them, and everyone sang the final chorus without a trace of reluctance.

> Oh!
> Puff the magic dragon
> Lived by the sea
> And frolicked in the autumn mist
> In a land called Honah Lee.

David struck several chords to end the song, and the children sagged against each other or their parents, exhausted.

"What's that?" said Dinah. "Oh, no! Look outside! Has Moonflower fallen? I see something glittering on the ground. I hope she didn't make herself too weak to fly! She did such a long dance, tonight! Someone go see!"

It was almost entirely dark, and as soon as the singing stopped, Vic had turned on the floodlights mounted on the roof to illuminate the backyard. The children pushed each other in their haste to get through the porch door. Right outside the steps they came upon a wide trail of silver glitter, and they stopped en masse, looking back to the lighted porch, uncertain what they should do.

Dinah joined them and bent to peer at the ground where they pointed. "I think it's a trail! I think Moon-flower must have left a trail for you. See if you can follow it to the end and maybe you'll find out where Moonflower comes from. No one knows. See if you can find her!" And the children dashed off, following the trail of glitter around the corner behind the house, until they reached the lilac bush that was strung with white lights and wound all around with garlands of gold braid and tied up with the golden crowns, the burnished doves, the bracelets and necklaces, and the tiny gilded cars. The children were stunned with excitement and exhaustion and sudden greed, and Dinah wandered back to the porch while they fell into squabbles about this or that prize. Greed among the children of other people didn't bother her at all, and she left it for them to sort out, knowing that each child would get something.

The parents watched in high spirits, too, enjoying having their children be so entertained. As the children began to make their way back to the porch, wearing a crown and beads or bracelets, David sat down on the bench next to Netta, who was leaning her head against the wall, looking out from under her brows at the whole event, which was winding down. The children's voices were less high-pitched, their movements less frantic.

Anna Tyson had been drawn into the singing circle of

children in spite of herself and was still out in the yard with some of the others. Netta was frowning slightly.

She turned her head against the clapboards to look at David. "I really didn't want Anna Tyson to get involved in this," she said, as matter-of-factly as if they had been in the middle of a conversation, but loudly enough so that Dinah heard her at the other end of the porch, where she was moving back and forth collecting glasses and paper plates.

"I meant to take Anna Tyson home before this all started, but I didn't want to get up in the middle of the singing and disturb everybody. But I mean, we don't do Santa Claus or any of that." She paused for a moment, considering. "Really, don't you think it's cruel in a way? I think it's wrong to lie to children, don't you? But Anna Tyson was really enchanted. I could tell. Now I don't know what to do when she talks about it. I'd be lying to her, wouldn't I, if I let her believe in all this when it's really just one more of those insidious ways that adults lie to children. Don't you think so?"

Netta didn't sound angry, only genuinely anxious for David's opinion. "It's bad enough just living in a town like this," she said with some scorn, "where kids are bound to believe that people are safe, that there aren't people dying on the streets, that there's no hunger in the world, no real poverty! Anna Tyson's whole life here is really a lie anyway, isn't it? And this sort of . . . *fantasy* . . . it's worse, because it's a calculated lie." She stopped again and peered at David intensely. "I don't mean that I think Dinah and Martin *intend* harm," she assured him and then drifted off into her own thoughts for a moment. "But you know, morally I think that may even make it a greater deceit, don't you?"

"I don't know. Yeah. I guess it's a lie. I don't know," David said, his voice bemused; he had never thought of this as any kind of deceit. "Actually, this is one of the best memories I have of my childhood." He spoke with a slight note of apology. "It was just for us, you see. Not like Santa Claus. And my mother always seemed amazed every time Moon-flower appeared. Her act was skepticism, so we had to convince her."

As David grew quiet, he was filled with affection for everyone in sight. Netta was so exotic to him that he hadn't paid much attention to what she was saying; he had merely been interested in the fact of her passionate ideas and her uncommon frankness. But at the other end of the porch, his mother was finally, in this day, enormously pleased to have been championed by her son.

CHAPTER FIVE

THE SUMMER HOUSE

EVERY YEAR WHEN THE college and the public schools released their faculty and students in early June, Dinah's house began to fill with people who came and went at all hours: her children's friends, various contributors to *The Review,* Martin's ex-students who wandered back into town with spouses or new children. The Hofstatters often dropped by, together or singly, as did other friends, neighbors, and assorted acquaintances. Any day of the summer Dinah might find herself drinking midmorning coffee with David's former best friend from eighth grade, who was only an amiable acquaintance of David's now, but had attached himself to the household in general.

Each summer teenagers who had first witnessed Moonflower on a long-past Fourth of July would drop by. They felt a special association with Dinah in the magical conspiracy she had engineered against their younger selves. And even outside her own house, anywhere within the town, they often confided in her. She ran into them at the grocery store or at the college pool. They told her about the repression of their own households, their foolish parents, their secret lives.

And yet, every summer Dinah was surprised when she wandered through her rooms and found them occupied, or when she was hurrying to get errands done and was helping the check-out girl bag the groceries and was suddenly involved in an intimate conversation about the girl's college choices, love life.

When she was pondering the cheese selection at The Whole Grain Elevator—a store displaced from the seventies—she found herself commiserating with a long-ago Moonflower devotee who didn't know how to tell her parents that both she and the boy they thought was her lover only had in common the fact that they were each involved with the same woman at their college. "Kate cares about us both, but sexually she's still ambivalent. . . . God," the girl said, "I really, really wish I were just one bit ambivalent!" She paused after drawing the wire cheese cutter through the cheddar Dinah had chosen. "It would be easier to be in love with Tim. And you know what? He's a much nicer person than Kate." She wrapped the cheese in brown paper and began tying it with twine. "But one of us is going to end up so unhappy." She handed Dinah the cheese and took payment for it, and Dinah left the store feeling sympathy for her, although Dinah had scarcely been able to place her and, at first, hadn't remembered her last name.

Dinah wasn't aware of encouraging or discouraging anyone who chose to confide in her. In fact, she didn't know such random intimacy was uncommon, but it was Dinah's instinct to ease any other person's anxiety in a conversation. Perhaps it was only cowardice masquerading as courtesy, because after cocktail parties or college functions she was often filled with self-loathing as she re-imagined her smiling, acquiescent self listening with apparent fascination to some fool pontificating about one thing or another. And she always despaired of herself when she realized that she had once again probably overwhelmed Christie with aggressive amiability in a desperate effort not to appear judgmental.

But her courtesy was a habit she could not break. Invariably, she inclined her head forward and raised her eyebrows in an expression of anticipation at whatever information or opinion was being divulged to her in any conversation. People were shockingly forthcoming now and then. It never occurred to her that they didn't speak this way to everyone.

She was surprised and discomfited every summer by her lack of privacy, but her restiveness in the warm weather merely became part of her own climate, part of her daily life, just as the animals were who moved with her from place to place, in and out of doors. When friends of hers or acquaintances of her children dropped by to chat with her, she treated them as visitors; she didn't understand that her house had become a haven to other people's children.

And the morning after Moonflower's visit, it became a haven for Netta, too, and her daughter Anna Tyson. Netta phoned at eight in the morning and spoke to Martin, who answered the phone out of a sound sleep, but the call also woke Dinah, who listened to his side of the conversation with mounting exasperation.

"What would you have said?" Martin asked in his own defense. "She started crying, for God's sake, and I was hardly awake. She said she's been up all night. You wouldn't have told her no." Martin was as irritated as Dinah, who had gathered that Netta had invited herself over for dinner.

"I'm exhausted, Martin! I've been up all night myself. I couldn't get to sleep until almost five-thirty, and I'm just exhausted. I really don't want any company." He turned his back to her and sank his head deeply into his pillow to shut out the light filtering into the room. He pulled the sheet up to the tip of his nose.

"I would have thought of some excuse," Dinah continued. She had turned to lie on her back, wide awake now. "I would have told her we were going out or something."

"She said she couldn't stand to be so lonely after being with people last night. For God's sake, Dinah! She's had an awful time, and she's going to bring a special dish for dinner, she said. She just wants to join us for leftovers. I'm no good on the phone. You know that. I'm not good at lying." Martin's words were muffled by his pillow and by the sleep that he was allowing to overtake him.

"Oh, God! Just because you don't tell the truth doesn't mean you'd be *lying,* Martin!" She believed this absolutely. "To protect yourself without hurting someone's feelings! That's called avoiding unpleasantness." She didn't expect a reaction, because she knew that Martin had sunk deeply into sleep again. For years she had suffered in restless aggravation while Martin turned his head to one side and slept, even in planes and trains and waiting rooms, and often in the midst of appalling circumstances. She had been in love with Martin, and now she loved him in a way that was simply a condition of her life, but there had been times when she had looked over at his sleeping face, loose in repose, his mouth slightly open, the muscles around his eyes and along his chin gone slack, and wondered if she *liked* him at all. Her own ideas or worries—thrilling or sorrowful, grave or frivolous—rarely relinquished their grip on her consciousness and never in any public place. Dinah thought of the sleep she got as coming to her in dribs and drabs, and not necessarily when she needed it.

Just as Martin and Dinah were clearing up after a late breakfast Netta arrived as she had the previous day, before lunch, and with Anna Tyson at her side. But she had brought a contribution, and she was agitated and pleased with the idea she had. "I thought that a really wonderful summer soup would be just right to go with sandwiches! You had so much ham and turkey left over last night. Oh, this is a wonderful soup. Bill and I used to spend Sunday mornings reading the *Times* and clipping recipes. . . ."

Her animation dimmed as she put down her two grocery bags. Her expression became somber as she unpacked ingredients: a plastic produce bag of three oranges and another one with several rubber-banded bunches of green onions, whipping cream, a quart of chocolate milk, and a medium-sized, rumpled paper bag, from which emerged masses of long, broad, muddy, red-veined leaves that shed droplets of brownish water all over the white counter and the cutting board next to the sink.

She turned to Dinah and held out her empty hands, as though to illustrate something. "Oh, God! It was all *planning,*" she said, and her eyes filled with tears. Anna Tyson was hanging on to her skirt, and Netta urged her along to the table and settled herself in the same spot she had occupied yesterday. She lifted Anna Tyson into the chair beside her own and appealed again to Dinah. "The only time I made this soup no one ever ate it. Anna Tyson ate some," she amended, with a little more control, her voice less tremulous. She leaned back in her chair and gazed at the table a moment, collecting her thoughts. "We had planned to eat it, and Celia was going to make dark bread. I don't know what happened. You know, that's what I can't ever understand. I just don't know what happened. I've always thought that people are fated to meet each other."

She held her hand up to stop any possible misinterpretation. "I don't mean anything mysterious when I say that. Well, I do believe in a kind of *particular* ESP, you know. A sort of instinctive selection. I met Bill because I had checked a book that he needed out of the library, and I'd forgotten all about it, so it had been out a long time. He came and *found* me! We talked for two hours, standing in the hall. I mean, other people were passing by. My roommates. After he left I went to the library and wrote him a twenty-page letter! You see"—and she bent forward to close the space a little between herself and Martin and Dinah so that they wouldn't miss the point—"I had met someone I *had* to talk to. You know that experience! I don't know how to say it, but it's as though there's an intention in the *world* that you reveal yourself to this other person."

To Dinah's astonishment, Martin nodded in solemn agreement. It heightened her edgy irritation with the direction the whole day was taking. She remembered the fleeting look of condescension that had crossed his face just last week when she had told him that she and the upholsterer, who was making slipcovers for the living room chairs, had some sort of shared sensibility. A shared sense of time. Something. Within the space of a week one of them had phoned the other at least five times to check on this or that, only to find the other had picked up the phone just before it rang. They had begun sentences simultaneously and with the same words. And yet, Dinah couldn't discover anything else they had in common. She, too, had always believed in some sort of ESP operating in the world, but she had assumed it would be dramatic or profound—just what Netta was describing. Dinah had never suspected it would be as indiscriminate as her experience with the upholsterer—a sort of mundane chemical function.

But Netta took heart from Martin's nod and went on. "It was the same with Celia. Since I was ten years old there was Celia. I was so glad when she and Bill had that same sort of . . . connection. I didn't even mind when Celia and Bill had a sexual relationship. I don't think that's what I minded. . . ." Her voice dwindled off into a silent musing, and Dinah took in the fact that David and Christie had come quietly into the kitchen from the garden, and that

Sarah was in her robe at the counter across the room, making toast. Sarah didn't seem to be paying any attention, but David had put his hand on Christie's arm to stop her from coming farther into the room and interrupting Netta by making their presence known. Netta was oblivious, in any case.

"I *did* mind that he wasn't having sex with me," she murmured, seemingly to herself but quite audibly. She put her elbows on the table and lowered her head to her palms in obvious despair. "Oh, God! That was so painful!" She exhaled the words as though she could not stop them, and then she straightened slightly and took in the room again, becoming more brisk. "Of course, I was pregnant when it all started," Netta continued in a stronger voice, with just a hint of weariness, as though she were gathering her forces against enormous odds.

Dinah got up from the table and went to the counter. She was sure she detected the unmistakably heraldic note of the beginning of a much longer story. "I'll put this chocolate milk in the refrigerator unless you want some now, Anna Tyson," she said, and she looked questioningly at Netta and Anna Tyson. "What do you have here, Netta?" Her own tone was light, and she lifted the paper bag a bit, which precipitated another rain of muddy water from the clustered greens. "Ah . . . beets. Well, I have a wide colander somewhere. You'll need that, won't you?" And she bent to search the lower cupboards. "And the kettle with the strainer insert. This soup? Is it borscht?"

One of the reasons some people stopped Dinah in the drugstore, or leaned nearer to her at a dinner party to tell her something they might not have told someone they knew much better, was that they instinctively trusted her to stop them from revealing too much. Dinah was always alert to the honesty of strangers. She had a horror of being held responsible for any part of their well-being later on, in case they remembered that they had told her more than they should have. To any person in distress she possessed the seductiveness of polite and kindly interest combined with an obvious reluctance to participate in any sort of overly intimate confession.

This morning, though, Dinah appeared to her family, whose attention suddenly shifted her way, not to be much interested in anything Netta said, not to be taking Netta's anguish into account. Martin glanced curiously at Dinah as she put the chocolate milk away and stood in the center of the kitchen pinning her hair up haphazardly to get it out of her face. David, too, shot her a speculative glance filled with censure. But Dinah didn't even notice; she was offended by Netta's emotional sloppiness, her almost obscene social naïveté. She was embarrassed for and disturbed by her, and she was also daunted by the prospect of the mound of produce Netta had piled on the cutting board.

"Oh, no, I don't think it's borscht," Netta answered, once again falling into that soft sibilance that marked her speech. She began to search through a canvas carry-all that was propped against her chair. Anna Tyson slid off her own chair to lean against her mother and peer inside it. "I don't think I've ever had borscht. This was in an article on summer soups. I've got the recipe with me here," she said, "and I would have done all the cooking at my apartment, but Bill has all the pans and knives—he even has the Cuisinart—at the apartment in Cambridge. Of course, he says I can come get anything I need, but I've been afraid to go alone. All I have to cook in is what was left by the former tenants of my apartment, and they didn't leave much. But this soup is so *beautiful*! I found everything I need to make it. Oh, but I couldn't find raspberry vinegar. Do you have any?" When Dinah merely shook her head, Netta smiled warmly, full of forgiveness. "Oh, well. Don't worry about it! This soup will be delicious anyway."

She finally fished out a piece of newspaper and unfolded it to reveal an entire page. She disengaged herself from Anna Tyson and showed Dinah the photo of the finished product, beautifully displayed in a soup tureen shaped like a dragon, under the heading "Soup for When It's Sizzling!" Dinah quickly scanned to the beginning of the recipe:

18 beets, boiled, peeled, and cut into ½-inch dice

And she stood in her own kitchen, on a nice day in July, and was overwhelmed momentarily by the idea that her life was going to be an endless round of chores and obligations for the rest of her days. She shut out the conversation going on around her as she carefully read through the long recipe. When she looked up, she saw that Martin had moved over to Netta and was frowning down at her, and David had come farther into the room to hear what Netta was saying.

"No, no," she was answering Martin, "I don't think he would actually *hurt* me . . . but he's so needy, you see. *That's* what I'm afraid of. I mean, I'm afraid of not being able to leave again. I got all the way to Cambridge one day and called the apartment to be sure he and Celia weren't there, but I couldn't make myself go in. I just stood across the street and couldn't stop shaking." This revelation seemed to surprise her. "I'm afraid of Celia, too. I mean, there are ways in which *I've* let *them* down. Well, I've got Anna Tyson. I couldn't have left if she hadn't been with me, but they need her, too."

"Maybe we could help you get whatever you need when we move David into his dorm," Martin said, and Netta glanced up at him and smiled a smile that was like her voice, wistfully sweet, the impression of it lingering for a moment after it had disappeared.

David stood against the counter. "We could go in anytime. We don't have to wait that long. You wouldn't even have to go if you could tell us what you want us to get."

"Really? Are you serious? Because that would be wonderful. No, I need to go, too, but that would just be wonderful, David, to have you and Martin help me. It's been so long since there was anyone I felt I could ask, because all our friends were *mutual*—Bill's and mine, I mean."

Dinah looked away and met Christie's gaze, which turned into a quick glance of pure appeal, but Dinah turned away from that, too, because she simply couldn't sort it all out. There was something disturbing in the air. It was startling to her to imagine David so separate from them that he could be helping strangers move in and out of apartments on streets Dinah had never seen, living a life of which she would not catch a glimpse.

Gradually everyone in the kitchen became involved with Netta's beets. She stood at the sink, watching water run over them in the colander, and finally Dinah moved over next to her, edging her aside, and began cleaning them with a vegetable brush.

"What should we do with the greens?" Netta said. "There weren't any beets at Price Chopper, so I went to The Whole Grain Elevator and they had these. Aren't they beautiful? But the woman thought I was buying them for the greens. She said they're delicious and don't have a trace of pesticide on them."

Sarah began to look through *The Joy of Cooking* for basic directions for boiling beets. "I can't believe this!" Netta had said when she had searched through various other books. "Even *Julia* doesn't say anything about how long to boil them. She says *canned* beets can be substituted in most recipes!"

Martin got out Dinah's stockpot, filled it with hot water from the tap, and put it on to boil.

"My mother always says that cold water comes to a boil faster, Mr. Howells," Christie offered from where she still stood right inside the back door.

"Right, Christie," David said. "That really makes sense, doesn't it?" David spoke as if he were teasing her, but there was an unmistakable edge of derision in his voice.

"I never said I could *cook,* David," Christie snapped back. The room went silent while the implication of what she might have said she *could* do hung awkwardly in the air. Everyone but Netta and Anna Tyson picked up on it and was embarrassed, especially Christie. "Well, I've got to go. But what about tonight, David? Are we going to the movie or do you want me to see if everyone can come over to swim?" Christie had lowered her voice and aimed her question only at David so that the rest of the family could pretend that any disagreement between the two of them had not been overheard.

"I don't know," David answered. "Why don't I call you later," and he didn't even look at her. She picked up a light jacket she had dropped on the kitchen counter and pushed open the screen door.

"I'll tell you what," she said with sugary exaggeration, pretending that she wasn't mocking David's rudeness, "I'm going over to Meg's and *then* I'm having a party at my house. I'll call you if we're short of guests."

Dinah looked at her in surprise. It was the first time she had discerned anything much about Christie's personality, and Dinah was startled to find that just as Christie let the screen door fall shut behind her, she glanced at Dinah again with some sort of mute appeal as she went off down the steps.

"It says here to 'chop the greens coarsely and let them simmer gently in the water in which they are washed,'" Netta read aloud from a dog-eared, spiral-bound cookbook she had found among the others.

"They're awfully sandy, Netta. Do you think it's worth it?" Dinah began to lift the severed leaves one by one under running water, while Netta dropped the scrubbed beets into the pot on the stove. Dinah was finding that she had to rub the sand away with her thumb, and even so she could still feel a persistent gritty residue. The entire sink and the counter around it were spattered with sand and mud and seeping red juice that exuded even from the cuts across the leaf stems. She was absorbed in this project for a bit until she looked up and realized that Sarah had disappeared, and that David and Martin were sitting at the table drinking coffee on either side of Anna Tyson, who had put her cheek down on the placemat in front of her and fallen fast asleep. Netta had drifted away from the boiling beets and was leaning on a chair, discussing some point of her article that was to be published in *The Review*.

"It's not my field, but I assumed that's what your intention was," Martin said.

"No," Netta said severely, and with a slight frown. "It is exactly my point that Foucault *doesn't* take into account—"

"I'll get out of your way here, Netta," Dinah interrupted. "Too many cooks, you know." She hated black coffee, but she poured a cup anyway, not wanting to linger long enough to scald milk. "I hope all those cookbooks aren't in the way. Sarah left them out, but you can put them back if you need the room. Where did she go? I need her to vacuum. And David, would you put away the extra chairs we set up on the porch for the party? You can stack them in the garage if you would. I'm going to straighten up the living room. We didn't quite finish last night. I could use a hand, Martin, taking the extra leaves out of the table. Do you want to help me now?"

Dinah walked off down the hall, stopping to take a sip of coffee while she waited for Martin. She had no inclination to treat Netta as a guest. Usually the disorganization of a party lingered in her household for a week or so because she wasn't a particularly ardent housekeeper, but this morning she launched into more than business as usual.

Martin stored the extra leaves of the table in the attic, and Dinah followed him up the narrow stairs to find the protective flannel sleeves that fit over them to keep the wood from being scratched.

The tension this year in their summer household unnerved Martin. He couldn't fathom Dinah's emotion; his sympathy was primarily with his son. The situation reminded him of his own leave-taking almost thirty years ago when his mother had unwittingly burdened him with the knowledge of her expectations of their continued connection. He had felt suffocated and guilty when almost everyday he had received in the mail from her some clipping from the local paper, a brief note of affection, or a recounting of the current gossip.

In his freshman year, when she had baked him a birthday cake and sent it on a Greyhound bus, he had discarded it right outside the station before any of his friends discovered it. He remembered her intimidating assumption of their familiarity, when, in fact, she knew nothing about his life as he had lived it at college. So many people—including his father—had warned him of the inadequacies of his Mississippi education that he had been afraid to unpack his trunk the entire first year of classes. He liked to know that he could pull his belongings together and leave in no more than ten minutes if it came to that, if he flunked out.

The summer before he left, when she had overheard his father warning him of all the pitfalls of an eastern education, his mother had waved her hand in dismissal of everything her husband was saying. "Oh, heavens, Theo, no school can possibly require more than *brilliance!*" But Martin hadn't been grateful to her; he had preferred his father's uncertainty about his abilities and his warnings against hubris. Because in all of her reassurance, in her faith in him, in her claustrophobic insistence of her knowledge of his character—in all of this—hadn't he sensed some kind of alarming idea of his *beholdenness* to her?

And it was still true, really. He had been irritated when Dinah had reminded him to call his mother over the weekend, and then he had been surprised that he was insulted when his mother had sweetly hurried him off the phone because her bridge group was meeting. He had been injured in the same way, although certainly not to the same degree, when his mother had seemed to take it as a matter of course when he had, indeed, graduated summa cum laude from Harvard.

He showered, and before he left to meet Vic at *The Review* office, Martin folded the extra chairs on the porch and stacked them away neatly in the garage because he had seen David's expression when Dinah had breezily issued instructions for the day. His whole face had tightened, his eyes becoming slightly hooded, his mouth drawn in—it was an expression amazingly like Dinah's when she harbored a resentment. He knew that David had no intention of doing anything his mother asked him this morning.

Dinah stripped the beds and found Sarah and set her to work with the vacuum. Sarah was surprisingly agreeable. "I think they invented Bremner wafers to make people look like pigs," Sarah offered as she unwound the cord. "Did you notice last night that everyone was covered with little flakes of white crumbs?"

But Dinah didn't even smile. She went off to straighten the guest bathroom and put out fresh towels. She was passing through the kitchen with a basket of dirty laundry, on her way to the washing machine in the basement, when Netta stopped her. She and David were at the table chatting while Anna Tyson had her chocolate milk.

"Oh, Dinah, I couldn't find the chopping blade for your Cuisinart. Don't you think that would be the simplest way to dice the beets?"

Dinah was struck by the bitter odor permeating the air. She could even taste it on the back of her tongue. "What's that smell? Is something burning?"

Netta got up and gingerly peered into a skillet that was steaming on a front burner. "Oh, I don't think these greens worked," she said, bemused. "They aren't burning, but they don't look very good, do they?"

Dinah leaned over to look at them. They were a slippery mass, all the leaves wilted around the prominent center veins so that they seemed mildly anatomical. "Maybe you should take them off the heat," Dinah said. "I don't think you should use the Cuisinart for the beets, Netta. I mean, it won't *dice* them for you, and you've got to peel them anyway."

"Oh, that's right. It was such a long time ago that I made this soup, I've forgotten what I did. How do you peel beets?" Netta was wearing another of her long, flowing skirts and a sort of little girl's blouse, the kind Dinah had worn at summer camp years and years ago, with short sleeves and one breast pocket. Netta's hair, in the steamy humidity of the kitchen, still frizzed around her long face, and she *was* oddly appealing, but Dinah didn't give in. She set the laundry basket down by the door to the basement and took the time to fix herself café au lait. She sat down at the table, crossing her legs as she settled back in her chair.

"I don't know," she said. "It's probably like peeling boiled yams. They have a kind of thick, soft skin." She wasn't going to offer another thing, even though she was aware of David's indignation. He didn't glance at her as he got up to lend a hand to Netta, who seemed to be bewildered as she stood looking into the pot of still-boiling beets.

"I'll pour them into the colander for you," he said to Netta. As he emptied the pot slowly into the wide stainless-steel colander, a pinkish mist rose in the air, tingeing the shiny white cupboards above the sink, and pink water splattered over the counter next to the stove.

"You know what?" Anna Tyson said to Dinah suddenly, with a note of challenge. Dinah shifted in her chair to look at her, not bothering to answer or even to assume an air of interest. She was wary of Anna Tyson. "My crown wasn't like anybody else's." She looked directly at Dinah, waiting for a response, but Dinah couldn't think of anything to say. She was sorry Anna Tyson had noticed the difference. Sarah had made the last-minute crown out of aluminum foil that had been applied to the cut-out cardboard too hastily, giving the finished product a forlorn, crumpled look.

Anna Tyson continued. "Netta told me that Moonflower and the spider are just puppets." At once Dinah was less sorry for Anna Tyson and mildly offended, as she always was when children called their parents by their first names; it struck Dinah as an unusually grating affectation. "But I know why my crown was different." Anna Tyson had lowered her voice to a tone of confidentiality. Dinah was so disheartened at the idea of explaining to this four-year-old that the charade of Moonflower was meant with every good intention that she didn't respond at all; she only looked off into the center of the room, hoping Anna Tyson would lose interest in the conversation.

"Moonflower knew that silver is the color I like best. Netta wouldn't let me be a silver fairy on Halloween. I went as a California Raisin. I wore a brown paper bag that Netta wrinkled up." By now Dinah was paying full attention, and Anna Tyson looked at her solemnly for a moment without saying anything, and then she continued. "But I wanted to get the silver princess costume they had at the store."

Dinah smiled delightedly at Anna Tyson. The little girl had developed the logic of one of life's survivors, Dinah thought, remembering the pathetic Reynolds Wrap crown with ANNA written on it in red glitter, so shabby compared to the gilded, sequined, gold crowns she had found for the other children. Nevertheless, she couldn't think of anything to say that wouldn't in some way legitimize Moonflower and therefore countermand Netta's instructions to her daughter about how to view the whole phenomenon of the party the night before. Anna Tyson gazed back at Dinah soberly and then smiled, too, leaning back and swinging her feet separately beneath her straight-legged chair in a rhythm that established a sort of skittering, satisfactory rocking motion as the chair creaked with her movement and inched minutely back and forth on the tiled floor.

Dinah was entirely satisfied for the first time in two days, and she swung her crossed leg from the knee to match the rhythm Anna Tyson had established. The two of them looked at each other and laughed at Dinah's silliness. And Dinah continued to swing her leg without even realizing it as she watched David and Netta across the room dealing with the beets. The counters, the chopping board, Netta's palms and fingertips, and David's T-shirt were stained with the oozing, beautifully rosy beet juice. The two of them looked harassed, and David seemed to be personally affronted. Netta made that gesture once again of shaking her hair back, and some of Dinah's contentment evaporated. It would be a terrible chore to remove the red stains from the Formica countertop, and it would be she who would do it. And the cutting board would retain the splotchy beet color until the surface wore away.

Franklin M. Mount
Dean of Freshmen
Harvard College
12 Truscott Street
Cambridge, Massachusetts 02138

Dear Mr. Mount,

David had an amazing imagination when he was a child. He and Toby, and eventually their sister Sarah, lived whole imaginary lifetimes every day after school and all through the summers in their own backyard or in the basement, where they built forts and cities with cardboard boxes and old rug samples if it was too cold outside.

I tried hard not to destroy the days' fantasy. I

really made an effort not to blunder into the amazingly detailed and ordered world they created, and I pretended to whatever role they needed me to pretend. Sometimes I was an evil witch who made them come to dinner and turned their macaroni and cheese into worms and their salads into man-eating plants. Sometimes I was a creature called Sweet Penelope, with a cotton candy voice, so stupid in my naïve good-heartedness that David and Toby had to rescue me from the various hazards and traps the monsters in that afternoon's world had constructed.

But I always, always knew to stop the game if, at age four or five, or even six and seven, the children's fantasy edged toward conviction. Well, you see, I always understood that the children were enchanted and excited by the *possibility* of their mother transmogrified, but that they would have been terrified had they believed in the reality of it.

But you know, I don't know what happens to the imagination of young children. By the time David was about eleven, if he had one of his friends home after school, he wouldn't play those games with Toby anymore. Sometimes, though, if he was just with his brother, he would still throw himself into the whole thing.

By the time he was twelve, it seemed to me that he didn't even believe he had ever invented a world for himself. Don't you think that's odd? I mean, it happened to all my children, but it must be that the energy that fired so much creative thought was just *diverted* somehow. I have no idea, these days, what either one of my children imagines.

Netta turned when she felt Dinah's glance on them,

and she smiled in a way that transformed her face. She held up a clear bowl of diced beets. "They're really *beautiful,* aren't they?" she said to Dinah. "There's such sensual pleasure in something so simple as this, isn't there? I've always thought that there's genuine beauty in something intrinsically basic." She turned back to dicing the beets that David was peeling, and David was less tense all of a sudden. He looked at her and smiled. "I mean, just this simple root vegetable," she said. "Domesticity has its own . . . oh . . . *elegance. . . .*"

Dinah watched Netta inexpertly cut up the remaining beets, now and then repeating that little habitual shake of her head. "You must have had your hair cut recently, Netta?" she said pleasantly enough. "I bet you had very long hair. I know how odd it felt when I had mine cut after college. It's like taking off skates after an hour or so of skating, don't you think? You still feel elevated. I had let mine grow below my waist. . . ."

Netta looked over her shoulder at Dinah, surprised. "No," she said. "My hair has always been short. It would be so much trouble to wear long hair."

The kitchen was quiet, and Dinah made no more attempts at conversation. She had that rather light-headed feeling that follows a night of intermittent insomnia. She merely sat idly, just resting, until she would have to rouse herself to clean up the kitchen when Netta was done with her soup. Suddenly she had a horribly intimate but vivid fantasy of Netta and her life before she came to West Bradford. She could see Netta's friend Celia and Netta's husband, Bill—both of whom had slowly taken shape in her imagination as those sort of wispy, grayish, thin people with stringy hair. He would have that long-limbed, hollow-chested, saintlike look, and Celia would have that starved look of knobby knees and elbows. The two of them had retired to the bedroom to have the kind of listless, sweatless sex that Dinah always assumed those passionless-looking people must have, while poor Netta earnestly battled the beets in some tiny kitchen in Cambridge.

The astonishing vision was gone in an instant, but Dinah felt absolutely convinced that that was why no one had eaten any of that soup—whenever it was that Netta had first made it—except Anna Tyson, who would have been so young that not much that happened would have affected her appetite.

CHAPTER SIX

BAD WEATHER

TOWARD THE MIDDLE OF this past spring semester, Professor Charles Beck's ten-month-old male cairn terrier had developed an incurable lust for Anton Vrabel's medium-sized mixed breed. Professor Vrabel's mutt appeared to be distressed and baffled whenever the tenacious little terrier attempted to mount her. She shook him off, dropped her ears, and slunk away, leaving the frustrated cairn to attach himself to whatever was nearby—someone's pants leg, a box of computer paper stacked against the wall, the newel post that turned the corner of the stairwell on the second floor of Jesse Hall. Several of Chip Beck's colleagues suggested gently to him that it was an unkindness to bring the lovesick cairn with him to the office, at which point Professor Beck approached Anton Vrabel in the beautiful old lounge in Jesse Hall during coffee hour and demanded that Anton leave *his* dog at home.

"You know the saying we had in Austria, Anton? 'You coop your chicks, mamma! My rooster runs free.'"

Like many of its faculty, Chip Beck was a man of some stature beyond the confines of Bradford and Welbern College. He had taken a prolonged leave several decades before to chair the President's Council of Economic Advisors, and more recently he had served as an adviser to a presidential candidate and done a brief stint in the Health and Human Services Department. He was a tall, bony, kindly-looking man who gave up his jovial tone in the face of Professor Vrabel's blank-faced refusal to agree that they had a mutual problem. There in Jesse lounge, beneath the portraits of deceased dignitaries of Bradford and Welbern College, he accused Anton Vrabel of harboring in his office "an ill-bred slut of a dog!"

Professor Vrabel was instantly enraged and accused his former friend of being no better than all the other "robot-like, cold-blooded economists who have done more to dismantle any decent social programs over the past years than any one of a half-dozen monster capitalist conglomerates would have dared to hope for!" In one moment amenities between two old friends ceased, and each aired all his long held hostile views of the other—their philosophical disagreements, their political antipathy.

Other faculty members, who were standing in clusters around the book-lined, paneled room or were sitting together on the dark red leather couches with coffee and doughnuts that the Jesse Hall receptionist, Mrs. LaPlante, set out each afternoon at three o'clock, fell into embarrassed silence when they could no longer ignore the raised voices of those two dignified, elderly men who were saying unforgivable things to each other, venting frustrations that had lain dormant for years under the weight of their mutual respect and the long-standing friendship of their families.

Three years previously, in fact, Katherine Vrabel—although suffering herself from rheumatoid arthritis—had taken Marie Beck out for long drives three or four times a week during the last year of her life when she knew she was dying but was forced, in Chip's presence, to assume a ghastly facade of wellness, because the thought of her death was unbearable to him. It was Katherine who eventually sorted through and disposed of all of Marie's clothes, straightened her neglected closets and cupboards, and re-arranged Marie's house with sensitivity and great sorrow for its surviving occupant. "For God's sake, Katherine," Marie had said, "please don't let Chip sell that house when I die! He loves that house. He designed it during all those years when we lived in those terrible, sterile, box-like houses on the outskirts of Washington. I know he'll be lonely. Oh, God! I can't tell you how much I wish now that we'd de-cided to have children! But make him get a cat, or some-thing."

Katherine had agreed to do all these things, even though the slow death of this closest of friends was a singu-larly debilitating torment to her, and she was careful to hide from Marie the signs of her own distress and deteriorating health. While Katherine cleared and cleaned the modest, modern cedar-and-glass house, Anton drove Chip up to spend several days sorting out and arranging the sale of the Becks' cabin on Lake Winnipesaukee in Moultonboro, New Hampshire. But that was some years ago and apparently all forgotten—or perhaps their sorrowful intimacy had been so wounding all around that it was too well remembered. In any case, the fury that mounted between the two men that afternoon last spring in Jesse lounge was terrible and ab-solute.

Three days after the disagreement, Larry Croft, who was Chip Beck's physician, had called Martin—breaking the time-honored doctor-patient confidence—to say that he had hospitalized Professor Beck for observation after an un-nerving spell of irregular heartbeat, and to ask Martin if there was any way at all to resolve tactfully the question of whose dogs were to be allowed in Jesse Hall. Dr. Croft was concerned about Chip Beck's angry belaboring of the subject. He was worried on several counts—it did not bode well for what Dr. Croft was beginning to suspect was his patient's deteriorating mental state since his wife's death, although he didn't mention that concern to Martin. He explained arrhythmia to Martin in general terms, and he expressed his worry over Professor Beck's excitability. Martin had gotten in touch with Jean Atwell, and on Monday of the following week the faculty found a slip of paper in their mailboxes.

Memorandum

From: Jean Atwell, Chairperson, Jesse Hall Users' Committee

To: All Faculty

It has come to the attention of this committee that several faculty members have complained of an infestation of fleas in the hallways and in some offices. Please make plans to vacate your offices between Friday at 4:00 P.M. through Monday at 7:00 A.M., removing any plants or other living things from the premises, so that the Buildings and Grounds Department can exterminate these pests.

Since the Jesse Hall Users' Committee deems it likely that these parasites are being carried into the building on pets accompanying their owners, we formally request that hereafter no animals be allowed inside the building. An exception will be made in the case of the fish and other marine life in the aquarium presented to Mrs. LaPlante by a student group from the class of '82.

Otherwise, the committee asks all faculty and

staff to observe this restriction for the sake of our mutual comfort and health.

> Sincerely,
> Jeanette Atwell
> Department of Philosophy

But now that summer was here, Martin disregarded the committee's regulation. Jesse Hall was almost empty and, besides, Martin liked Duchess's company as he strolled through the grounds of the school. He thought the grounds should be teeming with teachers with their dogs, teachers with their children, teachers on bikes. He thought men and women who wanted to impart knowledge should be available, visible, along all the paths, around every turn.

After his own graduation, Martin had discovered that he had loathed almost every minute of his years at Harvard, where he had learned a good deal but had been taught very little. And he had infuriated his graduate director, a distinguished man of letters—a scholar—at the University of Virginia, when he took the man's advice to enter academe, but at the first opportunity opted to teach at a school that claimed to cherish undergraduate teaching with an ardor equal to, if not greater than, that with which it embraced publication. Early in his career, in fact, Martin had turned down three separate offers from large and distinguished universities with prestigious graduate programs. He knew his zealousness about teaching was regarded by his colleagues at best with affectionate tolerance and at worst with suspicion, cynicism, and disdain. But he also knew that many of those men and women still harbored what he believed was the foolish desire to be famous people within their designated sphere. He accepted their condescension and regarded them, in turn, with some degree of pity.

Even Dinah thought that his devotion to teaching was

sometimes unthinking, that he was likely to be ill-used by the very institution that he served. Martin, however, had seen that happen to some of his colleagues, and he was cautious in his affection for the place. He was simply pleased for his own sake to be walking across the campus at a leisurely pace while Duchess nosed into a hedge, or stopped to examine a tree, or looked longingly after the complacent squirrels that chattered at her from the high branches.

As he had set off with Duchess in the late morning, Dinah had rounded on him. "Are you going to the office *today*? You're taking that silly dog? Well, for God's sake, please be home in time to eat this soup that the whole world has gathered to make in my kitchen."

"I have to meet Vic and Owen Croft to explain the summer assistant's job at *The Review*. I think it's something Owen can handle. I won't be long." He was trying to get Duchess to hold still while he attached her leash, and he saw her ears go flat when she heard Dinah insult her. He always felt compelled to defend Duchess against Dinah's occasional scorn, although within the household the dog was entirely devoted to Dinah, following her up and down the stairs, back and forth across the kitchen, always underfoot. Martin had never claimed that Duchess was a dog of noble character, but he also took care to point out that the dog's fearfulness and various neuroses required a certain degree of intelligence. "Any fool can be brave," he had said that morning in Duchess's defense.

"I think she was just weaned too soon," Dinah replied.

One of the pleasures of Martin's life was the long summer days he spent working at *The Review* offices while Duchess sprawled across the cool linoleum in luxurious security. Vic was usually in the adjoining office, but the rest of the building that housed the English and Philosophy departments was almost empty. Now and then the sound of someone else engaged in some sort of studious work would filter down the staircase—a file drawer rasping open, a pencil sharpener, the Xerox machine. These sounds were as comforting to him as Dinah's house was to her or David's garden was to him.

And occasionally he or Vic would come across something brilliant, a piece of fiction, an essay—like Netta Breckenridge's. Her prose was elegant, her thesis stringent, and her subject of interest. He had known only that she was a Fennel Doyle Scholar in her first year of a two-year appointment when he sent her a letter of acceptance for her article. Because of the ferocity of her prose, he had made a guess at who she might be during a faculty meeting. For several weeks after that, Martin had taken care to nod agreeably at a very tall, handsome, dark-haired woman with a severe face and a mildly aggressive nature.

One day he had been standing in the ten-item express lane at the grocery store, waiting to pay for a half-gallon of milk, when this same woman met his eye steadfastly as she approached him. "I'm in a frightful hurry!" she had declared, with a trace of a British accent, and he stepped back to allow her to go ahead of him, only to be dismayed when she trundled forth a cart full of groceries.

The check-out girl looked up to object, but began ringing up the items with a sigh when she met the woman's implacable gaze. When Netta had finally shown up in the office toward the end of the semester, Martin had assumed she was a student applying for the summer job which now, in fact, he and Vic had offered to Owen Croft. Martin had been enormously relieved at Netta's unprepossessing nature, and she further endeared herself to him by not being the fearsome woman of the express lane. He remained irritated in retrospect that he had so docilely surrendered his place in line to that mysterious person.

As he entered Jesse Hall today, though, he began rehearsing his greeting to Owen, the way in which he would carefully construct a channel of amiability between Vic and

Owen, in order to protect Owen from Vic's cynicism. But Owen had arrived ahead of him, and Martin had an unexpected sense of suffocation—really as though there were not enough air in the place—when he came around the corner of the corridor and saw Owen sitting, half turned, on the arm of the old wing chair in Vic's office. Owen twisted in his direction, and Martin nodded in acknowledgment, stopping in the doorway and fighting an unnerving queasiness while he unclipped Duchess from her leash.

Owen continued his conversation with Vic. "Hey, I think I can help you out, Professor Hofstatter! I'd like to do it." He was mocking himself slightly.

Vic leaned back with his hands clasped behind his head, swinging his swivel chair slightly from side to side, enjoying the banter.

"We'd count on you to pretty much use your own initiative to answer these letters," Vic said, getting down to business now that Martin had arrived. "I'll tell you how we usually handle it. Mrs. Krautz sorts the correspondence into fairly rough categories. We get letters from a variety of people that are essentially just 'letters to the editor,' but some of them require a reply. We don't publish any letters in *The Review,* so until Penny Krautz is back you'd better let us see all of those. There's no way you could know which ones need to be answered. But most of the answers fall into a sort of formula. How do you want to work this, Martin?"

Martin had pulled a wooden chair away from the wall and was sitting catty-corner between Vic and Owen. He couldn't help but think that Owen's wide-eyed expectancy looked a little stale, as if it were calculated.

Larry Croft had come to Martin in despair this spring. Larry had been embarrassed but desperate, and Martin had agreed to try to help Owen get a grip on his life. Larry continued to believe that Owen's emotional problems were due to his having been involved in Toby's death, and that any kindness that Martin could see his way clear to extend to Owen would be the only thing that might help him heal. Martin was willing to give it a try, but he had let several weeks pass before telling Dinah about Larry's request.

Martin began explaining the job to Owen. "Penny and I have about a half-hour conference every morning to run over the general answers to queries or comments." He looked hopefully at Owen, and Owen nodded. Martin was encouraged and went on. "There could be four or five letters that I could tell her to reply to with the 'Thank you very much for your suggestion, blah, blah, blah . . . We'll certainly consider it in the future.' Do you see what I mean?"

"Sure," Owen said, "but do you have some copies of her letters that can give me a general idea of the tone?"

Vic and Martin exchanged a brief, satisfied glance, and Vic picked up three files of letters from his desk. "I pulled these for you," he said to Owen, "but they're on the computer, too, so you can just alter them to personalize whatever form is suitable."

"Okay, okay. That sounds good," Owen said, growing animated. "But say some letter comes in that doesn't have a precedent. Look! Maybe I could do something like this. I could mark anything that I need to consult you about with green pencil, anything that seems to be a 'Thank you very much' in red, and a query that will be turned down in blue. I could leave them on your desk in the evening, and you could look them over in the morning before I type them up to send out."

"Great. That's a good idea," Martin said. "Don't worry too much about typos and so forth. Helen LaPlante will type them from your printout. We don't like to send out letters that look as if they were composed on a computer. Even when we print something 'letter quality,' it looks less personal than Helen's standard typewriter."

"Oh, yeah! That's good! That gives it a sort of personal

touch, doesn't it? I mean, it's like you guys are actually answering the letters yourselves."

Owen's interpretation made Martin uncomfortable, but Vic grinned. Martin realized that they *were*, of course, practicing a kind of deception, but he had never thought of it as a clever stunt—a slick idea—as Owen clearly did.

Owen had been sitting with his arms lightly clasped around his torso and his long legs stretched out in front of him, crossed at the ankles, but he dropped his hands to his sides and collected his feet beneath him as he bent toward Vic. "Well, this sounds good to me. I really do think it's something I'd enjoy doing. Helping you out until I can get things sorted out again. I've talked to the registrar. Bradford and Welbern's admitted me as a special student. I'm planning to finish my degree next year, so I'll be around, and I could always help you out if Mrs. Krautz is away. But it would be great for the rest of the summer."

Martin was unable to listen to Owen without feeling uneasy, and even physically his was a contradictory presence. Owen was tall and lanky and sometimes oddly menacing in his angularity, with a curious half smile and a habit of ducking his head in conversation so that his words tumbled down his long frame. Any listener was forced to lean forward and gaze up at him, as though in supplication, in order to catch a phrase. And anything he did say had an edge to it, slipped this way and that in intention.

At other times, though, he was endearingly gangly, with a subdued, self-deprecatory attitude in all his gestures, as if to illustrate that he was making every effort to rein himself in so as not to take up more space than other-sized mortals. And then, when he spoke, he was careful to meet the eye of his audience, and whatever he had to say was straightforward. At moments like that everything about him was sympathetic.

Martin realized that he wouldn't need to mediate between Owen and Vic, and Martin should have been relieved, but instead he was unaccountably apprehensive. Owen was still good-looking, with the beginnings of lines crinkling at the corners of his green eyes, but he had an almost tenuous presence. It was not so much that he seemed vulnerable as that he appeared to be already slightly bruised, a bit weathered for a twenty-three-year-old, as though he were the blunted edge of something that had once been quite sharp.

Judith and Larry Croft had come to Dinah and Martin in abject despair in the middle of the year following Toby's death, when Owen had been asked to leave Swarthmore. The school had been alarmed by Owen's alternately manic then utterly withdrawn behavior, and the Crofts felt sure he was suffering from the aftermath of having unwittingly caused such a tragedy.

"I wish they wouldn't involve us," Dinah had said to Martin then. "I *do* know they're frightened for him. And I know it's hard for them to ask *us*. . . ." Her voice broke and she had paused. "I think they expect more than I can manage," she said, finally.

That first year, though, Dinah's several meetings with Owen had oddly enough served to dispel, a little, the fog of constant distress that enshrouded her. Her surprise at feeling even a tiny bit of sympathy for Owen had served its purpose for a while, and her incessant sorrowing had lessened. She had even begun to break free of it for moments at a time.

Martin had noticed, however, that the better she got to know Owen, the less she cared about him one way or another. While she might pity him, she didn't like him. Dinah left Toby's death out of the equation. "Owen peaked at about age sixteen," Dinah had said several years ago when she had finally washed her hands of him. "It's a clear case of 'early bloom, early rot.' I always think of those people as having deteriorating personalities, but usually they just become boring. There's something a little scary about

Owen." She thought that Owen was doomed by his own nature, and therefore, as time went by, he simply didn't interest her much.

But now and then, when she knew Martin was going out of his way on Owen's behalf, her husband's insistence on such generosity of spirit wounded her in an obscure way. She said his continuing association with Owen was a forfeiture of judgment, a denial of pain, even an abdication of responsibility. And this morning she had said that the idea of his working with Owen on a day-to-day basis was a perfect blueprint for disaster.

What she didn't know was that when he had found out about Owen's initial breakdown at Swarthmore, and every time he heard about Owen's continuing problems, Martin envisioned himself in midair, launched at Owen in the damp gymnasium, tackling him and encompassing him with terrible guilt and responsibility.

For months after Toby's death, Martin had envied Dinah her ability to hold her grief in the forefront of her mind and move through it in all her sleepless nights, while his stupid body betrayed him and sought solace in sleep so deep and dreamless that each morning he had to become reacquainted with the actuality of the loss of his son. He would wake in the mornings rested, interested as always in the idea of the day ahead, only to be blindsided by the dismal task of discarding all the promising possibilities.

Martin felt compelled to seek out Owen's company, if only to test himself. He knew that it was the leap to unthinking acceptance of his son's death that had marked his transition from grief to sorrow, and he felt sure that he had hurdled across that abyss, but somehow it was necessary to turn around and see just how far he had traveled and be sure his footing was relatively secure.

When Martin returned in the late afternoon he settled in the kitchen with a weak Scotch and soda. Christie arrived shortly afterward, returning a sweater that David had left in her car. She stood by David's side as he worked with Netta at the stove. Anna Tyson grew restless and querulous, and Sarah took her in hand without even being asked, whisking Anna Tyson out to the porch while Dinah came in and out, setting the table, slicing bread, moving the things she needed in the cupboards with a clatter.

Sarah had seen the furrowed expression of concentration on her mother's face that generally foreshadowed familial disharmony, an explosion of bad temper, hurt feelings, misunderstandings, and she did what she could to forestall it. While Anna Tyson drew pictures at the table on the back porch, Sarah slipped away to phone her friend Elise and tell her that she wasn't coming over that afternoon. "I can't help it," Sarah said. "We have company for dinner." Sarah was like a seismograph within the family; she could register oncoming tremors.

But Martin didn't notice any discordancy in the household; he was simply relieved to be at home after spending the afternoon getting Owen settled into the little anteroom in Jesse Hall.

Martin took a sip of his drink and reveled in an almost smug pleasure at being in the company of friends, with all the easy time of the summer days still ahead that would fit into the rooms of Dinah's house. He had given the house over to her emotionally a long time ago. The interiors were however she had invented them—the pictures on the walls, the furniture placement. When he was preparing for a seminar to meet at home and she came into the living room while he was arranging things, she became truly distressed.

"For God's sake, sweetheart! You've lined all the chairs up straight. It's not an auditorium in here, you know. It's a real place. I thought that was the point of having the class here." He would leave the room while she rearranged the chairs he had brought in from the dining room, and it was a long time before he had understood that this was a gift she had: to arrange the rooms, to place the chairs, to hang the pictures, to maintain the physical equilibrium of their domestic arrangements.

Christie was scrubbing the built-in cutting board next to the sink, and David was washing the huge stainless-steel stockpot, which was encrusted with pink scum from the boiling beets. Netta went back and forth from one to the other, and finally she sat down beside Martin at the table. He found himself so filled with affection for his wife, his children, his house—even Bob, the cat, circling sharklike around his ankles, campaigning for an early supper—that Netta's narrow presence appealed to his largess. He wanted to extend to her his idea that serenity could be achieved only in this particular turmoil, this remarkable domesticity. He wanted urgently to explain the chemistry of families.

She was leaning forward, her chin cupped in her hand, her eyes lowered and ringed underneath by dark circles that made her look excessively fragile. Her fine hair was in its usual frizzled disarray, and her fingertips and nails were tinged bright red, as though she were bleeding.

He looked around the kitchen, shadowed now at the far end, where Dinah came back and forth from the dining room, stepping over Taffy who had settled stubbornly in the center of her path. He watched his wife as she navigated through the swinging door and around the hunched yellow cat without apparent thought, just habit, and everything about her exact passage to and fro seemed to him just for a moment to be an example that—if he could only articulate it—would be the explanation for everything. The answer to a search for God, a small instance of order in the universe, the plain fact of how every human, regardless of circumstances, will live the largest portion of his life—in pieces, in small, rote moments that are not *considered*.

He thought that Netta hadn't hit upon how to do it yet, how to live any sort of daily life with her daughter. He had felt sorry for her last night at the party, surrounded by families. He attempted to put himself in her corner so that she would pay attention to what he wanted to explain, would learn to give herself over now and then to action without consideration, would relax and lapse occasionally into the mundane. "You know, Dinah has always understood houses . . . the things in them, how we live in them," he said, unintentionally falling into a didactic cadence, persuasive and gentle, but deliberate—a tone and attitude that had an agenda. He gestured toward his wife, who was carrying a large soup tureen in from the dining room, and then he expanded the sweep of his arm to indicate the room, the house, the enclosure. "It's more important than you can understand at first. . . . Well, for instance, when my mother sent us some antiques that had belonged to my grandmother, it threw everything out of kilter."

Netta straightened as he spoke, sitting back in her chair with a resolute expression on her face, as though she wanted to say something, but Martin didn't notice and simply continued on conversationally. "I'm not sure how to explain it except that we had lived for years and years without these things, and suddenly we had to accommodate them, because they had emotional weight as well, you see. We just put the furniture here and there, wherever any piece would fit. But Dinah couldn't stand it. She drew all the rooms to scale on graph paper, measured all the furniture, planned it all so . . . *cautiously*. And finally she called in movers and put everything in a chosen place—I mean, she figured it out and rearranged the house. And you see, she knew how to do it. And I don't even think she cares much about visual effect." He paused to think about it for a moment.

"When the movers left she insisted that I follow her through the house, and she said, 'In case I die I've fixed it so you'll know where the furniture goes if you have to move it to clean, or something.' She'd marked the placement of everything with safety pins in the rug, or tape under the edge of a picture, or a pencil mark behind a desk. I thought it was funny then, you see. Alarming, too." And he glanced at Netta to be sure she understood that he was illustrating the profound with the ridiculous. "But the thing is . . . what she knew . . . was that to hold on to sanity it's absolutely necessary to believe that where the chairs go really is important. Do you see what I mean?" He leaned toward Netta enthusiastically, certain that she would understand. "There are ways in which each family defines itself. Not necessarily where the *chairs* go, of course."

Martin had thought of this often as he pondered the continuing functioning of his family after they had experienced a tragedy, and he had become ardent about his theory of the human tendency to define and cling to a structure of normalcy within one domestic unit. He and Vic or Ellen or Dinah had discussed and argued variations on this theme many times, expounding upon it, retreating from it. He smiled over at Netta, who had put both beet-stained hands flat on the table in front of her in preparation for what she was going to say.

But Dinah, who had overheard bits and pieces of Martin's conversation, was overwhelmed by a feeling of betrayal. She was astounded that he would reveal her most vulnerable self to this most literal of people, and she turned around and went back through the swinging door into the dining room, where she couldn't hear any more of what was said, so that she could collect herself.

She remembered the incident exactly. After the movers had gone, she had asked Martin to come with her into the living room. She had pushed a chair to one side and explained the solution she had come up with, pointing out to Martin the little golden, rustproof safety pins fastened to the heavy oriental rug they had also inherited from Martin's grandmother. He had laughed, and she had glanced up at him, surprised, and then laughed, too. But she hadn't been able to give it up, this insistence on order in—or control of—her surroundings.

For a long time Dinah had taken to readying things for

the rest of her family in case she, too, might die while she was still needed. She realized she had become obsessive when she would catch a fleeting look of exasperation as she insisted to Martin or David or Sarah that they pay attention. "Here's the shish kebab recipe written on the inside of *The Joy of Cooking* in case I die, or something."

"If anything happens to me, the red napkins and the red placemats are in the cupboard under the stairs. They're the only ones that will all fit on the table if you're serving twelve."

By now the compulsion had mostly dissipated, and she fought whatever remnants of it that remained, although only last week she had filled eight large aluminum pans with lasagna made from her own recipe, and carefully labeled and arranged them in the freezer as a barrier to catastrophe. Her lasagna, frozen and ready to be whipped out and heated up in the face of disaster, was a red herring. That's how she had really felt as she stocked the freezer. It was magic thinking. If she was ready for the worst, it might not happen.

As she stood stock-still in the dining room, with her hands to her face, which was flushed with embarrassment, she was visited with an image drifting across her sensibilities: Martin was driving a car, and Netta was in the front passenger seat, her hair shoulder length and blowing in dry wisps across her mouth. When she flicked her head to settle her hair on her neck, Dinah had a glimpse of David and Sarah and Toby sitting behind her in the back seat. The children were very young—Sarah's head didn't reach the top of the back seat—and Toby was leaning his forehead against the glass, mindlessly watching the landscape pass by.

Then the image was gone, as though a film had run inside her mind. She lowered her hands and stood alone in the middle of the room, dismayed and perplexed. What could it be that she was having? Not daydreams, which unwind logically from an idea, and certainly not flashbacks or premonitions, and not anything as full-blown as hallucinations. It was as if, in that supercharged state of insomniacs' exhaustion, some deep, interior part of her mind could not rest and was combining images, actualities and imaginings at random, and delivering them to her as waking dreams—flash-*ins*—as though she were party to an existence that *might* have happened.

When Dinah went back into the kitchen, it was so filled with various guests and activity that she was able to pour herself a glass of wine and slip out the screen door without getting involved in any of the conversations. She made her way down the slate stepping-stones, around the garden, and down to the bottom of the yard. She moved slowly, considering the cedar hedges and making a mental note, as she paused now and then to sip her wine, of just where they needed cutting back.

She couldn't decide how she felt about being overtaken by these persuasive little moments of impossible visions—that first image of Netta making soup while her husband and her friend retreated to the bedroom, and now this. It was pleasurable, in a way, to be visited with intimations of other realities, as though it were she who was imaginary and Netta, in her Cambridge apartment, or the children, so young in the back seat of the car, who were real.

She walked the long hedge all the way around before settling on the old garden bench that had deteriorated and been pulled around to the side of the shed just beneath the garden. She drew her knees up and wrapped her arms around them, putting her glass of wine down on the wide arm of the bench.

The evening wasn't hot, but the twilight was humid and heavy, and she didn't move when she heard the screen door slam. It might be someone looking for her, but she wasn't eager to be found. She assumed it was Christie leaving or Anna Tyson coming outside to play on the old swing set, but then she heard David and Christie in the garden. It was clear from the conversation that David was bending to tend to the plants, because his voice was muted, although she couldn't discern the actual words Christie spoke, either. Dinah really didn't care what they were saying. She simply remained where she was, not wanting to get up and muster cheerful small talk with the two of them.

She rested her head against the wall of the shed and closed her eyes. She was frozen in place just like that when Christie's voice suddenly rose in an anger so intense that her enunciation was chillingly precise. Dinah was trapped within earshot, having waited too long to make her presence known.

"What will you do, though, if I am?" Christie said. "I mean, just exactly how will you *feel* if I'm not just late? Those tests are just over the counter. I mean, they're not perfect. It could be wrong. I don't think you even give a shit about anything that happens to anyone else in the world anymore! I don't know what's wrong with you!" Christie's voice had gotten high and raspy against tears. "I'm not sure anymore about you, David! I'm not sure you're worth caring anything about. We've been going together for three years, and I won't be able to just *stop* caring! But I don't like you very much. And I don't want you to even think of me as a friend anymore. Not even that! Not even a friend!"

"You know you're all right, Christie." David's reply was devastating, because he wasn't angry at all. He sounded like someone trying to overcome a bone-deep weariness. He sounded like someone trying to be kind, and Dinah didn't want to hear any more. She tugged off her sandals and picked up her wineglass and slipped away in the soft grass as though she were a felon, carrying her shoes in her hand and hunched instinctively against being caught out. It was simply the last straw, she thought. She was vastly irritated. This was her own house, and yet she couldn't find anyplace at all where she could retreat. She felt vexed, petty as a child, enormously cross at living in a house in which there was no place for her.

She had finished her wine, and she let the glass dangle from her fingers by its stem while her sandals swung from her wrist. She traipsed her other hand through the cool, fleshy lace of the cedar hedge as she moved petulantly around the side yard, and only then did it dawn on her what David and Christie had been talking about, and she came to a stop and leaned into the hedge for support.

If they ever knew she had overheard that conversation, she didn't suppose David would have any way at all in which he could forgive her, and Christie would never look her in the face again. Yet, as she moved forward, pacing the perimeter of the shaggy hedges, she was struck with the idea of David and Christie having sex. Had she really thought they weren't having sex? Had she ever thought about it one way or another? In the abstract, the idea of her children's sexuality had never concerned her, but now she found her pulse quickening and her hands beginning to tremble at the idea of the stupidity of what they'd done. Oh, God! The incredible recklessness.

She heard Christie's car door slam, and a moment later had a glimpse of her red Toyota pulling out of the driveway, and Dinah turned and made her way very slowly back down to the garden, where David was bending to pull up weeds between the staked tomato vines. She stood for a moment without speaking, but he didn't look up to acknowledge her, and she kept her voice very level.

"You have no right to behave the way you are, David." She kept her voice even, but her anger was immense, terrifying, and gathering momentum. She stepped back a half step, afraid for just a moment, and hoped that he would say something, but David kept his face turned toward the earth. Her voice had a tremor when she spoke again. "I would never have thought that you were capable of cruelty like that. I never would have! It's amazing! It's just amazing! Oh, and you think you know so much. How could you do that to her?"

But David still didn't look up. He didn't move at all, and she could see only a slice of his profile, the corner of his mouth pulled taut, the particular shape of his lowered eyelid. She felt such grief all at once that she turned to one side and bent forward slightly with her arm across her waist, as if the pain were localized and physical. "And, oh my God, how could you do this to *me*? To your father? How dare you? How dare you? How dare you let me *know*? How dare you take such a stupid risk? You're too old . . . you're too old not to take care of birth control! And you're too young—Christie's too young. . . . My God, I don't see how you can do this to us."

Dinah didn't even try not to cry; she stood wiping at her tears with the backs of her hands. "We've taken care of you for eighteen years—oh, that's what we're expected to do, that's what we *must* do, and you have the *nerve* to risk your future and Christie's future! How come *you* get that right and we don't? How come, Goddammit, that you don't have to be responsible ever—*ever*—for how *we* are? If we're all right? If we're happy or sad or scared or lonely? My God! We've spent eighteen years trying to keep you . . . to keep you from putting a key in an electric socket! To keep you whole! To keep you well! To keep you . . ." And then she gave up; she was weeping too hard to be articulate.

David slowly stood and faced her, and his face was streaked with tears and blotchy with misery. "Christie's okay. She's okay." He sounded quiet and defeated, and then he suddenly made an odd, childish motion of clenching his hands at his sides and making an abrupt backward shake of his arms. It was a gesture Dinah remembered from David at age two—it was determined refusal; it was his childhood embodiment of NO! And his voice gained resonance. "But why don't you get a fucking life of your own?

This is not your business! You don't need to care about me!
I can't *stand* to have you care about me!"

Dinah stood there staring at him for a moment in
shock, and her anger resolved itself into a tight knot of
breathtaking outrage. "It may surprise you—I mean, it really may amaze you to know that I once *had* a life all of my
own. My own life! Everything revolved around *me*! Oh, yes!
Really!" And she drew that last word out in a nasty mockery
of her children's language, a powerful disavowal of its po-
tency. "Really!" She repeated with a pause, and then she
continued, all her fury still audible in her voice. "That's how
it seemed to me. And then I had *children*!"

"Oh, God! So now we've got to be your life!" David was
bent toward her belligerently, his voice raised. "There's no
way I can ever leave here, is there, without feeling like shit?
Without feeling guilty!" He was close to crying now, and
Dinah realized what they were saying to each other and was
horrified. She settled back on her heels and reached her
hand out to him in the beginning of an apology, in a gesture to halt him, but he didn't notice, and he went on. "And
especially me, because Toby's dead. He was always causing
some sort of trouble. You and he were always having some
kind of argument. You would have been so glad to have
him leave if he just hadn't died, and I could have gone, too.
But now . . . we both know that I was always the one you
counted on. I was always your favorite! So how can I ever
go away? How can I ever leave you alone?"

"Oh, no, David," she said, not in denial, but in a whis-
per of entreaty. She was appalled. He would hate himself
someday—if he ever had children of his own—for believing
these things about his brother, about her, about himself.
She moved toward him and embraced him, reaching up to
hold him lightly around his shoulders, and he leaned his
head down against the top of her head and horrified her
even further with the peculiar gasping sound of male sobbing. "Oh, no, David!" She thought about Toby and Sarah

and David and how terribly she loved them. She was assailed with the misery of her helplessly tenacious maternity. She wanted to be a better person than she was; she could not bear to be causing her child such pain. She wanted to explain herself to him, to relieve them both in some way of the injury they had done each other. "Oh, David," she said with an awful sense of desperation. "That's not true, sweetie! That's not ever how it was! You don't understand at all. You were *never* my favorite child." And they were marooned there, holding on to each other, baffled and heartbroken in the burgeoning garden.

CHAPTER SEVEN

LIFE AS A GIRL

ELLEN WAS SO PRETTY, Dinah thought. Years ago she had been intimidated by Ellen's beauty, but recently she had forgotten to notice what her friend looked like, and although Ellen was heavier now than when they had all first met over fifteen years ago, she had thickened sleekly. She wore her extra weight like velvet; her flesh flowed over her delicate bones with tiny ripples at the joints much like velvet when it is flexed. Dinah watched Ellen as she led the rest of them, all the while chatting back over her shoulder, her movements seemingly considered, all her gestures elegantly constrained and contained, a whole world described by the brief fanning out of her plump, tapering fingers, a shrug of her soft, round shoulders. Dinah felt ungainly by comparison, uselessly tall, too lean and overboned. Her own hands and feet and knees and elbows seemed to her grotesquely articulated and hazardous—likely to fly out in any direction uncontrollably.

Dinah had tried to salvage something of this day by including Ellen and Anna Tyson in place of Martin and David, and now Dinah and Sarah, who was leading Anna Tyson by the hand, followed in Ellen's wake through the crowds of people streaming toward the auditorium—the Shed—at Tanglewood. Ellen glided placidly against the throng, making way for the rest of them, nimbly avoiding being jostled along the path, her eyebrows raised in a sort of amused expectation that the masses would part before her. She was luxuriant, like a smug, spayed cat. Her pointed face, so delicately pink in contrast to her abundance of curly, loose, silvery hair, almost formed a double chin when she glanced back at them, but Dinah was charmed. And even if Ellen was a bit heavy, no one—not anyone at all, Dinah thought—would ever think of her as fat. Every move she made, and every facet of her manner—her soft, light voice, her intense posture while listening to someone else speak, her every habit—bespoke sensuality.

Dinah was mollified under the pale blue sky. She offered Sarah a tentative smile, which Sarah returned. It struck Dinah, too, that her own daughter was uncommonly pretty in her sleeveless, drop-waisted, midcalf-length linen dress that Dinah noticed was the current style for many of the girls between twelve and eighteen milling through the crowd. Dinah had tried subtly to discourage Sarah from wearing this intrinsically unattractive outfit, but as she took in the scene she realized that on these young girls the odd, dreary dresses only heightened one's awareness of the loveliness of their youth.

Sarah had added a wide-brimmed straw hat with a white ribbon around the crown and streamers down her back that mingled with her long, pale hair. Her face was bare of makeup and was not so much beautiful as it was endearing. Sarah had large, light brown eyes, wide set, with a slight droop of her right eyelid that was a sweet eccentricity of feature. Although her brows were far darker than her hair, they were finely arched, and the bridge of her nose was narrow and scooped as opposed to her brother's, which was broad and straight. She was slight, with fragile wrists and ankles, small hands with beautifully tapering fingers, and she was small like Ellen, only a little over five feet, not at all like Dinah, who was almost five feet nine.

Dinah towered over their group, with Anna Tyson holding on to Sarah's hand bringing up the rear, and she was unusually self-conscious. She felt tall and conspicuous, which was odd because she knew she was an attractive woman, and of all the insecurities she had ever had during her life as a girl, she had never been unhappy about her height. She looked around at the crowds, though, and lost interest in herself. She relaxed, slouching into a comfortable walk and ambling along behind Ellen as they struck out across the lawn, with all their picnic paraphernalia, in search of a place where they could settle onto the grass and eat their lunch.

It was Sarah's thirteenth birthday, and months ago Dinah had ordered box seats for this Sunday afternoon concert so that she and Martin and David and Sarah would have an unimpeded view of Seiji Ozawa conducting the Boston Symphony Orchestra and the Tanglewood Chorus in Bach's *Magnificat*. Afterward, they were to have a celebratory dinner at The Candlelight Inn in Lenox. But at breakfast Netta had appeared at the screen door like a wraith—such a common occurrence lately that Dinah no longer hurried upstairs to dress but remained in her comfortable, tattered robe and ducklike corduroy clogs.

David got up from the table and ushered her in, but she had only stepped just inside the room. Enshrouded by an air of urgent pathos, she gave the impression of a person always forced to remain excluded, a woman destined to cling to the verge of every occasion. Dinah had fought her rising irritation, because Netta was impervious to hints or even outright insults, and Dinah's vexation would only dou-

ble back upon herself. Besides, her mean-spiritedness toward Netta was truly unkind—Dinah knew it was so; Netta
was pitiful, literally to be pitied, Dinah had instructed herself, although she couldn't summon any sense of commiser-
ation. Netta's presence in her household—something about
her always askew, a bit bedraggled—evoked in Dinah a kind
of foreboding, a gloomy lassitude.

On his way to refill his coffee cup, Martin had taken
Netta's elbow solicitously and moved her along to the
table. When Dinah grudgingly took a good look at her,
even she was surprised at Netta's bleak expression, the
tense mouth, the shattered and bleached look around the
eyes. "Are you all right, Netta? Where's Anna Tyson? Is
everything okay?"

"Oh . . . Anna Tyson's in the car. She fell asleep on the
way over here. Bill called. Well . . . he called back every time
I hung up. He and Celia have probably already left the
apartment by now. They're driving in from Cambridge today, and they want to take Anna Tyson with them on a
camping trip up into Vermont this week."

Netta's whispery voice was flat and shocked, and Dinah
looked around the table at the plates of S-for-Sarah–shaped
pancakes she had put down in front of her family, each
stack of three with a lighted yellow birthday candle in it,
gutteringly aflame and burning down rapidly around the
tiny, curling black wicks. She bent forward and blew her
own out, concerned in spite of herself, especially on Anna
Tyson's account.

Dinah removed the candle and put her plate in front
of Netta, and got up to get her some coffee and start
more pancakes for everyone. As she passed behind Sarah,
who was sitting at the table with her unopened presents
arranged around her place, Dinah bent forward to embrace her in passing, leaning her cheek down to her
daughter's temple and hugging her shoulders in a brief
gesture of encouragement, meaning to assure her that

this was a day that would be devoted to her in just a minute. But Sarah stiffened slightly and shook her head in dismissal, with a peculiarly condescending half-smile tugging at one corner of her mouth. Dinah stood at the stove feeling unusually rebuffed and puzzled, wondering what Sarah meant to indicate.

"I told him no," Netta said. "I told him Anna Tyson was staying with me, and then Celia got on the phone and begged me to let Anna Tyson come. She even wanted to speak to her." Netta glanced around the table imploringly, as if she sought absolution. "But I said no," and her voice shuddered downward into an almost inaudible range. "And I didn't even tell Anna Tyson. I didn't even *ask* her. Well, she was asleep, of course. Bill phoned about eleven, and I've been up all night talking with him."

David leaned back in his chair and folded his arms across his chest. "That's ridiculous!" he said. "You don't have to agree to something like that. God! Why didn't you call here last night? It must have been terrible to be by yourself and get a call like that!" Dinah looked at David in surprise. Netta had somehow tapped into David's easily accessible outrage; he was furious, as if this had something to do with him.

"Netta," Martin said, "you don't even have a legal separation." He was calm, holding his knife and fork poised over his pancakes, and Netta gazed back at him vacantly. "What I mean is that I don't think you're obligated to do anything you don't want to about Anna Tyson until you've got all the legalities worked out. You should do whatever you think is best."

Netta slid her plate aside, resting her elbows in its place, and put her head down into her hands, swaying in a gentle negative. "I don't have the right to keep Anna Tyson away from her father. He loves her, too. She must need him. Oh, God! I don't have any idea what to do. The thought of seeing Celia and Bill . . . Oh, God! The idea of seeing them together is just overwhelming. I don't know. . . ." And although her face was bent toward the table, her voice was full of tears. "I don't think I can do it, and I really thought I'd be able to. I mean, I've imagined meeting them and talking things over. But I always thought it would be in Cambridge. I thought West Bradford was . . . oh, I don't know . . . a *safe* place. And I never thought it would be about Anna Tyson. I know that was stupid of me. I didn't want to think about it."

She had latticed and templed her fingers supporting her forehead and hiding her eyes, but now she lowered her head further, cupping her face from chin to hairline in her open palms. The room stilled at her resigned and inescapably poignant posture of being the sole source of comfort to herself. Netta sat at their table in a state of hopeless isolation while they regarded her with a kind of horrified awe.

But their mutual discomfort galvanized everyone at once. Dinah turned back to the stove to find that the skillet was smoking, and she moved it off the burner. Martin took a sip of his orange juice, and Sarah unfolded her napkin into her lap and looked across the table at David, who was so disturbed that he got up and stood for a minute and then walked out of the room, pacing the dining room and returning, still unnerved. "Well, Netta, you don't have to meet them when they come," he said. "I don't see why you have to be here just because they want you to. Why do you think you have to fulfill *their* expectations? Just leave a message on your answering machine, or something. A note on the door." He sounded angry at Netta, although Dinah realized that it was the same odd, hollow-voiced anger that he had fallen into off and on all summer; she didn't think he realized that he was angry at all, but Netta's head sank even lower onto her hands, and her shoulders shook with weeping.

"Oh, David . . ." Dinah said, finding herself in the perplexing position of protecting Netta from further anguish, "you know, it's really more complicated than that, sweetie . . ."

But David brushed her voice away with an abrupt flick of his hand. "Look, if *they're* coming *here* why don't we go get the rest of your things from the apartment in Cambridge. That way at least you'll know you won't have to see either one of them, and you never agreed to have them come get Anna Tyson anyway, did you?"

Netta stilled at the table but didn't lift her head from her hands. Dinah was appalled by David's proposal but waited for Martin to object. Anything she said to David these days seemed to be unbearable to him, but the moment stretched out in silence, and she realized that Martin was meticulously cutting his stack of pancakes into even-sized squares as he always did before he ate a single bite. He was gazing at his plate, attentive to his task, and all at once, after twenty-one years of marriage, this was a habit of his that Dinah could no longer bear.

"Eat the damned things before they get cold, Martin!" she snapped at him with a crack of her temper across the kitchen.

He glanced at her in surprise, and then looked down at his plate, mystified, wondering what had possibly angered his wife. "Oh . . . Well, I was just cutting them up so that there'd be syrup on every piece." His voice wasn't defensive or apologetic, only kindly explanatory in the face of her unreasonableness. He had been listening to the conversation around the table, but he hadn't let what they were saying catch his entire attention because everyone seemed painfully overwrought. He had puzzled out a method for equally sectioning the nongeometric S-shaped pancakes.

". . . and this would be the perfect day for you to get the rest of your stuff, Netta," David was saying. "The pans and things you need." He was less angry now but intense, back in his chair, leaning across the table toward her.

She had looked up at last, shaking her head backward in a reflexive movement. "I couldn't get everything in my car, though . . ." she said musingly, experimenting with the possibility.

"Well, we have the station wagon and Dad's car. Or one of us could drive the Hofstatters' van."

"I can't, David," Netta said softly, shaking her head and looking at him apologetically. "I'm just not up to it. I didn't sleep all night. It wouldn't be safe for me to drive. . . ."

"Look, we could even take some of my stuff in and leave it with a friend of mine in Boston so I won't have to make two trips when I move into the dorm. Dad and I can each take a car, and you and Anna Tyson can ride with one of us." David's anger had been transformed into enthusiasm, and Dinah didn't dare say a word; she still waited.

"Oh, David, it's a good idea, but Anna Tyson's exhausted, too, and I don't think I should take her back to that apartment without even explaining. . . ."

Dinah had looked to Martin again, but he seemed completely unaware of what was going on around him, while Sarah was watching David with her whole attention. Finally Dinah broke into the conversation as delicately as she could. "David, I know you've forgotten that this is Sarah's birthday, but we have tickets . . . we have reservations at the Candlelight. . . ."

But Sarah caught the brief expression of disdain that crossed her brother's face at his mother's words. He settled his shoulders against the back of his chair and crossed his arms tightly over his chest in a posture Sarah had come to recognize as his way of controlling his impatience toward his parents. She knew from watching him over the past year that their parents were often foolish, often absurdly sentimental, and that he was having a harder and harder time forgiving them for it.

She trusted his opinion even when she envied him, because in the small world of the teenagers in West Bradford—a world which she was about to join—it seemed to her that he was the recipient of so much approval. What she admired most was his indifference to the whole business. Sarah could see that he had achieved a kind of star status in his own realm, but either he didn't know it or he knew that it wasn't in the least important. Sarah knew it wasn't important, too, but she only *knew* it; she didn't believe it.

When she was with her friends at the college hockey game and David and Sam came in late, pausing for a moment to unzip their jackets and glance around the bleachers to decide where to sit, three high school girls sitting two rows down from Sarah had grasped each other's arms and leaned toward one another. "I swear to God I'm going to save myself for David Howells!" one of them said, and the three of them laughed together and continued to watch David and Sam as they found their friends in the stands. Various older girls had attempted to befriend her so they could come by her house to see David, but Sarah had carefully studied David's genuine indifference to his social status and pretended to it herself, which really did work; it really did enhance her desirability as a friend or girlfriend.

Now and then she could feel the atmosphere around herself become supercharged when a collective attention focused on her: a group of teachers in the school cafeteria suddenly glancing her way with beneficent expectations. Adults genuinely interested in her when she came through to pass the cheese and crackers at one of her parents' dinner parties. Her parents' guests didn't merely nod and thank her; conversation stopped momentarily and they turned to ask a question and listen to her expectantly.

"Another one of those gorgeous Howells children,"

she had heard a woman she vaguely recognized say to another when she made her way past them on the Carriage Street sidewalk. The limelight David inhabited in this last year he would really live in West Bradford was wide enough so that the soft edges illuminated her, too. There was no one, therefore, whose wisdom she trusted more than she trusted David's, because she knew from everything her parents had ever said that they would disapprove of her desire for popularity and acclaim. They would think her frivolous. But she also knew beyond a doubt that they didn't understand the real world of political life in which she had to operate.

"It doesn't matter about my *birthday*!" she said. "It's not a big deal. It's just a birthday! You know this is much more important, Mom. This is Netta's *real life*!" David met her glance with a surprised and dazzling smile that entirely opened his expression, lighting his face with a look of unusual pleasure. In someone less sternly featured, it would have been a cartoon smile, with the corners of his mouth curling up, his eyebrows lifted in delight. Ever since he was a child, that smile had been an amazing transformation of his strong features, but these days its appearance was more and more rare.

"Goddammit, Sarah!" Dinah finally exploded. "Your birthday is *your* real life! This is the only day you'll ever turn thirteen! We've planned this for *months*! All of this . . ." and she gestured around the room with a sweep of her arm to indicate the overheated atmosphere, ". . . this is *not* your responsibility!" She leaned across the table toward her daughter, unconsciously venting all of her aggravation on Sarah in what she thought was Sarah's behalf.

But it was Martin at whom Dinah was really angry, so angry that it made her face tingle with suppressed rage. When she had told him about the conversation she had overheard between David and Christie, a pained expression had crossed his face as he looked away from the baseball game he was watching on television and absorbed what she was saying. They had been propped in bed, side by side, late on the same evening of the afternoon when Dinah had overheard that conversation. She had been trying to read, or at least to appear to read, while she considered how to tell Martin that Christie might be pregnant. Dinah had still felt bruised from her confrontation with her own son that afternoon, still baffled, and she was both horrified and terribly saddened at the situation Christie and David might be in.

Martin had turned to listen to her as she began relaying Christie and David's conversation, but he had glanced back toward the television for just a second when a roar arose from the crowd at Fenway Park. He hadn't turned fully away from her—he had merely been distracted—but she reached over and flicked off the remote control and the screen went black. He had started to say something, perhaps to apologize, but she had glared at him, and his face had set in resignation as he heard her out.

"Oh, Christ!" he said, but quietly with a note of resignation. He rubbed one hand beneath his jaw, running his fingers along the sides of his face and brushing his thumb over the cleft of his chin as though he were assessing his need of a shave. Dinah was familiar with that gesture from other times in their lives, moments of anxiety and pain. "Jesus Christ! How could they be so stupid? I mean, it's hard to think of David being so irresponsible!" And she could hear that he was as anxious as she. Then he dropped his arm and lifted both hands helplessly, palms up, and she immediately felt abandoned. "Well, Dinah . . . I don't know what we can do unless David asks us to do something. It sounds like Christie hasn't told her parents anything yet. It seems to me that most of all it has to be *her* business."

"What the hell do you mean? You mean it's all *Christie's* fault?"

He gazed levelly at her for a moment, and then spoke with pained elaboration. "For God's sake, Dinah. Of course I don't mean that. I *mean* that it's her body, her choice whether to tell us anything about it. It may turn out that she's fine, and she might be mortified that we had ever known anything about it. And not only that, it seems to me that *you* would normally be saying exactly the same thing."

"Normally! Oh, right! Well, normally David hasn't gotten anybody pregnant! Sweetheart, Christie might be pregnant with *David's* baby." Her anger had turned into a sort of pleading. "How can you not care about that? I can't think about anything else! I wouldn't even know what to suggest they do about it. Oh, Martin, I can't believe you're not on my side. At least you could talk to him!"

"He knows we know about it," he said to her reasonably, "and my whole point is that I don't think you and I *have* a side. David's eighteen years old. I don't think we have the right to make this our business."

"How can you possibly believe that?" She was truly astonished. "Christie's *not* eighteen, you know. She's only sixteen. But Martin, no matter how old he is, David's still our son! We still owe him some sort of guidance . . . or . . . protection!"

"David is like an explosion getting ready to happen this summer. We've got to give him his privacy, too," Martin said. "And we owe him some dignity. He knows he can come to us if he needs help. I think Christie knows the same thing. I mean, I think she would come to us if she wanted us to help! Or if she wanted us to know about it."

To her own frustration Dinah had started crying. "God damn you, Martin! Goddammit! You have so much trust in *reason*! In *logic*! This is too much for anyone to handle in some sort of orderly way you seem to think exists in the world! You are so *stupid* sometimes that I can hardly believe you're smart!"

"Dinah." He sounded worn out. "Why don't you talk to him if you want, but I think . . ."

"God! That's the whole point, dammit! I can't talk to him anymore about anything. *You* need to find out what's going on!" She hadn't been able to stop crying, and she wiped her eyes repeatedly with Kleenex, dropping them in scrunched puffs into her lap. Martin put his arm around her and they simply sat leaning against each other for a while, Dinah waiting to see what Martin would come up with. But Martin hadn't replied. He had hugged her toward him comfortingly, and within half an hour or so, when she had let her head fall back against the headboard and had closed her eyes, he had reached over and flicked the game back on, keeping the volume low.

And in the kitchen on Sarah's birthday, as he did nothing to stop the celebration from slipping through the cracks, she had wanted to turn to him and say that he had been loved too well for all of his life and it had left him diminished. Today, for the first time, that's what she believed. It was not so much that he lacked empathy, but she thought he misdirected it; he never *considered*, he refused to be reflective. With Netta's presence this morning and almost constantly over these summer weeks, Dinah had been too constrained ever to get anything sorted out within her family, and time was suddenly out of control, flying by, her family separating from her as though she were the whirling center pushing them away by centrifugal force.

But in that exact moment, when a new way of knowing her husband had clicked into place, Martin looked over at David and spoke calmly and in a reasonable voice. "David, I can't believe you expect us to give up what we've planned for Sarah's birthday. I don't understand how you could be that thoughtless. I really don't." He was sincere and rational in the wake of Dinah's impassioned outburst. She began to clear away the mixing bowl and baking powder from the counter. Martin spoke between bites of pancake, which he alone seemed maddeningly determined to finish. "Netta, you need to get this settled with Bill. . . ."

David's brows drew down, and he tucked his chin into his chest, his shoulders lifting and falling in a long, resigned sigh as he rocked back on the legs of his chair. Sarah watched him carefully; she was attuned to every nuance, and she was overcome with sorrow at his frustration—she felt a kind of grief that she was too inexperienced to name; she was only able to translate it into anger.

"My birthday is not a big deal! Okay?" Sarah said, each word deliberate, her tone scornful, a verbal sneer, her fists knotted alongside her plate. "It's only a big deal to you! You're the one who made all the plans!" she said across the room to her mother.

Dinah was startled. "What? But Sarah, I asked you what you wanted. . . ."

"I know. But I didn't really care what we did. I know you and Dad like to go to Tanglewood. I mean, it was fine with me whatever we did, but obviously this is much more important." Dinah settled back against the kitchen counter and crossed her own arms in an unconscious but exact replication of her son's posture, cocking her head at her daughter and staring her down in the face of the huge injustice of what she was saying. Sarah was hoping to intern at Tanglewood in voice when she was sixteen, and it was for her sake that Dinah always bought box-seat tickets—so that Sarah could see the stage.

And Sarah did flinch away from her mother's gaze and back down a little. "I mean, I really think this is great. These pancakes and everything. But this is just more important!" She looked to her mother for a signal, but Dinah didn't give an inch, and Sarah's own anger flared. "And, besides, wouldn't we really all have a great time with you in the mood you're in! I'll baby-sit with Anna Tyson, Netta, if that would help!" She left the table abruptly, her pancakes uneaten, her presents unopened, and her face far less defiant than her words had been.

Martin sat still, with his elbows on the table bracketing his plate of neatly partitioned pancakes, miserable at the unpleasantness that suddenly pervaded the room. David straightened in his chair, all at once evasive and uncertain. Netta remained oblivious, her face glazed with exhaustion. Dinah was bewildered, wondering how, once again, her championship of her children was so unacceptable to them.

Generally New Englanders believe that their favorite time of year is summer, when the days are long and gentle and the mountains are verdant. But as the days lengthened, Dinah felt a sort of frantic distress when confronted by the abundance of green, the warmth, the excessiveness of everything growing. By late July, she was overwhelmed by the cloud of seasonal expectations as persistent and bothersome as gnats.

Martin said that she resented enjoying herself, and Dinah thought that it was quite possible that her disposition simply wasn't suited to it, but it irritated her that Martin had so easily categorized her.

"I *do* enjoy summer, Martin. I just don't think I should *have* to. But you're right. I resent it. I do resent having to be so cheerful all the time! I hate the . . . *forced* spontaneity in the summer. The articles in any magazine you pick up at the dentist's on how to have 'your pantry stocked for that unexpected guest.' My God! I'd have to hang a side of beef and keep a poultry farm and plant an orchard." This was what she had said to him in her own defense on the day that Netta had dropped by to make soup. Dinah wasn't always so cranky, but by midsummer she was in the midst of her worst emotional season.

Now and then she consoled herself with the fact that at least she hadn't grown up in California, where there wasn't any weather at all according to Ellen. Just sunshine and eternal flowers, or so Ellen recounted frequently. Dinah didn't think that she herself could make it through the year without January and February, with their severe clarity, their freedom of *non*-celebration, and their confirmation of the fact that fluctuations of mood were necessary, were natural.

But, to her surprise, this day that had begun so inauspiciously had come together quite nicely, genuinely spontaneous, and Dinah luxuriated in her lack of responsibility for the success of the rest of the afternoon. Wandering through the beautiful grounds of Tanglewood, she was delighted with the summer air and the crowds of people spreading over the lawn with their picnic baskets and folding chairs. One couple had set up a little table with candles and flowers and china plates arrayed with avocado and shrimp, varied lettuces, and pale white cucumber fans. It was a bit of showing off they were doing, of course, but they were delighting in the attention they received from passersby, the acknowledgment of their unabashed romanticism.

The mood of the afternoon was buoyant. Dinah was caught up in it all around, and she thought with pity rather than disdain of those friends of hers who were such purists that they wouldn't come to Tanglewood but waited to go to Boston to hear the orchestra in Symphony Hall.

Dinah loved the tourists who enthusiastically applauded between movements, who always leaped to their feet during Handel's *Messiah* for the "Hallelujah" Chorus, despite the tactful plea in the program guide not to do so. It was clear that many of them had never seen a major orchestra before, and it delighted Dinah to spot someone in the audience who was as overwhelmed as she had once been at witnessing the astonishing mutual effort of all the disparate elements of an orchestra and the chorus to produce a miraculous sound. It was newly breathtaking to Dinah every time despite twenty years of acquiring a little musical sophistication. After every performance, she was angry the next morning at Matthew Bardwell, whose reviews in the paper pointed out inadequacies she hadn't noticed, and whose dour recounting of a concert diminished the memory of her pleasure. She had privately decided that Matthew Bardwell had no capacity for joy.

At the end of the school year one of David's closest friends, who had been away for his freshman year at Harvard, had unexpectedly joined Dinah in the auditorium at West Bradford High School while she was waiting for the seniors' musical recital to begin. "Jay!" Dinah had exclaimed. "How brave of you to come back and sit through two hours of this just to hear David play."

"Oh, great!" Jay had replied. "Actually I didn't know David was playing. I really wanted to hear the xylophone player. She's great!"

Dinah had laughed and hugged him, and gone on to ask him about Harvard, about what David could expect *his* freshman year. Jay was one of David's friends whom she dearly loved. He was interested in everything, sophisticated but never smug. She was delighted to be in his company. And she was astonished when, indeed, a xylophone was wheeled onto the stage midway during the evening, and a girl she didn't recognize approached it with seeming trepidation and played quite a complicated piece. Dinah had thought Jay was kidding, but she clapped loudly along with him when the girl stepped forward to take a bow.

"Isn't she terrific? God!" he said. "Isn't that fantastic? She didn't miss hitting a single note!" He was jubilant, and Dinah had remembered his pleasure and recognized it in herself every time she watched a singer, a quartet, a choir, or an orchestra. She and Jay shared the disproportionate admiration of the musically nongifted for any of these performers.

This afternoon, with the concert still ahead of her, as

she and Ellen and Sarah and Anna Tyson made their way across the Tanglewood grounds, she was even feeling sorry for Martin and David and Vic, who had taken Martin's car and the Hofstatters' van into Cambridge to help Netta pack up whatever she needed from her apartment.

Dinah and Ellen spread a blanket under a tree near the building in which the chorus was rehearsing. Ellen had taken charge of unpacking their picnic, and Dinah walked over to the hedge surrounding the grounds to peer out at the landscape, which fell away down the steep sides of the Stockbridge Bowl where a lake glimmered flatly, like a pewter plate, unshadowed by clouds, before the mountains rose again in gentle folds until they met the horizon. She stood for a bit in mindless and entirely pleasurable contemplation of the view, and then she came back to their blanket and began to open out the webbed lawn chairs they had brought.

"Okay, tell me the truth, now, Ellen! Don't you *really* think"—and her voice was light and sweetly teasing—"in your heart of hearts, at the core of your being, that Sarah is absolutely the *loveliest* girl in the world?" Dinah pulled her daughter to her in an amiable hug. "And the most *pleasant* company!" Ellen was sitting on the blanket arranging plates, and she smiled up at them, but Sarah pulled away, with Anna Tyson still attached to one hand, and Dinah grinned an indulgent apology toward her daughter for having embarrassed her with a public display of affection.

"I'm going to take Anna Tyson to get a T-shirt at the gift shop," Sarah said, and only when she was well away from her mother did she suddenly feel the pressure of tears behind her eyes and a long aching in her throat. She was sorrowful all at once at not having responded to her mother just now, and she was also overcome with some amorphous disappointment that was almost like being homesick. At the Glass House, where souvenirs were sold, she bought a T-shirt for Anna Tyson, and before she turned away from the salesgirl, Sarah asked for a Tanglewood poster and bought it for her mother.

When she finished arranging the plates of sandwiches and fruit and cheese, Ellen leaned back on her elbows on the blanket with her eyes closed, her face tipped up toward the sun. Her thick hair fell in loose waves just above her shoulders. Ellen was the adult Dinah knew better than any other except Martin, and she studied her with admiration and then hazarded a soft comment.

"You know, I don't know what to do about David these days, Ellen. What to say to him. He can hardly stand to be in the same room with me." She spoke matter-of-factly; she wasn't even sure Ellen was listening to her. "And now Sarah . . . Well . . . Oh, God, Ellen, you can't imagine how painful it is to realize that sometimes your own children really don't *like* you!"

"Umm. No, you're wrong. I imagine that it's very hard. But you know, I was talking to Vic this morning. It seems to both of us . . . well . . . you can't *expect* so much from Sarah and especially from David. Frankly, I think you're behaving very badly toward your children, Dinah."

Dinah was astonished. She swiveled around to stare at her friend, but Ellen was still basking in the mild sunshine, eyes closed. "I can't even imagine what would make you say something like that to me when you have absolutely no idea . . ." Dinah didn't raise her voice; in fact, her tone was softly plaintive, but she was quite angry.

Ellen interrupted her, though, by a continual shaking of her head, her hair swinging behind her, her eyes still closed, and her face tilted away from Dinah. "You've got to understand, Dinah, that you simply aren't allowed to *need* anything from your children! It's the greatest unkindness you can do them. And we probably shouldn't even discuss it, because you won't get any pity from me."

Dinah sat completely still with shock and anger, and

Ellen, who could not see her, mistook her silence for reluctant acquiescence, and she began to elaborate on the subject. "I know the situation too well from the other side," Ellen said. Her voice was soft with pained amusement. "My parents were impossible. You know I was in therapy for years, of course. But you have no idea ... I can't tell you the enormous relief I feel whenever I remember that my parents finally died. Oh, my God! The *freedom*! I started writing.... Well, I suppose I also feel guilty, too, in spite of myself, at feeling that relief. But still ..."

Without opening her eyes, Ellen stretched full-out on the blanket and put her hands behind her head, turning her face to the side slightly so that Dinah only gazed at her profile. Dinah was too dumbfounded to reply. No longer than three minutes ago she had thought of herself as the mother of two children who sometimes, and in varying degrees, seemed to dislike her, but now she saw quite clearly that she was a woman whose children—perhaps unwittingly—eagerly anticipated her death. It was quite a lot to absorb in the soft air and under the gentle sky.

She glanced in appalled enlightenment at the clusters of picknickers around them. There was a woman nursing an infant, and another mother in irritable pursuit of a gleefully fleeing toddler, but when she caught up to him and swung him into the air, he crowed exultantly, and the woman laughed, too. Nearby an elegantly dressed couple talked between themselves while their teenaged sons threw a Frisbee back and forth. Dinah studied the boys carefully, putting their ages between fourteen and sixteen. As the younger boy ran backward several steps and raised his arm to grasp the lip of the descending Frisbee, Dinah saw, in her mind's eye, the slow, uncurling motion of his arm and a mighty and precise snap of his wrist, which sent the Frisbee in a lethal path in his par-

ents' direction, striking them simultaneously where their
heads were bent together in pleasant discussion. Without
a sound the two of them crumpled toward each other in
a quick and painless death. Dinah experienced a reflexive
recoiling from the blow in the same way that one awakens
with a start from a dream of falling. As she came back
into the moment, the younger boy released the Frisbee
in a high, short arc in his brother's direction, and they
both moved farther away where there was more space
and fewer people. A taller boy in a Boston College
sweatshirt called out to them, and the older brother sent
the Frisbee spiraling in his direction. A fourth boy joined
them so that they formed a loose square. They were
attractive young men, laughing and calling to each other,
and Dinah felt sure, all at once, that not one of them
was brooding about the fact that his parents were still
alive. The idea gave her faint hope and renewed her
anger at Ellen. The notion of Vic and Ellen discussing
her over their morning coffee flashed through her
thoughts.

"Ellen! For God's sake! What are you talking about?
I don't want *anyone's* pity! That's not the point at all. Of
course I need things from my children. Every parent
needs things . . . which, granted, is not to say that I'll *get*
them." She wanted to put an end to this discussion. She
was amazed at herself for having taken it up with Ellen,
who had no children of her own, and who fancied that
by occasionally borrowing the Howells children for an
outing or a weekend that she could comprehend parent-
hood. She had once explained to Dinah that she wanted
to take the children into New York, that it would be
helpful to her poetry. Dinah had thought at the time that
only someone with Ellen's vanity could even imagine such
a thing. But because Dinah liked Ellen's poetry very
much, Dinah had decided that other people's children
might well serve as triggers to Ellen's own younger self.

The act of writing was mysterious to Dinah, and she had great respect for Ellen's talent; but her arrogance, her presumption this afternoon was galling. Dinah meant to speak patiently. "Every parent in the world needs at least the illusion of returned affection. . . ."

Ellen remained stretched out on the blanket with her arms crossed behind her head, but she opened her eyes very wide when she recognized Dinah's indignation. She seemed mildly amused. "No. Absolutely not. You can't need anything!" She watched Dinah alertly, and Dinah sputtered back at her, "Ellen, you don't know anything about living with people you love unconditionally! I need just what they need from me. . . ."

"You don't get to do that, you know," Ellen said calmly, "especially if you're anyone's mother."

"Of course you do. It's not a question of *getting* to do it! It's simply the way it is. I need affection . . ."

Ellen was shaking her head again, and Dinah's voice rose imploringly.

". . . and kindness. That's just reasonable! Courtesy . . ."

"If you really need all those things—if you can't survive without them—then you'll become a monster," Ellen said, closing her eyes again, ending the discussion.

Dinah moved to one of the lawn chairs and sat gently massaging her neck, seeing no point in reminding Ellen of what she and Martin—and Sarah and David, too—had already survived. She did not say that the murkiness and intricacies of family life sometimes bewildered her with the things that could not be, were not under any conditions said to each other. Dinah would not admit to her friend that sometimes she felt she held on to her humanity only by the very tips of her fingers.

Franklin M. Mount
Dean of Freshmen
Harvard College
12 Truscott Street
Cambridge, Massachusetts 02138

Dear Mr. Mount,

Do you think it's true that people don't reach adulthood until the death of their parents? Erik Erikson said that, and I have no idea how he meant to define adulthood. I don't even remember where I learned it. Some people never become adults no matter how old they are and even if both their parents are dead. I think other people are adults at age six or seven. But I'm trying to understand what he was getting at. I wonder how old Erik Erikson was when he decided that. I wonder if his own parents were still alive, and also if he was an only child. Is adulthood what we're all striving for? Do you think it's a particularly desirable condition, or did he only mean that it was inevitable? He may have meant that adulthood is regrettable.

Our daughter Sarah just turned thirteen and still needs us, and I think that she probably knows it. I think that she needs her father right now more than she needs me, but in some ways she would never recover if she lost either one of us at her age. What I've been thinking, though, is that it seems possible to me that David could survive contentedly without either one of us. I do know, of course, that in all sorts of ways he would feel grief at our absence, and he would miss us terribly, but I'm no longer sure that our existence is necessary to his living a successful life. I guess it's true that in the ordinary way of the world it may be that parents simply live too long.

When Sarah and Anna Tyson reappeared, and all four of them were eating their lunch, Ellen told them about the problems she was having with her writing.

"I worry and pace," Ellen said. "I glance at the final poem and compare it with the *shape* of the copy I tape up across the room. It all seems wrong. The *real* poem—I mean, when it's written out—seems to me to be only a sort of shadow of the literal shape I've intended. Oh, well . . . but now that Owen Croft is in *The Review* office, Vic wants me to help weed through some of *those* poems. I don't know if I can cope with the distraction."

"What do you mean?" Dinah said. She was helping Anna Tyson slip the Tanglewood T-shirt over her dress. "What does Owen's being there have to do with your helping?"

But Ellen had lost the thread of what she was saying while Dinah was struggling with Anna Tyson's puffed sleeves. Ellen had turned to watch Sarah, who had taken off, then put back on, her wide-brimmed straw hat, arranging her hair with a toss so that it fell across one shoulder. She had grown restless where they were sitting—at the far edge of the lawn. They had Shed tickets and hadn't needed to eat their lunch among the multitudes in order to establish a place on the lawn close to the orchestra. Sarah would have much preferred to be in the middle of a crowd. She was covertly watching the boys who had been throwing the Frisbee and wondering if they had noticed her and also wondering how old they thought she was. She absently fiddled with the poster she had bought for her mother but had forgotten to give to her, unfurling it slightly and letting it snap to like a spring.

"Aha, Sarah! We've succeeded in boring you to death!" Ellen said with seeming delight. "But that's wonderful! Oh,

Sarah, you should be so bored by the two of us that you will simply trample us under your feet to get to what you believe in, or to do what you have to do. Whenever it is. Whenever that happens!"

Dinah saw that her daughter was embarrassed at being caught out in inattention and also by Ellen's drama, and perhaps even by the fact that she *was* bored to death with this company on her thirteenth birthday. But Dinah couldn't think of anything to say that would ameliorate Sarah's discomfort, and just then the first warning bell rang. They all turned their attention to gathering up the remnants of their lunch.

Finally the four of them made their way to the Shed as the third warning bell began to sound, but they were stopped by an usher, who reminded them that no child under six years old was allowed inside during a performance. Dinah felt a surge of relief. "I'll stay outside with Anna Tyson, Sarah. You and Ellen go on in. I'll give these other two tickets to someone out here."

Sarah and Ellen both began to protest, but Dinah forestalled any objection.

"No, no. I've seen the BSO perform the *Magnificat* in Boston. I'd really rather be outside, anyway. It's a beautiful day."

Dinah threaded through the crowd with Anna Tyson in tow and exchanged the box-seat tickets with the couple who had set up the lovely little luncheon for themselves just outside the Shed. She settled in one of their lawn chairs, and Anna Tyson climbed exhaustedly onto her lap instead of sitting in the other chair. Dinah settled her comfortably, with Anna Tyson's head against her shoulder, and pushed the little girl's damp hair away from her forehead. She didn't happen to glance up and see an expression of pure yearning cross Sarah's face as she looked back at her mother through the crowds of people, and witnessed that mindless caress as her mother's hand brushed across Anna Tyson's forehead.

In fact, Dinah didn't see Ellen or Sarah at all. She was idly stroking Anna Tyson's forehead and thinking of Ellen in that beautifully austere room of her renovated farmhouse where she sat at a window and composed her poems, working anxiously, filled with uncertainty. The picture of Ellen that Dinah conjured up embodied a high-level sort of anguish. Clean despair. It was too bad, Dinah mused, that her writing cost Ellen so dearly. She had such talent, and she was almost belligerently honest, for which Dinah could do nothing but admire her. It was also a shame, really, that she had let herself get so fat.

CHAPTER EIGHT

TRAFFIC

FOR THE THIRD MORNING in a row, Martin was awakened instantly and unnaturally early by the hammering of a woodpecker in the metal guttering at the corner of the house. The first gray daylight only smudged the screens, and in the dusky bedroom the windows themselves could scarcely be discerned except by the outlines of their white woodwork. He felt nearly tearful under the onslaught of morning—the maddened woodpecker and all the rest of the wretched din of morning birdsong. He pushed aside the rumpled sheet and lay still in the slight breeze produced by a careful and precarious arrangement of window and oscillating fans. Usually once during the night a sudden wind or a wandering cat brought the box fan, balanced on the windowsill, crashing to the floor, and by now its propeller was so askew that it tick-ticked with every rotation. The oscillating fan, which Martin had arranged with careful deliberation on a chair placed strategically at the foot of the bed, whooshed and whirred as it made its slow sweep back and forth. All night he and Dinah slept fitfully with the sound, but not the feel, of rushing air. The artificial breeze was teasing; it was very nearly a torment.

Dinah reached over and touched his hand, although she didn't grasp it, she simply made contact, and they looked across the expanse of white sheet between them and gazed dumbly at each other. Her hair was matted and spiked around her face; she had thrashed from side to side during the night, turning her head against the pillow, while her hair was damp from sweat. She ran her hand through it with a grimace.

"My God! That damned bird. I can't get up now," she said. "Can you?"

"He's not going to stop."

"I know. It's not even five o'clock, though. I believe I'll just lie here and languish and suffer." It was a phrase caught up from a long-ago telephone conversation with Martin's mother when she was asked how all the relations in Sheridan were faring during yet another parched summer. "Oh, we're all just fine," she had said to Dinah, "except, of course, we're just languishing and suffering in all this heat." Even David and Sarah used the phrase, although they probably didn't know its origin. It was part of the family's shorthand, conveying a determination to endure cheerfully.

Martin offered Dinah a weak smile, and then he closed his eyes briefly, contemplating the possibilities of the day as the woodpecker began another barrage above their heads. He thought about breakfast and the wonderful, piercingly bitter smell of the only two cups of real coffee he could drink during a day without becoming shaky and nauseated; when he was in his twenties he could drink coffee all day, even ten minutes before he fell sound asleep. On the other hand, given that he was heading downhill, what difference would it make if he had some bacon after a night like this? The idea of sitting in the relatively cool kitchen with the aroma of coffee brewing and bacon cooking was comforting. He glanced over at Dinah, but he couldn't see her face; she had withdrawn her hand from his and was sheltering her eyes from the light with her forearm.

"What if I fix bacon and eggs? You want some? Or pancakes?"

"Oh, sweetheart, I really can't get up now. I'll feel tired all day."

"I can't get back to sleep," he said. "I think I'll go over to the office and get some things cleared up."

Dinah had turned on her side, away from the windows, and she only murmured, but he came around the bed and kissed her lightly on the temple before he pulled on a seersucker robe and padded barefoot downstairs and into the kitchen.

In cycles during all the years of the Howellses' marriage, there was never a subtraction from the deep core of genuine affection each held for the other, even when they were irritated at each other, even when they were desperately angry at each other. But after the first several years of the giddiness of unrestrained sensuality, and with the birth of children, their lust had generally become more companionable than romantic, friendly, and accommodating more often than it was frantic or demanding. And it had become a habit since the children were small that the mornings were the time Dinah and Martin most enjoyed making love. While the children were still asleep, but past any nighttime crisis of midnight fevers, dreaming terrors, croup, or alarmingly severe nocturnal stomachaches, Martin and Dinah could indulge in the drowsy luxury of sex.

As the children grew up, Martin and Dinah were less physically but more emotionally exhausted by evening, and the habit of lovemaking in the early morning had persisted. But this was not their climate, and they both were awake in the early dawn with the exhausted, fuzzy sensation of never having slept at all. When Martin left the room, Dinah slowly fell back into a sticky sleep and unfolded her long arms and legs across the whole breadth of the bed in an attempt to be cooled by the sluggishly churned air.

The first week of August had settled heavily over West Bradford with temperatures and humidity in the nineties. It was the kind of weather that made Martin the most unhappy. He fought an intellectual battle against the visceral panic that overtook him in hot weather, because at some basic level he did not believe that the duration of such heat would be relatively short. His body remembered the claustrophobic and seemingly endless summer days of Mississippi, which dulled the spirits of all but small, school-free children. It was weather that was bearable to people like most of his neighbors, who only experience such blatant heat a few weeks out of the year. And it was these infuriating native New Englanders who most irritated Martin with their exuberant embracement of this enervating weather. It was the only time of the year that Martin could not shake pessimism.

After breakfast he showered and pulled on nylon running shorts and a short-sleeved gray T-shirt emblazoned with a red and white logo that read BEER NUTS. He had gotten the shirt for only two dollars and two proofs-of-purchase labels from bags of peanuts he had picked up at the store when he was in the check-out line. To have ordered the shirt was the sort of thrift scorned by his whole family, but the shirt had held up for three years, and both his children had tried to take possession of it. Even so lightly dressed, by the time Martin got to *The Review* office, with Duchess ambling slowly behind him, her head drooping like an old horse, he was already sweaty and discouraged. His bare arms and legs were plastered with fluffs of fur that the poor dog was shedding for her life. But he was sure that at six-thirty on a Monday morning, he would have the office to himself and could clear away a lot of work that should have been done already.

This morning, though, as had been the case whenever Martin arrived at his office, Owen was already settled into his own little cubicle. His long legs were stretched out in front of him and his feet braced against the uppermost interior edge of the knee-hole panel of his desk, and he leaned backward from the waist to the full extension of his flexible office chair so that he was almost horizontal. He was absolutely still, except for a slight flick of the sheaf of papers he was holding before him and peering at intently, although he could scarcely have been unaware that Martin and Duchess had arrived. Martin allowed himself a glimmer of an image of Owen grabbing up those papers and assuming his careful pose the moment he had heard the heavy door of the building squeal open two flights above him.

"God, Owen! What are you doing here at this hour?" Martin heard his own false note of hearty good humor and wondered if he could ever in his life be comfortable in Owen's presence. When Owen lowered the papers he was reading, ostensibly taking a moment to refocus his attention and absorb the fact of Martin's being there, Martin had a terrible urge to reach across the desk and shake him out of his stupid pretension.

"When we get this great summer weather I always get up about four-thirty to go for a run. I decided to come on in and get these letters out. But, now, Martin, I need to talk to you about these letters of Vic's. . . ."

Martin held up his hand for Owen to stop, and he felt—as he always did—rising anger as well as a sense of prevailing and mysterious shame whenever he confronted Owen. "First let me get some things on my desk cleared away, Owen. This is the deadline if we want to take an excerpt of Brenner's new book, and I haven't had a chance to finish reading it yet." Owen was blond and lanky and unruffled by the weather. Just to get past what Martin had come to think of as the daily hurdle of overcoming Owen's ghastly bonhomie and his jovial assumption of shared authority made Martin feel gray and tired. He was beginning to think that Owen's insistent chumminess bordered on aggression.

As Martin attempted to bypass Owen's desk with no more than a greeting, Owen was on his feet in an instant, leaning forward and smiling triumphantly, full of urgency, and gesturing at Martin with the papers he'd been working on, which were exuberantly covered with green pencil markings.

Owen's initial suggestion for using a system of varicolored markings that would hasten Martin's or Vic's understanding of what was required had impressed Martin, but he flinched this morning when he glanced at the four or five pages liberally marked in the color that designated the need for a consultation.

"Give me an hour, Owen. I want to finish Brenner's manuscript."

"Right, right," Owen said, falling back into his chair and swiveling back and forth restlessly. "But I was looking through these letters that Vic left for Helen to type. I'll tell you, you know, Vic really should go over these himself. I mean, this prose . . . these are *rejection* letters, right?"

"One hour, Owen. An hour and I'll take a look." He was unusually disheartened at the prospect of going over this correspondence, because Vic had decamped and was answering many of the letters that Owen had been hired to handle, and Owen made it clear at every opportunity that he thought he could do a better job. Martin was unhappy about the whole situation. Several weeks ago Vic had entered Martin's office stiff and angry, restrained even in the way he moved.

"You know, Martin," Vic began mildly as he settled in across the desk, "I finally asked Ellen to read these poems"—he waved a sheaf of papers in the air—"and she agrees with me that they're really good. I don't think I *am* reading more into them than there is. I think they're extraordinary." He had grown more adamant and defensive by the moment, and Martin had been baffled.

"Whose poems are you talking about? I don't remember that we disagreed about any poems."

"Elizabeth Melrose's. I think they're some of the best things we've seen." Vic was shuffling through his papers looking for them.

"You know," Vic said, as he came up with the pages he wanted, "you're always saying that I see more in a piece of writing than there is to find. I don't understand how you can miss these . . . terrible *laments*! What is it you think I'm reading into them?"

Martin had reached for the poems without answering, and Vic had handed them across the desk and waited for Martin to reply. Martin read a page quickly and looked up at Vic. "I haven't even seen this, Vic. I'd like to take some time. . . ."

"Shit, Martin!" Vic had leaped up from his chair. "Owen put these back on my desk. When I asked him about them, he said you didn't think they were very interesting. This is just crazy. Every time I have to give him some sort of directions it turns into a marathon session. You've got to fire him!"

"You fire him!" Martin said. "You were right there when we explained the job to him. You seemed perfectly happy about it then. You fire him!"

"Oh no," Vic had said. "I won't do it. Owen's your problem."

And Martin had tried various subtle ways of firing Owen. When he had suggested to Owen that they simply didn't have enough correspondence to justify the position, Owen had volunteered to stay on for free. When Martin had asked Owen pointedly if he really thought he was suited to this job, Owen's face had twisted alarmingly into an agonized expression. "I'm trying *everything*! Every day! I'm trying to get this right!"

So Vic had set up office in the living room of his old farmhouse while Ellen worked in her study upstairs. It was where Martin and Vic had often worked in the summers in the early years of *The Review,* and Martin was suddenly filled with yearning for the fledgling enterprise, for the long afternoons by the pond.

Vic and Martin had an administrative assistant, complex financing, budgets, and even a little clout; but Martin could barely remember what it felt like to be ambitious, and clout didn't interest him at all anymore. In the beginning he must have possessed a kind of naïve hopefulness that was the fuel of ambition. He supposed he had thought that there was some sort of anonymous admiration to be earned that would please him, a limited but high brow sort of fame. It was a quest that approached or replaced religiousness, and the striving for it had been an easy way to live his life. But it still surprised him to meet so many people his own age or older who could sustain aspirations of eminence in the face of the real lives they led.

He unclipped Duchess from her leash, and she sank down to the cool floor exactly where she was, resting her chin mournfully on her front paws. Martin thumbed through the book manuscript to find a section that would be effective as an excerpt. He tried to concentrate, but even through his closed door he could hear Owen drumming his fingers along the stem of his arched desk lamp. Martin knew exactly what the sound was, because he had seen Owen swiveling restlessly in his chair and tapping his fingers along the flex of the lamp in the rhythm of the drums of a marching band:

> da-da-da-da . . . dum . . . dum
> da-da-da-da . . . dum . . . dum

Other times Martin would hear a soft, muted thrumming that he had eventually identified as the reverberation of the frantically tapping heel of one of Owen's rubber-soled deck shoes. And Martin had often passed by Owen's desk and seen him propped forward in thought, with his elbows resting on the desk top, sitting eerily still and unblinking except for his hands, which were pressed palms hard together, while his fingers moved in a rapid fluttering of silent applause.

Martin put down the manuscript and lowered his head into his hands in frustration. He could feel his blood pressure rise, and he told himself that Owen was as unwittingly irritating as the mindless woodpecker that attacked the gutter each morning at dawn. Martin also remembered that he would gladly have taken a gun and blown the woodpecker to bits if only he had a gun and had known how to do it.

Upstairs the huge door to the entry of Jesse Hall swung open, and Martin heard feet on the stairway. He went back to his manuscript, relieved that the day of the building was beginning. In the outer office Owen stopped his drumming and presumably went back to the exercise of his green pencil. Martin read in peace, absorbed and excited. At least an issue of *The Review* should be devoted to a long excerpt of this book, and he glanced at his watch to see if it was too early to call Vic. He decided to wait those few minutes until nine o'clock, just to be sure not to wake either of the Hofstatters; he and they were so tentative with one another these days. Meanwhile, he would go over the rest of the correspondence with Owen.

Owen folded himself into one of the chairs across from Martin's desk, his elbows resting on the wooden arms and his hands clasped loosely.

"You might want to make some notes," Martin said, passing a legal pad and a pencil across the desk.

"Oh, okay. Right." Owen seemed surprised and a little amused, as if Martin were taking some game too seriously, but Martin pressed on.

"There's a bunch of straightforward rejections and

then this one acceptance to Peter Hosley." He held up the paper-clipped essay to show Owen and set it apart from the material being rejected. "But ask if he's willing to wait, because we want to use his piece in our summer issue. He might want to send it somewhere that will publish it before then." Owen didn't make a single notation. Martin scribbled hastily across the margin of the Hosley manuscript, writing down exactly what he had just said. "Now these four only need responses to suggestions, but be sure to check the letterheads and get the titles exactly right. People are touchy about that." Martin paused, feeling better as Owen bent over the yellow pad. "Okay, there are three points you need to be sure to include in each of these letters," and once again he paused. He could not help but see Owen numbering the lines down the margin of the page:

1._____

2._____

3._____

4._____

5._____

6._____

7._____

"Just three points. And in whatever way seems most appropriate in each case," Martin said. Owen glanced up expectantly. "Well. And they're not so . . . rigid . . . that you need to number them." Owen nodded indulgently, his pencil poised over the pad. "I mean, Owen, you can phrase these yourself. I want to make sure that we don't lose contributions from these people." And Owen wrote something on the line he had numbered *"1."*

"That's not part of the letter," Martin said. "If you want to, you can mention something about it, but don't put it quite that way. 'We've always appreciated your generosity, etc.'" And as Owen hastily moved on to line 2, Martin hurried on, despairingly. "Just tell them that we're glad of their continuing interest, that we try to be unbiased about every political issue, and that we welcome their further thoughts about . . . whatever."

Seeing that Owen had strung out brief notations all the way down to number 7, Martin was apprehensive. He considered how he could find out what Owen intended to write, because Martin had learned from experience that to ask Owen directly would get them nowhere. He was slithery under specific questions; one had to approach him sideways. His blond, open expression concealed a passion for secrecy. Owen would leave for lunch and offer to bring back something for Martin from the deli on Carriage Street, and Martin would work along at his desk with the pleasurable anticipation of a thickly layered corned beef sandwich. But Owen would return an hour and a half later with a cold hamburger and fries from the McDonald's on the other side of Bradford—a twenty-mile drive. Once Owen had offered to get Martin tickets through a friend for one of the Theater Festival's productions that was sold out, but several days later he had shown up with two tickets to a Sunday afternoon reading by Blythe Danner of the poetry of Marianne Moore in the auditorium of the Freund Museum. If Martin pressed him, Owen became belligerently sulky.

"This is great, Owen," Martin had said, when he studied the tickets, "but what happened to *Suddenly, Last Summer?*"

"Were you serious about that? Bad Tennessee Williams?"

"It's not so bad. And the cast . . ."

"Right! It's all the cast! They're fabulous," Owen agreed. "So I got you Blythe Danner. Her performance is incredible."

This morning Martin was worried about the message Owen was going to send, and he flexed back in his chair and stretched his arms up behind his head to relieve the tension in his shoulders. Just as he had reached as high as he could, the door opened a crack and Netta peered in, looking flustered and anxious.

"Oh, Owen." Her words were light and whispery as usual, exhaled in relief, and she paused for a moment, smiling. "Hi, Martin. I won't bother you. I wanted to say hello while I was here." Her hair had tightened almost into ringlets in the humidity, and she looked even more childishly vulnerable than usual. Martin brought his arms back to his desk and his chair snapped forward.

"How are you, Netta? Have you got your apartment settled? Everything unpacked?" She had filled the entire van and the whole of his own car with boxes and plants in Cambridge. Martin had driven back to her apartment in West Bradford, and he and Vic had taken David up on his offer to help her move all her things upstairs. They had unloaded the car in the parking lot, and left David to unload the van.

"Oh . . ." She paused and lapsed into serious consideration. "I've left a lot of things in boxes, you know? I start to unpack them and then I end up just sort of walking around the box. Don't you think that unpacking takes real concentration?" She had stepped farther into the room and was leaning against the open edge of the door, looking at him inquiringly. "I mean, it's sort of an increase in the momentum. . . ."

Martin had only meant to inquire politely, but Netta was pensive and endearingly trusting in giving away strange little intimacies of her life in the innocent assumption that people wanted to know these things.

Martin felt callous in the face of her ingenuousness. "I do think so," he said, trying to think about it seriously. Netta was so earnest that he wanted to protect her from the discovery that most of the questions people asked her, or many of the comments they made in passing, were merely social niceties. "I know what you mean. Taking on possessions *is* a kind of responsibility . . . making room for their emotional weight. Well, remember when I told you about how desperate Dinah felt when my grandmother's . . ."

"No, no, Martin." Netta, suddenly severe, brushed her hand through the air to dismiss the idea. "I'm not talking about *owning* things!" Her gaze had turned almost fierce, and Martin was baffled but at the same time not especially interested.

"Oh," he said. "I didn't understand that."

Netta remained in the doorway for a moment, then smiled at him forgivingly and turned away. "I've got to get Anna Tyson to day care. She's waiting in the car." And Martin didn't have to reply, because she had already left the room and Owen followed her.

Martin heard her say something to Owen, her feathery voice too light to catch, but he heard Owen's reply. "I left a message on your machine. Maybe the tape was full."

"Owen." Netta's voice was strained as she drew his name out into a sort of sigh. "I told you you could stop by. You don't have to call. You did know that, didn't you?" Martin didn't hear Owen's reply, but there was a long silence, then Netta spoke. "Do you want to meet me for lunch at the Union? David Howells said he would come over tonight to help me with all this unpacking, but we could use your help, too. Or you could come over later."

Owen didn't answer her, and the two of them moved away from the door. Netta's words were indistinct, but they formed the sound of a short, soft plea. A moment later Owen's chair creaked as he sat down, and there was a long pause before Netta spoke. Her voice was unusually clarified and flat. "I've got to go. I left Anna Tyson in the car." And Martin heard the office door close behind her.

Even though *The Review* office was in the basement, it wasn't cool, it was only marginally less hot, and Martin decided not to phone but to drive out to the Hofstatters' to talk over the excerpt from the manuscript he was reading. He gathered the chapters together and left his office, and Duchess climbed wearily to her feet, raising herself leg by leg, and ambled after him, but he was intercepted on his way out by Owen, who stopped him with an agitated flutter of the green marked pages.

"I'll read you this little bit, Martin. I mean, I really don't think you can let this out of the office," Owen said. "We're sending these letters out all the time. We're sending these letters out to *writers*. It's embarrassing. . . ." Owen's consternation, his proprietary distress, was unnerving, and Martin realized that it would be easier to hear him out than to argue that Owen should take it up with Vic. Martin nodded at Owen to go ahead and read to him from a letter Vic had left for Helen LaPlante to type.

"Okay, okay!" Owen was agitated, scanning the pages for what he wanted. "Here! Now what do you think? I could hardly believe it." And he held up a page and began to read aloud:

"This particular story is, in substance and also in style, reminiscent of much of the work of Alicia Smith, who is widely published and whom we've published often. While there is much about this piece that is fully realized and compelling, we think that it's not quite strong enough to stand on its own as a piece of fiction. We do hope that you will think of us again and let us see more of your work."

Owen broke off for a moment to glance at Martin with a conspiratorial smirk. Martin thought briefly that Owen was *mean,* in the way that word had summed things up in childhood, but the thought was transient, and he listened patiently as Owen continued:

> "We hope you will understand that due to the dynamics of a small magazine such as ours, which only publishes six to eight stories annually, we try very hard to maintain diversity."

Owen let his arm drop to his side and shook his head slowly with an air of resigned bemusement, as though he had encountered an inevitable disappointment. Martin stood for several moments, waiting for him to explain, but Owen seemed to think the letter spoke for itself.

"I don't see the problem," Martin said at last. "That's sort of a form letter we send to any writer we think has some talent but who's submitted a story that's not very good. And the story's usually not very good because it's a pale imitation of a *good* writer who's established a certain voice." Martin was pleased at his own kindly patience, but Owen waved the letter over his desk in agitation.

"Oh, Christ, Martin! '. . . the *dynamics* of a small magazine!' What the fuck does that mean?" Owen was practically shouting at him. "It's verbiage! It's *garbage!* Is it *General* Dynamics? Is it *fluid* dynamics? Someone has to pay attention to what these words mean. . . ."

All at once Martin was overwhelmed with weariness, and he shook his head at Owen, lifting both hands in a gesture of surrender. Finally Owen wound down. "Owen. Listen! I don't have the time. . . . This is hopeless. You just can't work here. Don't come here anymore. I'm sorry. I can't do anything about this anymore."

Owen's whole torso arched in surprise, and he slumped backward in his chair. He splayed his fingers at his temples and ran his hands back into his hair, flexing his chair with a sigh.

"No, no," Owen said mildly and with a look of delibera-tion. "I'm trying to learn to curb my perfectionism. I'm in Miracle Therapy, you know? I know better than this. I do. I know better than this. Anger is only emotional energy. I'm really trying. The point is to learn how to be *open* to goodwill instead of suspecting evil and unkindness." Owen spoke matter-of-factly and with resignation. He gazed up at Martin composedly, but nothing in the world would have induced Martin to inquire about the nature of Miracle Therapy, and after a moment Owen continued. "I want you to understand that I mean every word I say when I tell you how sorry I am that I didn't channel my anger. I'm only just learning to trust people and to love them. And I have real love for you, Martin. And for Vic. But I can't expect either of you to fulfill my need for perfection."

Martin stood in the reception area and looked back at his own office, which had been a retreat for so many years. It had been a place where he could suspend melan-choly and weed through submissions that might be dull or esoteric to other people, but that absorbed him en-tirely. He unwound Duchess's leash, and she shambled over to him and stood patiently while he fumbled with the retracting hook. "I'm going out to the Hofstatters'. I won't be back in the office today." Martin was defeated, and he escaped.

When Martin pulled into the long drive that led up through a meadow to the Hofstatters' house, Duchess, terri-fied of car rides, was crowded against him, her head next to his above the steering wheel. The interior of the car was filled with the warm, tidal scent of dogs in hot weather. Catching sight of Vic in a bright blue shirt down by the pond, Martin pulled over and parked in the drive, flinging open both the front doors, so Duchess wouldn't trample over his lap in her desperation to leave the car. She col-lapsed in relief on the verge of the drive while Martin let the car air out. He retrieved the manuscript from the trunk, where he had put it so the dog wouldn't destroy it in her frantic scrabbling from the back to the front seat during the drive. Martin was relieved that Vic was sitting out by the pond, because if Ellen was working upstairs he didn't want to disturb her.

Ellen's study was a renovated, low-ceilinged gabled attic at the top of the house. Years ago she had sketched out an arched window, vaguely Palladian, and taken the drawing to Milltown Patterns in Bradford to have one custom made for herself. Vic and Martin had installed it at the far end of the room under the peaked roof during weather exactly like this, and they had scarcely been able to be civil to each other by the end of the day. But Ellen had come upstairs and stood elated in the center of the room, pointing out to them how the light from the setting sun was broken into elongated squares across the old pine floorboards. "Mr. Aldenbrook at Milltown Patterns couldn't understand why I wanted to go to all this trouble. He thought it would be a lot cheaper to order a regulation plate glass window, but look how the mullions divide the light! This is a wonderful room."

And Martin had felt much better. It was impossible not to be pleased to have fulfilled the eccentric precision of Ellen's expectations. Dinah had arrived with sandwiches and beer and a jug of wine, and the four of them had had one of the most pleasant evenings of their long friendship, sitting on the floor in the near dark, eating sandwiches and drinking too much.

But Ellen had told him just the other day that she was seeing windows like hers all over town now, in the most unremarkable, solely cosmetic, renovations. As a result she had literally turned her back on the window in her own study, rotating her desk so that instead of looking out at the wooded mountains, she now worked with the light falling over her shoulders. He understood that it was unbearable to Ellen to think that anything in her life was not rare and superior—in that it was her own original invention—but he was disappointed at her tactlessness in telling him of her disenchantment with something that, in its way, had partially been a gift from him.

With Duchess close at his heels, Martin made his way along the slate path that meandered through a space of controlled woods; he had helped Vic hack away the impassable underbrush the summer after Ellen's window. There was a fine stand of towering walnut trees and flowering wild honeysuckle bushes and then a slope of open meadow that Vic and Ellen had gently terraced down to the pond, where Vic sat at a white wrought-iron table under the willow trees.

He put some papers aside when he saw Martin approaching, and Martin had the momentary sensation, as he came down the hill, that the vivid colors of Vic's blue shirt and aged yellow straw gardening hat under the heated light, the barely wavering tendrils of the sweeping willows, and the quality of Vic's stillness were permanent on the earth, were beyond the reality of the progression of time. Then Vic called a greeting, and the image in Martin's head shattered into the separate fragments of the ongoing day.

"I've got Brenner's manuscript," Martin said as he settled in a chair across from Vic. "I was thinking that we might want to devote an issue to it, but I wanted to talk to you first, and I decided to drive out. I was afraid it might be too early, though." Martin turned to watch the dog in case she was seized with one of her occasional fits of exuberance and headed off for the trails in the far woods. But Duchess merely nosed around the edge of the pond and flung herself down in a muddy spot along the bank.

When Martin turned back, Vic was standing looking across the pond with an irritated expression. Martin thought that perhaps he *had* arrived too early. "At least one issue," Vic said, clearly annoyed.

"You think we should take that much of the book?"
Martin's voice was pleasant; he had no idea why Vic was so
exasperated.

"I think we should take the whole book. I attached a
long memo when I gave the thing back to Owen. Netta
brought him out to swim one afternoon, and I thought it
would save me a trip into town. But he said you hadn't
seemed excited. That you thought Brenner's agent sent it
to us as a courtesy because we had published part of his last
book when the magazines weren't interested. I don't know.
This new one's a strange book. Hard to excerpt, really. I'm
not sure he could place it that easily." Vic sat down again,
squinting slightly into the distance. "But suppose we devoted all four issues to the entire book. It would get some
publicity for the book. And for *The Review*. You can't think
his *agent* sent it as a courtesy! Give me a break! But if you
think Brenner insisted because he feels beholden . . . I
mean, if this has something to do with your idea of
honor . . ." he said wryly, raising an eyebrow. "But, Christ,
Martin, he can always turn down the offer."

Martin slouched down in his chair and let his head fall
forward while he massaged the back of his neck with one
hand, his eyes closed. He was remembering the memoless,
slightly gritty, water-rumpled manuscript that Owen had
left on his desk. Owen must have put it down on the floor
of his car and piled his and Netta's wet towels on top of it.
"Ah, God," Martin said, not loudly but with resignation.
"Well, I fired Owen this morning."

Vic perked up. "You did? You fired him? What did he
say?"

"He said he has great love for you and me."

"So? You mean he's not going to *be* fired?"

"He avoided it, I think. And I can't leave him fired,
anyway. Penny will be back in four weeks, and if we fired
him the whole town would hear about it. I feel sorry for
him."

"He's an asshole."

"Yeah," Martin said, and continued massaging his neck, turning his head slowly from side to side to stretch the muscles. "But he's a *pathetic* asshole. Maybe he *won't* come in tomorrow," he said. "And I really don't know how to get rid of him if he does come back. I feel terrible for Larry and Judith." Martin was filled with dread at the prospect of explaining the situation to Owen's parents.

"You know, at his best he's real good at being charming in a sort of bumbling way," Vic said. "That's how he was when he came out to swim. He's like a Doberman in a golden retriever's body. Ellen thinks he might be manic depressive."

"Do you think so, too?" Martin slid down in his chair, stretching his legs in front of him and closing his eyes as he rested his head as comfortably as he could on the iron scrollwork. He was genuinely curious. He had always thought that Ellen was overly severe in the conclusions she drew, but there was something elusive about Owen. Maybe she had it right.

"I don't know. Maybe it's drugs. Maybe it's just Owen."

Martin was groggy and stunned from the heat and from lack of sleep, and he stayed just as he was in the white chair under the trailing willows, mulling over the facets of Owen's personality. Martin let various suppositions drift across the surface of his mind, and he grew drowsier and more and more indifferent. He couldn't even summon the energy to open his eyes when he heard Ellen join them.

"I brought a pitcher of iced tea," she said as she approached, "but the ice has already started to melt. I should have put it in the Thermos. It's sweltering in my study. I thought I'd take a swim," she added, and Martin looked up and smiled at her in greeting. Ellen smiled, too, and then turned away and walked down the gentle slope to the edge of the pond, where Duchess only opened her eyes to see what she was doing. Ellen stepped into the water ankle-deep. "The water's not cool," she called back to them, "but at least it's wet." She shrugged out of her terrycloth robe and tossed it behind her on the bank, wading nude into the deepening water, spreading it outward with her arms as it reached her waist, and launching herself gently forward so that her silvery-gray hair floated out behind her as she turned her face into the water and began to swim toward the far end where there were no shallows.

Vic and Ellen always swam nude, and Martin never expected to be taken aback, although he was every time he joined them. Dinah thought their whole posture of casual nudity was an affectation, but Martin could never decide what to think. Years ago, when Ellen was slender and high-breasted, he had liked to believe that she wanted him to admire her. Now, however, that she had aged and thickened, he realized that there couldn't be much of vanity in her nakedness. But he liked to watch her all the more, because there was something erotic about the pleasure she took from the contact of the water with her soft flesh, and she was a voluptuous, pretty woman still. He wondered, though, what she could be thinking. She was his closest woman friend, but did she imagine that he could sit there and not think of her sexually as she dawdled in the clear water, carrying on a perfectly normal conversation while slowly scissoring her legs and stirring the surface of the pond gently with her arms to hold herself in place and keep her head above water? Did it not occur to her or did it not matter?

"What did you think of Philip Brenner's book, Martin?" she asked him from where she lounged in the deep water at the far end of the pond.

"That's why I came out," he said, loudly enough that she could hear him over the distance and the soft splashing of her movements. "Vic's probably right that we should take the whole book if we can."

She nodded in approval and then let herself sink under

the water, pushing off from the bottom of the pond so that as she broke the surface, with her head tilted back, the water swept her straggling hair flat against her skull into a smooth cap. Martin thought fleetingly that he was relieved that the Hofstatters hadn't had children; Ellen wouldn't have hesitated to nurse the baby wherever she might be, and he would have had to pretend that he was entirely comfortable watching a child suckle Ellen's breast.

"The water's much cooler at this end where it's been in the shade," she called out to them as she turned to swim toward them, and Martin let his head fall back again so he wasn't looking directly at her. No one had ever explained the etiquette of this situation to him. He let his eyes close again as he heard the steady splashing of her strong legs as she swam laps, and he fell into a half-sleep in the muggy air. Ellen was sitting with them, wrapped in her robe and briskly toweling her hair dry, when he came completely into consciousness again.

". . . and I feel *deprived* having toast without butter, or even worse, just imagine eating a tomato sandwich without mayonnaise," she was saying to Vic. She bent forward and wrapped the towel turbanlike around her head, then settled back in her chair. "Martin, I baked bread this morning because I couldn't sleep. But I can't touch it, because I've really got to lose some of this weight." She patted herself fondly on the thigh. "I'll make the two of you some sandwiches for lunch, though. You'll stay, won't you? I'll come down and sit with you. It's so much cooler down here than in the house."

"Ellen's dieting." Vic ran his hand along the top of her leg where it emerged from beneath her robe, and she grinned, which was always a surprise. Her features were delicate and secret and feline, and her smile was usually composed, seemingly considered. When her whole face opened into a grin, it was so revealing of her pleasure that it was very much like being exposed to another aspect of her nakedness.

"He can't stand it," she said to Martin, "because when we don't have company I begrudge him every bite he takes."

"I just don't see the point," Vic said. "Being hungry makes you so miserable."

Ellen had lost interest in talking about food, however, and she looked at Martin with her face careful once more. "You think the Brenner book is good enough to devote four issues to?" she asked.

"I'd love to do it, but I just got hold of the manuscript three days ago, and today is the deadline his agent gave us. I'm sure he'd rather sell it for real money."

Ellen frowned at him, and readjusted herself, crossing her legs and looking prim with disapproval, but Vic intervened.

"I sent it back with Owen," he said. "You remember when he and Netta were out here to swim? It took the long way round back to Martin." Vic dropped his air of injury and laughed. "You know, Owen read the manuscript before he passed it on to me, and he could hardly wait to tell me that he thought it was needlessly obscure. He said it was time someone put Brenner out of his misery." And Vic couldn't contain his laughter, waving his hand to convey his helpless sense of the absurdity of what he was trying to say in long gasps of breath. "God," he continued, "Owen was in a state of *outrage*. Just plain beside himself. He said someone should deliver Brenner to a taxidermist. Preserve him as a national monument!" Vic broke into laughter again, but Martin was overtaken by an unwelcome surge of pity for Owen, much like the misery he felt for some vocal but wrongheaded student in any seminar he taught. "He told me it was a piece of shit," Vic said, still amused, but Ellen looked solemn.

"I guess it gives him some sort of feeling of power to do that," she said.

"Well, Martin fired him this morning," Vic told her.

"Oh, I'm so glad, Martin!" Ellen said. "I'm uneasy around Owen. I don't quite know why. I would have thought you would have noticed how he was with Netta, Vic. You and Martin are so protective of her, but you don't seem to notice how Owen treats her. I'd almost call it abusive, but it's not quite that extreme. He *bullies* her, though, in some way. He does it by being . . . oh . . . sort of sullen and moody. Sulky." Vic shook his head to signify that he hadn't noticed anything odd in Owen's behavior toward Netta. "I'm so glad you let him go, Martin," she said.

"My firing him and our being rid of him are probably going to turn out to be two different things," Martin said, but Ellen's enthusiasm wasn't dampened.

"Oh, that doesn't even matter, you know. Penny Krautz will be back in a few weeks. But we've been so worried about you." She paused for a moment and glanced uneasily at Vic, whose face remained impassive. She went on, almost shyly. "For the past few years it's seemed to us . . . Well . . . It's been too long a time that you've tried to forgive Owen, Martin." Her voice was soft with her sorrow for him, and he didn't know what to say. He was taken aback and unprepared. The connection between Toby's death and Owen Croft had been far from his mind.

She got up, and no one said anything while she fussed with the sash of her robe and unwound the towel from around her head, shaking her hair free in the sun. She crossed the few feet of grass to Martin and bent to embrace him in a fierce hug. "It's been awful for us to see you try so hard to be generous." She released him and stood up, running her fingers through her hair in an attempt to untangle it. "Martin, you shouldn't ever doubt yourself, you know. I mean, in the very best sense of the term, you aren't *capable* of being anything other than an honorable man."

So Martin knew that some long discussion about him had taken place between these two closest of his friends, and he felt defensive and resentful. But he couldn't speak to object; Ellen's sorrowing on his behalf had brought him surprisingly near to tears.

"I'm going to shower and then I'll bring lunch down," Ellen said, kindly freeing him from the obligation of a response. Vic got up, too, and urged him to come for a swim.

In the late afternoon as Martin drove through Bradford, stopping and starting in the afternoon traffic and restraining Duchess in the back seat by holding his right arm straight out as a barrier, bits and pieces of the day floated through his mind. He felt less and less unnerved by the idea of the Hofstatters' probable discussion of and conclusions about him. Naturally they would speculate about him and about Dinah, just as he and Dinah did about them. Ellen had fixed a wonderful lunch and eaten her share, deciding that she would start her diet the next day, and Martin remembered her round arms and dimpled elbows, her heavy hips and thighs as she merged languidly into the water of the pond. He didn't think there was any reason for there to be less of Ellen—or of Vic—two people he liked as much as he could like any people he didn't love. He had for them an acute *fondness*.

He sat at the traffic light in West Bradford, and was ashamed not to have disabused Ellen and Vic of their notion that his behavior toward Owen Croft had anything to do with his idea of himself as an honorable man. Martin had never been able to blame Owen for Toby's death. Martin had often awakened to alternate realities: that he had only dreamed the accident, that his car *had* been struck from behind, but Toby had been all the way across town when it happened, running to intercept the soccer ball downfield, that his own car had executed a neat turn, and Owen's car, unnoticed, passed on through the afternoon traffic. And hundreds—perhaps thousands—of times, he had supposed other possibilities: if he had stopped at the convenience store to buy milk first, before he picked up his sons at soccer practice; if he had been going a little faster; if he had been going a little slower . . . But Martin was, in fact, a practical man, and he repeatedly assured himself that Toby's death was only horribly random.

CHAPTER NINE

PACKING

IT FASCINATED DAVID TO watch Netta approach the task of unpacking the boxes that were stacked on the kitchen counters and table and strewn along the walls through the rooms of her apartment. He had dropped by to lend her a hand three afternoons in a row after he got off work, and yet they had made almost no progress. She would start a conversation, open a beer for them both, stop and fix something for dinner. Anna Tyson and he and Netta would sit in a row on the one unencumbered futon in the living room and eat the dry sandwiches that Netta made—two pieces of the hard French bread she bought at The Whole Grain Elevator and a slab of hard cheese between them. David admired these hastily put-together sandwiches, even though they weren't good to eat. They required nothing in return. The meal was a bit of business, served without comment or ceremony. And all the while Netta ate her dinner, she talked about her work, her ideas, sketching them with both hands, waving the partially eaten sandwich in the air. She asked him about himself.

"What are you planning?" she asked David. "I mean, I hope you know *why* you're going to Harvard. So many people who get in just go there because it's the next step. You know what I mean? It sounds good to them. To go to Harvard. But I taught three sections, and the freshmen don't have the slightest idea why they're at college. It was such a waste of my time to try to interest them in anything. One of the T.A.'s thought all the freshmen should be required to take mandatory deferments and not come to Harvard until they were twenty-one." She laughed, remembering this, and David smiled. "But I really do think taking a deferment is a good idea. I should have waited a year before I went to Swarthmore. Have you thought about it?"

David hadn't, and he shook his head in reply, because Netta was filled with ideas and was rushing ahead. "I still wish I hadn't just flung myself straight into college. I shouldn't have had to decide so much so soon." She looked at him imploringly, to be sure he sympathized, or at least that he understood. "I was trying to be too many people, I think." She fell silent, contemplating that idea, testing it in her own mind for validity.

Eventually she set to work, drooping languidly over the contents of this or that carton, unhinging the four flaps of a boxtop so that they fell open like wilted petals, and she would pick up one thing or another and scrutinize it. She held up an eggbeater to show him.

"Look at this!" she said to David, who was sitting with Anna Tyson and helping her break her cheese into small pieces. "I bought it at a flea market in Arlington. It's probably about seventy years old. Isn't it an elegant shape? See how it's elongated? People have forgotten how to look at things."

He nodded in agreement, although he had never paid attention to the shape of an eggbeater. But he could imagine himself perusing the long tables at garage sales with

Netta, finding other treasures as amazing as her eggbeater.
Netta rotated the handle, absorbed momentarily in watching the ratchet turn the looped blades. She opened a deep
drawer next to the sink and placed the eggbeater in it before looking again into the depths of the carton. "Oh, it's
all this silverware," she said, sounding disappointed after
her discovery of the eggbeater.

David got up and took a look. "Listen, why don't I go
get some of those plastic trays they have at Farrell's Store
that have dividers for forks and spoons? You could fit two
of them in this drawer and it would hold all this stuff. Farrell's is open until eight."

Netta considered the drawer, which was a little gritty
with crumbs and so far contained only the eggbeater.
"Oh . . . I don't know. Here . . ." and she took a random
handful of silverware and dropped it in the drawer. "Let's
just leave it loose. I mean, anyone can figure out which
ones are the forks or knives or spoons, right?" She up-
ended the box and dumped the welter of stainless steel
flatware into the deep drawer where it fell in a jumble
like pickup sticks.

For a moment David was taken aback, but then it was
clear to him that her gesture and idea were wonderful. It
dawned on him that all the time he had taken over the
years to put the silver away in little pockets of the appropriate size had been wasted. It was absolutely true that
even Anna Tyson could sort out whatever utensils she
might need, and for the first time he realized that any
sort of domestic order was only whimsical, not necessary,
as the arrangement of his mother's kitchen seemed to
suggest. Netta dropped the box to the floor with satisfaction as she closed the drawer. She rested against him
with her head in the niche of his shoulder, and he was
so surprised that he almost stepped backward, away from
her. She moved off and began to sort through the cartons
on the table, removing things randomly, not box by box,

dropping folded towels at her feet, unearthing cutting boards and measuring cups.

He began unpacking a box on the kitchen counter that contained Netta's Cuisinart and all its blades, which were packed within the carton in boxes of carefully fitted Styrofoam. When he glanced at Netta, he was struck by her fragility, the movement of the muscle and fragile bones in her wrists and arms as she stood on tiptoe to reach into the bottom of a deep box and strained to pull out a bundled, heavy down quilt. He was intrigued by her narrow, delicate torso, with small breasts but slightly wide hips for her tiny frame. He didn't understand—nor would he have cared—that the fascinating play of bone and muscle and sinew of Netta's arms as she hefted the puffy green quilt was the beginning of the loss of the elasticity of youth; the slightly widened hips and small curve of her stomach were those of a woman of twenty-six who has had a child.

Netta moved back and forth carrying armfuls of towels and sheets, stuffing them unceremoniously into the linen closet in the hall. "There's no point in folding all these, is there?" she said rather breathlessly, standing still for a moment with her hands on her hips. "Do you know that my mother actually irons her sheets? It's such a waste of time since it all just has to be done all over again." He nodded, but he was astounded by the eroticism of watching Netta dispatch all her possessions to their most likely storage space with such blithe practicality. It was a way of having a household that he hadn't seen before, and she stood amid the rubble of scrunched newspapers and Styrofoam packing bubbles that clung to her long skirt with static electricity, triumphant and more arousing than anyone else he had ever encountered.

He was impressed by all her ideas, by her absolute certainty about her profession, her household, her person. She never bothered with makeup or gave any thought to her clothes or hair, as far as he could tell. And not until tonight had he realized how pretty she was, and how unusually sexual, with her soft, soft voice and deliberate, thoughtful questions, her attention to his answers. He felt toward her a kind of considered desire that was new to him. It didn't cross his mind that if he had passed her as a stranger on the street he wouldn't have noticed her one way or another. David was so young, he didn't quite understand that, for now, there were bodies to be found everywhere; he didn't understand that he was really interested in Netta only for her mind.

Anna Tyson was lying on her stomach on the floor, working with her crayons on a large pad of drawing paper that Dinah had given her the last time Anna Tyson had been at the Howellses' house. David sat down beside her cross-legged and asked about the picture. He was too embarrassed to pay any more attention to Netta.

"That looks like a really nice house," he said, and Anna Tyson flipped over and lay on her back to study him. "Are you going to put any trees in the yard?" He didn't have his mother's assurance with small children. He had unconsciously slowed the rhythm of his speech as if Anna Tyson were dimwitted, and she narrowed her eyes and pinched in her lips disapprovingly. "No," she said.

"You could put some flowers in the yard," he said, trying to speak to her as he might speak to anyone, but she wouldn't be engaged by him. She held out the brown crayon she had been drawing with.

"You do it!" she said.

"Okay. Why don't you help me? We could make some red flowers or some yellow flowers, maybe." She didn't comment. She merely rolled back over on her stomach and propped herself on her elbows to see what he would do.

"Okay?" he asked, looking at her for permission but unnerved by her steady observation. "I'll just draw some flowers over in this corner," and he replaced the brown crayon in the shoebox of crayons, arranged much like Netta's drawer of silverware, and searched for a red one. Netta was standing behind them, unfolding a brightly woven blanket over the back of the futon, but she stopped what she was doing to watch the two of them on the floor. All at once she swooped at David and snatched the box of crayons away, stooping down between the two of them. She looked at him with amazed and gentle reproach, holding the crayon box tightly against her chest.

"You weren't going to draw on her picture, were you?" she asked him plaintively.

"I was just going to help her put some flowers in . . ."

"David!" She seemed scarcely to believe him. "You wouldn't really have done that." And he had no answer at all, because he wasn't sure what mistake he had made. Netta sighed in disappointment and sat down on the floor, putting the shoebox aside and picking up the drawing. She studied it for a moment, and then leaned over to show it to David, resting her shoulder against his arm as she held the paper up in front of him. "You see, this is Anna Tyson's whole idea of what she wanted to create. She's thought of this very carefully. Look at the smoke coming out of the chimney. She's imagined a room inside this house with a fireplace where someone has built a fire. Lit a match, ignited the wood. Who built this warm fire inside the house, Anna Tyson? It must be cold outside, since the people who live in the house had to build a fire." Her daughter was now stretched out on her side, pillowing her head on her outflung arm. Anna Tyson only shrugged one-sidedly, her eyelids drooping slightly. Now that her mother was talking with David, her own attention began to wander.

Netta looked back to David, gesticulating with the drawing. "If you inhibit a child's vision by imposing your own ideas . . . it's almost like stealing," she said pleadingly, trying to make him understand. He looked at the picture of a square brown house with two windows and brown smoke rising from the brown chimney. He didn't know what to say. He was remembering the drive to Boston, with Netta tense and fragile for an hour or so until she had collapsed against the door in such a complete sleep that she had fallen forward against the shoulder harness with her head bowed against the window and her chin almost reaching the door lock.

"Children can be so easily crushed, David," Netta said gently. "Anna Tyson's only four years old, and she's just beginning to develop faith in her own convictions. She's just beginning to *form* her own convictions." Netta was leaning against him from shoulder to hip, although she was gazing at Anna Tyson's picture. She let it fall to her lap and sat quietly, deliberating. Anna Tyson clambered up from the floor and stood for a moment, and Netta absently hugged her around the waist until Anna Tyson broke away and went off down the hall to her room.

"You see what you would have been doing if you'd added anything to her picture, don't you? It would have been an invasion of her imagination, which is so fragile at this stage. She's just beginning to understand what's real and what's imagined." David looked down at Netta. "I mean, I know you would never have intended anything like that, it's just that . . . oh, well. But you should have thought about the damage you could have done," she said, glancing up at him to see if she had made her point.

David bent down and kissed her before he even realized what he was doing, and eventually they moved to the futon. Netta left him for a moment to check and see that Anna Tyson was asleep, and then came back to the living room wearing only her white cotton bikini panties and bringing with her a foil-wrapped condom, which she handed him with a little shrug of embarrassment. They made love uncomfortably on the narrow futon, and it didn't occur to David to compare Netta and Christie in any way, except that when the thought of Christie crossed his mind he felt guilty. He fell briefly asleep, balanced precariously on the edge of the hard couch, and he came abruptly awake with Netta's arm draped limply around his neck, his chin balanced against the top of her head. He felt relaxed and unanxious.

When he and Christie made love—even though she was taking birth-control pills and he always used a condom—she became uneasy and nervous almost immediately afterward. And because of her anxiety, they were edgy toward each other until her period started. Twice she had driven to Bradford to buy a pregnancy test kit at a drugstore where she wouldn't see anyone she knew, but each time she had doubted the results. David was pleased to think that Netta wouldn't worry about any of this. He was pleased with everything at the moment. He relished his inclusion in Netta's chaotic household; he could imagine himself leading a comfortable life in such a haven.

When he got home that night at 10:30, his father was making popcorn in the kitchen. "I didn't know you'd be home so early," Martin said. "The Red Sox are tied in the bottom of the seventh." He raised his eyebrows in an invitation to David to join him.

"I'm really tired," David said, and passed by his father on his way to his room. Martin watched the popcorn fill the plastic dome of the popcorn popper, and worried about what might be happening between his son and Christie, wondering if he ought to follow David upstairs and ask him about it. But when Martin heard the roar of the water in the pipes as David turned on the shower, he decided to leave things alone for the time being.

Netta lived two doors away from The Whole Grain Elevator, where almost everyone in town shopped for nice vegetables and fresh fish. Her apartment was half of the upstairs of a large house right off Carriage Street, along an unmarked, graveled lane called Marchand's Drive that had become a shortcut to River Road. Only a few people in town still remembered the Marchand family, who had occupied the large house in the lane and had owned the thirty-five acres behind it. Their drive had been extended long after they were gone from West Bradford. They had sold the house and much of the acreage to the college and a few home builders. Netta's apartment was fashioned out of the bedroom and study and dressing room of L. J. Marchand, who had come back to West Bradford after World War II.

Saturday morning Nat Kaplan, an older colleague of Martin's, had picked up the *Times* at the news room and was glancing over the headlines as he made his way to The Whole Grain Elevator to pick up two loaves of bread and to see if there was any fresh asparagus. His wife, Moira, was hoping to serve it to their guests for dinner that evening. When he reached the curb of Marchand's Drive, he folded the paper and tucked it under his arm and looked up at the house. For a while L. J. and Amelia Marchand had been great friends of his and Moira's.

When he and Moira had first moved to West Bradford, they had been delighted with and in awe of L.J.'s and Amelia's sophistication. Amelia, who was British, was amused at everything American. She was delighted at what she perceived as a quality of uncritical innocence, and all her new friends played up to her expectations. The Marchands had been almost fifteen years older than the Kaplans, and yet Nat and Moira had been adopted by them more or less. L.J. doted on his wife, not only commending her humor but recounting incidents that illustrated her discriminating and meticulous sense of the ludicrous, her remarkable intelligence. These were things that Nat admired in his own wife, and it often seemed to him that he learned from L.J. the reasons and all the ways in which he loved Moira.

The Marchands had been his example of how it was possible to live a married life, although a few years after they had arrived in West Bradford it turned out, to everyone's surprise, that they weren't much good at it themselves. They had divorced amid surprising rumors of violent brawls between the two of them, one spilling out onto the lawn of their house and being broken up by their dinner guests. Suddenly stories had abounded of L.J.'s indiscriminate and particularly inelegant affairs, and there had been a good deal of speculation about Amelia's involvement with various other men. All this gossip had been very satisfying to those friends of theirs who had been confronted with their own failures in the face of the Marchands' smug unity. But it had saddened and disappointed Nat, although their breakup hadn't disillusioned him. The model he had perceived when observing the Marchands at the best of times was valid, even if its practitioners had failed. He had learned much about the strengths of his own marriage, which had left him and Moira estranged for years from his Jewish family and her Catholic one.

After the divorce, Amelia had gone back to England, and Moira and she had kept up a brief correspondence before eventually losing touch. L.J. had moved away almost three decades ago to Connecticut, where he had remarried, and Nat had come across his obituary in the *Times* about seven years ago.

Nat Kaplan was unaware that every time he passed that way he glanced up at the profile of the house, now laced with exterior wooden staircases after being turned into four units of college housing. Saturday morning, when Nat looked in that direction, Netta Breckenridge and David Howells were standing on the little porch at the top of her staircase. Netta leaned forward and ran her hands from David's shoulders to his waist, resting the tips of her fingers just above his hips. She was apparently instructing him in some way, because he nodded and turned and hurried down the steps.

Nat looked away, embarrassed not to have been minding his own business. But two nights later, when he and Moira were crossing the street on their way to the seven o'clock show at the movie theater, Nat noticed Netta once again under her porch light, this time with Owen Croft, who was lounging against the railing. When Nat stepped up on the curb and turned to give Moira his arm, he saw Owen reach forward and pull Netta toward him so that she disappeared entirely from Nat's sight, since Owen's back was to him. Nat was bothered and distracted by the scene all during the movie. He considered the unhappy connection between David Howells and Owen Croft, and he didn't like what appeared to be their mutual association with Netta Breckenridge. That night, before he went to sleep, he mentioned both incidents to Moira.

"Oh, I don't see how that could mean anything. I think David Howells is only a junior or senior in high school," Moira said. "I think he's going with Meg Cramer or that Douglas girl. Netta Breckenridge must be ten years older than he is. He was probably helping her with something or doing an errand for her. She has a little girl, you know. He might have been baby-sitting." But both Moira and Nat thought about David Howells and Netta Breckenridge and Owen Croft now and then over the next several days. They remembered the terrible years the Howellses had endured after the death of their second child, and they were both uneasy.

When Moira and Ellen Hofstatter were sorting through boxes of donated books Tuesday evening for the library's annual used-book sale, Moira grasped the opportunity to mention the possible situation lightly to Ellen, as though it were Moira's own foolishness even to imagine there was any significance to the little tale. But Ellen's face puckered in thought as she listened, and she didn't respond except to sigh and tuck one wing of her extravagant hair behind her ear.

When Ellen got home she was brutal in her fury at David and Netta when she told Vic what was going on. "Netta's just spooky, but I'm crazy about David. He's acting like an absolute fool, though, and he's making Dinah miserable! I don't know whether to say anything to Dinah or not. I mean about David and Netta. But I think you'd better warn Martin. The whole thing could turn into a real mess since Owen's involved."

Vic did tell Martin the next day, when they were alone in *The Review* office, and Martin gazed blankly at him for a moment. "Ah, shit. Christ!" And he passed his hands over his temples and into his hair, swinging his chair away slightly at an angle to Vic. Neither of them said any more about it.

Shortly after David had received his letter of acceptance from Harvard this past spring, he had also received a booklet called *Living in Freshmen Dorms*. He had put it aside, but Dinah had read it thoroughly and had made detailed lists of things he would need: 3 wool blankets; extra-long twin bed sheets; 1 trash can; 1 chair; 2 lamps, desk & standing; 8 towels and washcloths. It was suggested that he bring an umbrella. A raincoat. Dinah reeled through all the images she could summon and couldn't recall ever having seen a Bradford and Welbern student wearing a raincoat. Sometimes they used umbrellas, especially the girls, but she was certain she had never seen a single person on campus under the age of twenty-one in anything she would have called a raincoat.

"A raincoat, David. You'll need a raincoat at Harvard." She had followed David to his room and was standing in the doorway while he was leafing through a stack of garden catalogues. "What kind of raincoat are you going to get? I mean, I wouldn't think you'd want the London Fog kind."

"Don't worry about it, Mom," he said over his shoulder. "I don't need a raincoat."

Dinah had left him alone, but she had continued to brood about it. It seemed unlikely to her that Harvard would bother to print up this booklet and list things that David would *not* need.

The next morning at breakfast, she had urged Martin and David to bring Martin's old trunk down from the attic and put it in David's room so that he could begin gathering together the things he would be taking to school in September. This was only a small chore she asked them to do, a task that would take them perhaps ten minutes, yet it was a request that washed through their house like a wave, receding and leaving behind the emotional detritus of a thousand other domestic disagreements, accommodations.

Although they did as she asked, both of them made it clear that they were irritated, each in his own way. David merely tightened his expression, his eyebrows drawing down, his lips tightening against making any spoken objection. Martin had put his coffee cup down and set aside his toast in pained resignation. "Dinah, the attic is filthy, and I've got an appointment with the dean at ten," he said. That morning neither David nor Martin had been gracious about being inconvenienced; they thought it was unnecessary, before David had even graduated from high school, to wrestle the foot locker down the narrow, doglegged staircase from the attic.

And neither one of them said aloud that he knew too well what Dinah's air of urgency might portend. Unexecuted plans, lists of tasks not done—any loose ends—were a torment to Dinah. Her husband and her son dreaded three whole months of her impatient preparations. What *she* did not say was that David and Martin always made plans in a slapdash fashion, and then made only desultory, un-thought-out forays into the practical world to do what was necessary to carry them out.

She understood that David loathed the notion of *non*-spontaneity; he romanticized the idea of a kind of school-yard, pickup existence. He seemed to be alarmed at taking the future into account, and so, this past spring, Dinah never said to him that there was nothing less spontaneous than his careful garden. When she passed by his room and saw him plotting his garden on graph paper, surrounded at his desk by a welter of books and seed catalogues, she had hoped that this might be a project that would literally and figuratively ground him. As for Martin, he simply went through life without great anxiety, sure that those things that needed to be done would get done.

And so it was she who, years ago, had found someone to substitute for her at the Artists' Guild shop, and dashed out to drop off David's forgotten running shoes or soccer shorts, or to get the leather shoelaces for the hiking boots he had bought without laces. It was she who frantically rinsed and arranged the dusty china coffee cups and sau-cers, and made both coffee and tea to accompany a birthday cake that Martin had bought at the bakery to be a surprise for Nat Kaplan at an impromptu committee meeting Martin had called for the same evening. It had not occurred to him that he couldn't serve the cake with beer. The loose ends she picked up were the unimportant ones; they earned her next to no gratitude, and the very fact that she continued to do them maddened Ellen.

"Why do you do these things? It's not fair to either Da-vid or Martin. They take it for granted. Leave them in the lurch a few times, for God's sake. They'll learn to do these things for themselves. Why do you feel your time is less important than theirs?"

Dinah had never been able to explain it to Ellen. Not for a moment did she believe her time was less valuable than anyone else's on earth. Dinah felt that she was, in fact, rather selfish, and that she rarely did anything she didn't choose to do. In Martin's case Dinah knew he did his share; the two of them had settled into an equitable division of labor, and she relied enormously on his wholehearted optimism and his good nature in taking care of the things that fell into his domain within their marriage. She didn't begrudge him any of her time. She found it comforting, in fact, to be attached to the world by any activity that had a bearing on the real life she lived. She might ponder black holes, anguish over the extinction of yet another species, the depletion of the ozone layer, the implacable movement of the universe, the inevitable chaos and tragedy bearing down hard upon the tiny earth, but she also remembered to take all of their skis to Rudy's Sporting Goods to be tuned before Thanksgiving.

And David. "You can't possibly understand how vulnerable any teenager is unless you have one of your own," she had finally replied to Ellen, not unkindly, since it had been Ellen's own decision not to have children. "We've all repressed memories of our own misery at that age. Or we've *edited* the whole experience so that we can bear to remember any of it at all." But Dinah gave up the effort of explaining when she saw Ellen's expression of suppressed disagreement.

David *was* so vulnerable because he had made an apparent success of his childhood. He was one of those children whom most adults come to believe they once were themselves, the sort of person they unwisely urge their own children to be, as though anyone could choose his or her nature. It was perfectly natural that the anxious parents of West Bradford, when they considered what appeared to be David Howells's easy progress through the years, didn't understand that his talent for growing up would not necessarily have any bearing on his success at being a grown-up. They had, of course, reinterpreted their own history in the context of their current lives; otherwise the contradictions were unsettling, were too illogical.

David appeared golden in his small pond because he had such easily recognizable talents, scholastically and socially, but he had a naïveté that only his parents understood. It seemed to his parents that David's faith in the logical progression of his own life was unaccompanied by any understanding that he would have to shape its direction. Eventually he would have to make invidious comparisons, unpleasant judgments, difficult choices. He accepted his existence at face value, with very little cynicism. Dinah didn't know how to protect him from his own innocent expectations; for the time being, she did her best to guard him from disillusionment by covering his tracks and anticipating his failure to plan ahead.

But it was true that morning in May, while she cleared the way for Martin and David to maneuver the trunk into the bedroom, that she became increasingly angry at both of them. She didn't think they had the right to pass judgment on her request, to patronize her by their mutual air of condescension. She had sensed she was being ganged up on. Didn't they remember all the requests they had made of her over the years that were whimsical, foolish, or a consequence of their own forgetfulness or lack of foresight?

She hadn't said any of this; she merely nurtured her resentment icily in the old farmhouse, which had been filled with the light of spring when the leaves were still only sparsely sketched on the trees and the interiors of the four-windowed rooms were bleached with a shadeless profusion of unshifting sunshine. She had remained silent. She could not have said to them that if David was leaving in three months, she needed to begin to believe it at once.

And now, in August, the trunk still sat empty, so while David helped Netta sort through the things she had salvaged from her marriage, filling the cupboards and bureaus and bookshelves of her apartment on Marchand's Drive, Dinah rummaged through all the closets of her own house, collecting whatever items she had on hand that David would need. Sarah would have made up her own lists competently, needing very few reminders, and Toby would have had his trunk packed by mid-July. He had planned ahead with a sort of desperation and had never seemed to be able to relax entirely into whatever pleasure was to be had in the immediate moment. Whereas Toby had always been wary of the immutable onslaught of his own future, David's talent was to navigate the present with brilliance.

Dinah had glanced out the window one afternoon years ago, when Toby was in third grade, and had seen David emerge from the schoolbus and turn to continue a conversation with a friend through one of the bus windows. Finally Toby had climbed down the steps and trudged past David and even Duchess, who abased herself before him, wriggling and shambling around him in a humble plea for affection. He didn't pay any attention to the dog or to his mother when he passed her in the kitchen, except to acknowledge her with a monosyllabic greeting and go on his way up the stairs to his room. After a while Dinah had gone to find him there, where he was stretched out on his bed.

"Are you okay, sweetie?" Dinah asked. "You feel all right?"

He was quiet for a moment, thinking it over. "Matthew thinks that if me and Anne and Jason are all lawyers we could have a good business, because he's black and Jason's Jewish and Anne's a girl, and she's a Catholic." He looked away from her after explaining this and didn't say anything for a moment. Dinah was so taken aback at such sad precocity that she was struck dumb. "And I guess I'm a Christian. That's what Matthew says."

He looked at her for confirmation, but she was searching for some way to discourage this whole line of thought. He went on. "Jason's going to go to Columbia, and Matthew's going to Yale, and Anne's going to Vassar, and I'll go to Harvard." None of this was cute or amusing to Dinah, and it was clear it had filled him with anxiety. "But if I can't get into Harvard I don't know what I'll do. I don't even know how I'll get a job."

"Toby, you're only eight. . . . It's tokenism. . . . Why are you. . . ? Well . . ." She had paused to marshal her thoughts, to think of a way to discourage him wisely. "Look at Ellen! Or your Aunt Isobel! Neither of them even *finished* college! God, Isobel didn't even start . . ." She was sputtering with frustration. Where had he even heard of these schools? What could have put this into his mind? She made an effort to collect herself, and sat down on the foot of Toby's bed. "Listen, most of the people in the world don't go to Harvard or Yale or Columbia or Vassar, and they have jobs. *Most* of the people in the world don't go to college at all! And there are lots of fools out there who did go to those schools and *don't* and *shouldn't* have jobs!" She had been surprisingly angry—not at Toby, but at this suffocating set of expectations he had set up for himself when he was only eight years old. For a few minutes she thought she had assuaged his fears about his life as an adult, because he settled farther into his pillow and gazed out the window.

"You mean, even if I go to Harvard I might not get a job?"

And over the years whenever Martin and Dinah took the children into New York, Toby had trod after them moodily through any museum and lagged behind them along the frantic sidewalks. Once when Martin had persuaded David to go again with him and Sarah to the Museum of Natural History, Dinah had begged off, and Toby had simply refused, so he and she were having a sandwich at a deli they frequented whenever they were in the city.

For as long as Dinah could remember, there had been a bearded, disheveled man who stood or sometimes sat in front of the deli and never spoke, but became upset and insistent when customers approached, leaning forward aggressively and thrusting toward them a jar that already contained a few coins. Dinah always had some change ready to give him, and she took his presence in stride after so many years. But that lunchtime, when they had not gone to the Museum of Natural History, Toby had pulled his mother back as they approached the deli.

"What, Toby?" she had said, but he hadn't answered her. He had only been in the fourth grade, but his pull on her arm and his braced feet and locked knees had brought her to a standstill. He wouldn't answer her, though. "Come on! I'm hungry, and it'll be too crowded for us to sit down if we don't go in now." She had disengaged her arm from his grasp and moved ahead, and he had, indeed, followed her to a booth, although he refused to have anything to eat. She didn't attempt to chat with him; she concentrated on her own lunch.

"I'm never going to be like that," Toby had said to her. "Even if I'm really poor. I'd live out in the country."

She had tried then and many times afterward to persuade him of all the desirable, likely, and secure possibilities between the extremes of being lost and adrift in society and being a Harvard Law School graduate, but without success. He noticed the people huddled in doorways, or wandering with their possessions through Grand Central Station, or the man outside the deli, and without fail he imagined himself in their situation. All the ordinary people in the streets in their suits and dresses or jeans and T-shirts might as well have been invisible.

In all his life Dinah had not been able to figure out why Toby had so little faith in his own abilities. She didn't think she had ever been able to reassure him adequately, and now, on a warm August day in the heavy air of late summer, it occurred to her that David might eventually complete a cycle that Toby had hoped to begin. Neither she nor Martin had ever wanted David to go to Harvard, hoping that he would choose a four-year undergraduate college. Her resentment of the whole institution—admission to which, in all its imagined unattainability, had loomed gloomily over much of Toby's life—resolved itself into a thin fury as she sorted and folded and marked sheets and towels. She was tense with a shaky, febrile anger at Mr. Franklin M. Mount, who had suggested that Harvard students would need raincoats to carry on their rarefied lives.

As Dinah was bending over David's bed, where she was carefully lettering HOWELLS in the bottom right-hand corner of each one of eight towels with a laundry pen, she heard Ellen call up to her from the kitchen. People in West Bradford hadn't locked their doors until recently, when several women's purses had been stolen from kitchen counters right inside their back doors. Dinah still didn't lock her door. For one thing, she was rarely parted from her purse. Even when she was in her robe or nightgown, she went from room to room with her old Coach bag slung by its strap over her shoulder, where it functioned as a kind of portable office. She often used it to brace her checkbook while she paid the plumber or wrote out a check at the grocery store while standing in line, and the tan leather was marked and dotted with black squiggles of ink from hurried moments when she had struggled to tear off the check before capping her pen. But besides that, she had no idea where her house keys were, and she never remembered to take Martin's and have them copied. So people came and went all year at the Howellses' house. Friends left a jar of soup or a plate of cookies on the kitchen counter if they found no one home. The man who read the gas meter made his way through the house to the basement, and workmen left their bills propped against the sugar bowl on the kitchen table.

"I'm up here, Ellen," she called down. "I'm in David's room."

Ellen was one of the few people whose voice Duchess recognized, and she went to the top of the stairs, wagging her tail enthusiastically. Taffy stayed where he was, lolling on David's pillow, but the gray cat, Bob, disappeared like a wraith beneath the dresser.

"Vic and Martin are going to be at the office until about seven. I thought we could get pizza," Ellen said, zigzagging around Duchess, who impeded her way excitedly. Ellen sat on the other side of the bed and idly scratched Duchess between the ears. "Would that be okay or would you rather go out?"

"No. That'll be fine," Dinah said, although she wasn't in the mood to be sociable this evening. "I don't even know who'll be home for dinner. I hadn't planned to cook. But God, I really want to get this done. Why don't you make a salad if you would." Dinah had looked up when Ellen came in to smile a greeting, but she had seen right away that Ellen was in one of her purposeful moods, in which she would be likely to be bossy. Dinah had deflected her intention, and although Ellen cast a disapproving eye over the trunk, into which Dinah had folded sweaters and blankets and sheets, she didn't comment.

"I hate washing lettuce," Dinah added conversationally. "In the summer I feel like I devote my life to washing lettuce. You make the salad and the pizza will be our treat. David and Sarah both have friends over, and no telling how many people will be here for dinner."

"Will David mind if I take what I need from the garden?" Ellen asked.

"Oh, no. He hasn't done much work in the garden the past few weeks. I imagine the lettuce needs thinning." Ellen shot her a speculative look to see if Dinah intended irony, to see if she knew what David *had* been doing in the past few weeks. Clearly, though, no one had mentioned to her David's probable involvement with Netta, because Dinah continued earnestly marking the last of the washcloths. Ellen went off, clattering down the stairs in her clogs, with Duchess fast on her heels.

By the time Dinah had arranged the towels and sheets in David's trunk and showered, the house had filled up. Sarah and two of her friends were out on the porch, talking with David and Sam Albergotti, whom Dinah had scarcely seen this summer. Netta stood in the porch doorway, with Anna Tyson leaning back against her knees. Ellen was slicing cucumbers, and Martin and Vic were sitting at the kitchen table over a stack of papers.

"Have you ordered the pizza yet?" Dinah asked when she came into the kitchen.

"We're trying to sort it all out," Ellen said. "We think two large 'Vegetarians' and two 'Combinations.' One 'Deep Dish' and one 'New York Crust' of each. What do you want?"

"I don't care. I'll have a piece of either kind. Will Anna Tyson want something plain, though? Should we get one 'Small Cheese'?"

Ellen didn't want Netta and her daughter to stay for dinner, and she grimaced at Dinah with urgent intent, but looked away as Martin glanced up to speak to his wife. He was distracted and frowning slightly. "Sweetheart, Netta and I are going over to the office and see if we can finish the editing on her article. Is that okay with you? We'll pick up something and take it over there. It goes to the printer tomorrow morning. Vic, are you coming?"

Vic held his hands up, palms outward in surrender, shaking his head. "Not unless you need me. I'm done in."

"No, that's fine," Martin said. "I don't think it'll take us more than about an hour."

David had come into the room, and Anna Tyson had sidled over and was slouching against his legs while he rested his hand on her shoulder. "Netta's not going to eat with us?" David asked lightly, looking down at Anna Tyson for her nod of confirmation. "Well, Anna Tyson and Netta can come with me and Sam to pick up the pizzas and you can follow us, Dad."

People began to mill about, getting Diet Cokes or beer or wine, finding places to sit. Sarah and her friends appropriated the table on the porch, and Vic got up and put napkins and plates on the kitchen table; but Dinah suggested that he and Ellen and she have their dinner in the living room.

When the three of them were finally settled there, sitting on the floor around the coffee table, drinking wine and waiting for David to return with their pizza, they didn't worry much about keeping up a conversation. This gathering was familiar and undemanding.

Ellen put her glass of wine down after taking a sip and sat back against the edge of the sofa, contemplating something. When she spoke, her voice was careful, the way people speak to patients in hospitals.

"Dinah," she said cautiously, pausing, "I know that it's impossible for you to be openly rude to someone." She stopped, considering, and her voice was soft, not instructive. "But doesn't it ever occur to you that you don't have to be nice to every waif who crosses your doorstep? I mean, Anna Tyson might as well just move in here."

"I don't mind Anna Tyson," Dinah answered, mildly enough, but with the sudden hope that Ellen wouldn't say anything more.

Ellen picked up her wine and swirled it gently, studying her glass with concentration. "Anna Tyson is hardly the problem though, is she?"

A shadow of doubt about Martin and Netta crossed Dinah's mind, but she held it off. She listened for the sound of the car, wondering why David was taking so long to return with their pizza. She rose and went to the window, looking out to see if he was in sight. She noticed the rather nasty aluminum aftertaste of the cheap red wine she bought in jugs and usually mixed with orange juice and drank over ice.

"This wine's awful," she said to Vic and Ellen. "I'm going to dump mine and get a beer. Can I bring either of you one?" She left the room when they both demurred, and she heard Vic ask Ellen something about their storm windows as she carried her wineglass down the hall to the kitchen.

Franklin M. Mount
Dean of Freshmen
Harvard College
12 Truscott Street
Cambridge, Massachusetts 02138

Dear Mr. Mount,

I've pretty much done all that I can do. I'm sending expensive sheets for David's bed because I couldn't find any reasonably priced sheets that were extra long. How many parents do you think have these things lying around? It seems to me you would think about the expense and inconvenience. I bet there's not a single freshman coming to Harvard next year who has an extra-long bed in his own house. And how many of us have an extra trash can, for instance? Or lamps? *Two* lamps?

The thing is, Mr. Mount, I'm losing too much. I'm having to let go of things that I need. I'm giving too much away. I've always thought that in the long run—if you could look at the whole picture—I am a generous person, even a fatalistic person. I've let a good many things go out of my life without bitterness, with no thought of revenge. But I'm being pressed to the absolute limit, and it seems to me that Harvard College ought to take this into consideration in the future.

CHAPTER TEN

A CRY OF ABSENCE

WHEN DAVID PULLED IN behind his father's car along the curb in front of the pizza parlor, Netta was talkative and amused. "I can't believe this place," she said, gesturing out the window in the mild evening. "It's great, isn't it? It could even have been Minuteman Pizza and Sub *Shoppe*. With an extra *p e*. You know, like all those terrible *cute* places they've built out on Route Two." She was delighted. "I hadn't realized how provincial I'd become in Cambridge. I'd forgotten that this kind of irony existed outside of Harvard." She smiled in fleeting self-disparagement and grew pensive. "In spite of everything—I mean, even living in a place like West Bradford—I think it's been good for me to get away from the whole Harvard thing."

David and Sam exchanged a glance. The two of them and Socs Trangas's youngest daughter, Irini, had waited tables for Socs one summer, and he was a morose man who lacked any trace of a sense of irony. Neither Sam nor David had ever considered the absurdity of the logo in the win-

dow, which depicted a stalwart Minuteman in his tricor-
nered hat, clasping his musket across his chest with one
hand and with the other holding aloft a steaming pizza.
That same logo decorated the countless cardboard flats that
Sam and David and Irini had spent many hours folding into
carry-out boxes.

In 1977, Socrates Trangas had moved his wife and
three daughters from Greece to Albany, New York, where
his older brother Connie lived, then finally on to West
Bradford in 1979, when he and Connie had a final falling-
out. Socs hadn't spoken to his brother since. He had chosen
to locate in West Bradford because it was a college town
with no cheap restaurants, but when his fledgling attempt
to make a success of a modest place serving Greek food had
failed, he had turned it into a pizza and sub shop in 1982.
It still rankled, though, the failure of his restaurant, and he
avenged himself somewhat on his clientele, all of whom
were regulars since there was no other place to get a pizza
in West Bradford. He begrudged and rationed each piece
of pepperoni, each chunk of green pepper, every slice of
mushroom that he dealt out as fast as cards onto the waiting
rounds of fresh dough.

He rarely socialized with his customers while they
waited at the counter for their orders, but he was fond of
the Howellses, who had expressed real regret when he had
given up serving avgolemono soup, spanakopita, pastitsio,
moussaka, and assorted Greek pastries, and had built a long
counter across the back of the room to facilitate carry-out
orders of Italian subs and pizzas.

The Howellses had been almost nightly customers in
the fall and winter of 1983, when the renovations to their
own kitchen had taken two months longer than they had
expected, and Socs always came out of the kitchen to chat
with Dinah when she came in to pick up an order. One
evening she had listened with sympathetic attention when
he told her about the disagreement with his brother in Al-

bany. When he had looked down and realized that the box with her pizza in it had grown cool to the touch, he dropped the conversation and handed it over to her at once. At the door she turned back, with a short wave.

"So long," she had said, but he misheard her and hesitated uncertainly for a moment while she stood with her hand still raised as she pushed sideways against the door. "Right. Okay." And he paused once again. "Shalom," he replied, raising his own hand in a peaceful dismissal. When Martin Howells came in to pick up an order in mid-December of that year, Socs had presented him with a bottle of Wild Turkey in its holiday box and a card with Chanukah greetings. Neither of the Howellses could think of a tactful way to set the misunderstanding straight, and it didn't matter as long as they were careful not to order pizza on any of the Jewish holidays, when Socs would invariably make a point of greeting them appropriately. They were uncomfortably trapped into false pretenses because they had left it too long ever to explain.

Now Sam and David only exchanged a look; they didn't want to appear foolish themselves by revealing to Netta their own innocence—that the anachronism of a Revolutionary War pizza had never occurred to them. They followed her into the restaurant, where it took a little while to get the order straightened out.

Netta came back to the car with them to be sure Anna Tyson was fastened into her seat belt in the back seat, and to give her a quick kiss. Then she moved to the driver's window and leaned in and kissed David lightly on the cheek. "Thanks for baby-sitting. I'm sure I won't be long," she said, before going along to get into Martin's car where he had pulled in ahead of them at the curb.

Once Netta and Martin arrived at his office, Netta cleared a place on the desk and put the pizza box down between them. When she discovered that the wedges hadn't been sufficiently severed one from the other, she took up a pair of scissors laid out on Martin's blotter and snipped the gooey pie into neat triangles. He was unusually impressed; Netta had always seemed so removed from practical concerns.

"That's great," he said. "You just cut along the dotted lines. We always use one of those roller things. It never works, though. All the cheese runs together." He was surprised, as he always was, when one of his family's habits turned out not to be universal. But as she stretched her arm across the desk, Martin noticed dark, smudged bruises where her short sleeve pulled away from her upper arm, and another fading bruise along her collarbone. "Netta. What happened?"

She looked up from the pizza to see what he was talking about, and when she saw her arm exposed, she let it drop to her side, the scissors in her hand falling against her skirt, where they left a smear of oil against the pale blue print. She sat as she was without answering, and then she gestured with her free hand in a brushing-away sweep of her arm, as though she could push the question back to Martin. When her eyes became glassy with tears, he realized that she was going to confide to him so much more than he wanted to know.

She settled into the chair across from his and looked down at the scissors she was still holding, idly clicking them open and shut. She let out a gentle exhalation of breath, not quite a sigh, and shook her head backward with her customary flick. It was a preparatory gesture, Martin decided unhappily.

"It's true," she said, "that I'm not sure how to handle the whole thing anymore. I mean, I know I've done a lot of good, and I've never met anyone who's so . . . I don't know . . ." And she paused to consider, and to gather her forces. "Owen's so *needy*. So sad. I don't think I've ever met a person as lost. I mean, there's a lot of denial going on in that whole family, I think. The Crofts are very controlling, especially Judith. And they've refused to let him move home." She snapped the scissors shut, putting them on the desk, where the blades, resting on the absorbent blotter, left another feathery spear of oil.

Martin didn't have anything to say; he was unmoved. What Vic had told him about *David* and Netta crossed his mind. The thought of Netta's victimization, even possible brutalization, by Owen Croft offended a kind of fastidiousness in Martin.

She looked directly at him in appeal, holding her hands out slightly, almost in supplication. "I didn't want Owen to hurt himself. I can see now that he just couldn't stand it. He just couldn't be hurt anymore by . . . by any sort of *censure*. Oh, God! He grabbed one of my knives down from that magnetic rack. We were standing right there in the kitchen."

Her eyes filled with tears again, and she glanced away in an attempt to compose herself. "He's just so emotionally injured, and I'm the only one he can come to. At least, I can offer him a *moral* base. Do you see what I mean? He has to count on someone. I don't think anyone can live in the world with . . . well . . . a total *absence* of trust. And I do think there's a person there with so much value. But then *I* seemed not to trust him!" Tears were running down her face, and she wiped them away with the back of her hands the way a small child would; she was clearly filled with regret at the memory of her own behavior. "And . . . well, we were both pretty drunk. I should have just left him alone. He had his wrist over the sink. I don't know if he really would have cut himself. I don't know. I just don't know. But of course he didn't mean . . ." and she gestured to the bruises on her arm. "He didn't have any idea what he was doing. He only wanted me to leave him alone."

She had been bending forward toward Martin in an effort to make herself clear, and suddenly she seemed to deflate. She settled back in her chair, and she was such a small woman that she appeared to shrink within her clothes in an attitude of despair. Her downslanted eyes were swollen, the fragile flesh beneath them was shadowed, and across her cheekbones and along the graceful stretch of bone from ear to jaw, her skin was taut and luminous. She was so slight, so small and vulnerable, sunk deeply into her chair just across the desk from Martin. She was utterly and obviously defenseless.

Martin was appalled. Martin was repelled. He hadn't wanted to imagine the scene she described. He hadn't wanted to get further involved, and although he was rarely unkind, he knew he was about to be ungenerous to Netta after all she had revealed to him. He sat there studying the pizza, noting that the cheese had gone cold and opaque, and closed the box, putting it aside. He placed Netta's manuscript squarely between them, shuffling through the pages to see where it was marked. When he finally looked up at her, he smiled in apology. "Well," he said, "be careful, Netta. Take care of yourself."

Anna Tyson sat at the kitchen table with David and Sam, tucking her legs beneath her to give herself enough height to reach her piece of pizza and her glass of chocolate milk. Without even thinking of it, David used her as a foil to avoid Sam's questions about Christie. Why didn't David care, Sam wanted to know, that after three years of going out with her, he was hurting her feelings so much? David got up to dampen a napkin so that Anna Tyson could wipe the tomato sauce from around her mouth.

David was hardly able to pay attention to what Sam was saying; his head was filled with the thought of Netta, and he was sluggish and stunned by the amazing eroticism of the time he spent at her apartment. He was dazed by the combination of sex and the luxury of guiltless, irresponsible domesticity. Even while Sam was talking to him, David couldn't distract himself enough to think much about Christie.

Finally Sam gave up. He was tilted backward, and he let his chair fall forward with a thump. He took a piece of pizza and began to eat it as he got up and made for the door.

"I've got to go," he said. "I told Meg I'd pick her up after work. I'll see you."

"Yeah. Okay," David said. He looked up just as Sam reached the doorway, and David experienced an abrupt sense of loss, then, just for a moment. It moved over him like a shiver, and he didn't want to see Sam go out of the kitchen into the dark, his shoulders still stiff with reproach. "I feel bad about Christie," David said. "But she's so young. And next year . . . I mean, I don't know what's going to happen next year. I'll talk to her, though."

Sam was silhouetted in the doorframe beyond the light of the kitchen, but David saw the white flash of Sam's quick grin. "That'll be good," Sam said, and then the screen swung to and Sam disappeared down the back steps.

But while David sat with Anna Tyson, who was concentrating in silence on the piece of pizza she was eating, the thought of Christie slipped out of his mind. He had helped Netta arrange furniture in her apartment the previous afternoon, and she had begun fixing supper for the three of them. David had read a story to Anna Tyson while Netta made noodles Alfredo from a packaged mix, peeled carrots at the sink, cut three apples into eighths on a wooden cutting board, and set the table.

All the while that David was reading *Frog and Toad Are Friends*, which he remembered from his own childhood, he couldn't help but be aware that later on, after he washed the dishes and Netta had put Anna Tyson to bed, he might again have leisurely access to Netta's body. Maybe they would unpack another box of books, or her records, and then they would sit and talk for a while. But eventually, he was sure, she would stretch out next to him on the futon, or maybe on her bed. Netta wasn't so young and so ardent as Christie. And Netta didn't urge him toward her with her arms and legs wrapped around him; she merely cradled him. But neither did she become agonized or guilt-ridden. It all seemed another amazing part of a normal evening.

He would rummage through her refrigerator, if she asked him to, and bring something back to bed for them to eat—two plums, or a box of raisins, or two plastic cartons of yogurt. So much sensuous freedom numbed his intellect; he was sated and stuporous with the dailiness of it all. It was an easy leap of his imagination to think of the days continuing in just this way.

David realized that it was true, as Netta had explained—as she had cautioned him—that he had no idea why he was going to Harvard in a few weeks. He had applied and been accepted; it hadn't occurred to him that he should have a reason to go, a sense of purpose. The idea of deadlines, classes, roommates, communal meals—the work of being a student—depressed him and made him anxious. Certainly it filled him with wonder that he had so cavalierly planned to do such a thing. He thought of his undemanding, routine job waiting tables at the café, and realized that it would be even easier in September when the tourists had gone. And also, to his surprise, he felt a powerful melancholy at what he now realized would be his departure from all that was familiar to him. He had been excited about going away, but now the thought of it frightened him.

David would sit next to Netta in her twin bed while she leaned back against the wall, stirring the blueberries up from the bottom of her yogurt, telling him about one thing or another, and he would sometimes fall into a dazed sleep for moments at a time. Eventually she would get up and start to dress, urging him to do the same, hurrying him out.

If Anna Tyson were to wake up in the night, Netta explained, she didn't want him to be found there.

The long evenings he spent after work helping Netta unpack had led to their having sex together only three times in about as many weeks, but the familiarity of such easy householdery enhanced David's idea of their intimacy. He spent a lot of time in Netta's and Anna Tyson's company, lending a hand whenever Netta had to attend to some chore or other. He went with the two of them to the Laundromat, for instance, and hefted the heavy baskets of wet clothes and sheets and towels into the back seat of Netta's car. If he didn't mind carrying them, Netta said, she much preferred to bring the laundry home right out of the washer and hang it to dry on the communal clothesline in the backyard of her apartment, but the baskets were too heavy for her to lift alone. She handed him clothespins while he pegged up blouses and skirts and shorts and towels on one of the three lines, strung between tall poles, which were hard for her to reach.

They went to the supermarket in Bradford, where David wheeled the cart with Anna Tyson facing him in the fold-out compartment of the basket, eating animal crackers while Netta stocked up on paper towels and canned tomatoes—items that were overpriced, she said, at The Whole Grain Elevator.

"Your mother told me that she didn't think it was worth the trip to come all the way over here, and that it was depressing, too. It *is* sort of like a warehouse. Pretty grim. But it's so much cheaper. It seems strange to me that Dinah would spend so much money just for cheerful surroundings. Especially since she does such elaborate cooking."

"She doesn't really," David said, not knowing what prompted him to say that, and feeling uncomfortable. "She doesn't have much time for cooking." He knew that his mother cooked dinner every night, often cooked breakfast if she was around when any of the rest of the family got up, and he didn't know why he felt compelled to deny it. In his own kitchen, though, one evening later that week, when he was opening a can of frozen orange juice concentrate, he stopped abruptly and glanced at the price stamped on the top. He turned to his mother, who was reading the paper at the kitchen table. "Don't you think it's a waste to spend so much money on this stuff when you could get it for almost a third less in Bradford?" But his mother hadn't answered him; she only looked up at him briefly with a bewildered expression.

He didn't know, either, that in the past two weeks there had been moments when he was lugging baskets of Netta's and Anna Tyson's wet laundry out under the clear sky while his own mother was dividing the laundry at his house into separate stacks of colors and whites. He didn't know that, once, at the very moment he was impressed by Netta's idea of wanting Anna Tyson's T-shirts to dry in the fresh air, Dinah, in his own house on Slade Road, had taken up a handful of his shirts—damp and musty-smelling from having lain in a moldering pile that she had repeatedly asked him to do something about—and tossed them all into the wash together, the navy and red and white polo and T-shirts intermingled. "What the hell," she had muttered as she slammed the top down and set them to run on "Warm/Cold."

The fact of Netta's involvement with such mundane things as buying and cooking food, ironing, hanging her clothes out on a clothesline never failed to surprise and intrigue David. It didn't cross his mind that anything of the kind went on at his own house.

Dinah spent the rest of the week making repeated trips to the mall in Albany or to outlet stores in the area in search of various things that David would need for school. But she was vague and forgetful and slightly disoriented. She could not shake Ellen's warning about the association between

Netta and Martin, but she didn't want to consider it head-on just now.

She was driving along a familiar stretch of Route 7, on her way to a small store that sold Pendleton blankets, when she began to feel she couldn't get her breath. She was flushed and clammy and panicky by the time she brought the car to a stop on the shoulder of the road. She rested her forearms against the steering wheel and lowered her head into her hands. Her breathing slowed, but she was nauseated with the visceral acknowledgment of the feeling of abandonment. It seemed to her that she was being left to fend for herself on every front, and yet she wasn't at all sure what it was she was fending off.

Ellen had dropped by early that morning and joined her once again in David's room as she was just finishing packing David's trunk. Dinah sat on the lid while Ellen closed the hasps. "You've packed enough towels and sheets to carry this child through middle age," Ellen said as she strained to fasten down the second latch. She glanced up when Dinah didn't respond.

"Oh, Ellen, you know, this is just so incredibly hard," Dinah finally replied, embarrassed to find herself near tears.

Ellen concentrated on the clasp and snapped it home. "Yes, it must be. Remembering David's first step, and all that."

Dinah nodded, although she couldn't, in fact, remember David's first step or his first word; she was not particularly sentimental. She did not grieve over visions of David as an infant, a toddler, a little boy—she could not even successfully place herself back in that time and experience. She could, of course, recall innumerable happy occasions of all her children's early lives, but in recalling them she didn't reexperience the happiness.

What was haunting her was the memory of the condition of unqualified, unguarded, untentative goodwill between her and her children. She remembered the assuredness—even when they were in the midst of some furious argument—of unconditional love. She had thought there would always be an enduring conspiracy among herself and her children in the face of the world. But even the idea of attempting to explain this to Ellen filled Dinah with a sense of futility.

Now and then, in unguarded moments—in dreams, coming out of snatches of sleep—she was overtaken by the most suffocating apprehension. If she could not keep militant control of her emotions, sorrow encroached on all of Dinah's sensibilities. She could not eat, she could not sleep, she could not read. Her attention was diverted utterly to the prospect of losing David, and this puzzled her because, love him as she did, right now she didn't much like him. She didn't like the way he was choosing to leave, cold and aloof to his parents, ignoring his friends, apparently superior to any sentiment.

That morning, when they were sitting at breakfast, she and Sarah and David and Martin, she had sipped her coffee and watched David finish an English muffin. It was rare these days that the four of them were at the table together. As she got up to get some more coffee, she leaned over and gave him a quick kiss as she passed behind his chair. "You know, sweetie, it's going to seem so strange when you aren't here next year. We're going to miss you."

Dinah hadn't understood that she was hoping for reassurance from the last person who could give it to her. The best response David could have made was to say that he would miss them, too, but he was far too endangered to say such a thing. She had no way of knowing that he was full of alarm on his own behalf. He had no practice at leaving behind every familiar thing in his life. But she was astounded when, after a few moments, David had given her a quick smile and said, "Right, Mom. The empty nest syndrome, huh? When Sarah leaves that'll be it. Just you and

Dad." His tone was bantering and brittle, and she turned to look at him, but he had folded the newspaper into a rectangle and was reading the baseball scores, and Martin was smiling at her rather absently. Dinah was hurt and taken aback at being so diminished—as though she were just anyone at all and not connected to these two smug males sitting at the table. She had refilled her coffee cup and left the room without another word.

But now, as she sat resting against the steering wheel at the side of the road, no longer able to avoid considering the possibility of Martin's betrayal, she was overwhelmed by an appalling and sorrowing . . . lackfulness. For a good part of her life, she had had so much, and then that remarkable abundance had begun to dwindle.

A car pulled onto the gravel shoulder ahead of her, and a tall girl was getting out of the driver's seat and heading back toward her. Dinah straightened a little as the girl approached her window.

"Are you okay?" the girl asked, bending considerably to gaze in at Dinah, a look of concern on her pleasantly long face, her thick hair swinging against the metal window frame.

Dinah nodded. "I think I'm fine, now. I just felt nauseated for a minute. You're so nice to stop."

"You know," the girl said, "maybe you ought to see if it would make you feel better if you had something to eat. Or maybe a Coke. I'll follow you. The Red Hut is right up the road."

Dinah was embarrassed. The intense sensation that had swept over her had dissipated somewhat, and she felt better. "Oh, I'm not even going that far. I'm just going to Carmichael's Outlet Store up ahead. I really am fine, and you were awfully kind to pull over." Dinah hesitated for a moment, wondering how to say what she knew she should say and not sound churlish. "You know, though, you really shouldn't stop when you see a car parked on the shoulder.

There've been some terrible incidents. . . ." She fell silent because the girl was nodding at her in agreement.

"Oh, I know, but I've been behind you for about ten miles, and I noticed when you began to slow down. I could tell you were having trouble. Actually, I've figured the odds on these things. Grown women in Volvo station wagons are not a big risk. I think it's the middle-aged guys in those kind of anonymous green sedans who worry me most. Those cars that are always dusty and dented. I mean, it's like they're designed that way. Born to be a heap. You know? And some guy's driving who has on a white T-shirt and his elbow out the window. . . ." The girl straightened away from the car and mimicked a man slouching at the steering wheel. She pretended to take a long drag from an imaginary cigarette while steering casually with the other hand. Dinah laughed, and the girl dropped her arms to her sides and grinned back at her. "Why don't you pull in front of me and I'll follow until you turn off? In case you don't feel as well as you think?"

Dinah pulled ahead, and in a few miles turned off into the graveled lot at Carmichael's, flashing a wave at the girl, who tooted her horn and accelerated up the long grade of the mountain. While Dinah sorted through the heavy wool blankets, she felt sure that the girl who had stopped to offer her help had parents who had no idea that they had a daughter so kind, so clever, so responsible in the world. So adult. Dinah let herself think about the incident, but she didn't allow a single thought of its cause to enter her mind. The memory of the girl loping back toward her along the highway cheered her through the rest of that day, and she completed every chore on her list.

In the next few days she was at loose ends. Until David had enough time off work to try on his jeans and slacks and shirts and jackets, to see if they needed to be altered, there weren't any more preparations for his leavetaking with which Dinah could busy herself. She made a halfhearted

attempt to get back to a book Ellen had persuaded her to review for a new local literary magazine, but she knew she
would do the author a disservice if she read his book now.
Her attention was vague and indirect, having the quality of a
pointillist painting. At the end of a day she had a memory of
a cohesive unit of time, but, in fact, during that day each moment registered more or less out of context. She was reluctant
to allow herself periods of long, uninterrupted musings. She
wasn't sleeping well, and she put her fuzzy-headedness down
to that.

She began to think it was important—perhaps only for
herself—that there be some sort of occasion to mark David's
transition from living at home to a life of his own. After all,
David would leave them only once, and it seemed to her
imperative that the family do something together, something that David could enjoy and could add to the picture
of how his life had been. It was possible that David was taking leave of them with such ease because he simply didn't
understand how much they loved him. He would be able to
think back and say to himself that when he had gone off to
school his freshman year, his parents and his sister had . . .
and Dinah was at a loss. She couldn't think of anything appropriate, and one part of her unkindly wanted David, at
about age thirty-four, to look back and think, "When I went
off to school my freshman year . . . I was an ungrateful little
shit." This was not in any way admirable, Dinah knew that,
but she had come to a flinty peace with herself these past
few months over the fact that her maternity was not selfless.

She considered a surprise party, but most of David's
friends were going off to school also, and she imagined
each family would mark the transition in its own way. She
thought briefly of the customs of some of the early Irish
immigrants to the United States. The families held an
"American Wake," on the night before the final leave-taking, to give form to the agony of the coming separation.
They had accorded dignity to the grief of having to live on

as childless parents and parentless children—an unnatural condition because the lost children and absent parents were alive in the world, but lost forever to each other. For almost five minutes, one late afternoon, this appealed to Dinah as an appropriate ceremony, but then she snapped out of her gloomy reverie and decided she didn't really think any sort of celebration was worth the trouble, given David's current state of mind.

She didn't allow herself to ponder what connection there might be between Netta and Martin—that seemed to her a separate issue altogether, and certainly boded a different sort of regret. The very evening Ellen had first mentioned it to her, when they had all sat around eating pizza, Netta and Martin hadn't returned from the office until long after Vic and Ellen had gone home, and Dinah had helped David put Anna Tyson to bed in Sarah's room. When Netta and Martin had arrived, David had offered to drive Netta home so he could carry Anna Tyson up the steep stairs of Netta's apartment.

"I'll drive them, David," Martin had said, uncharacteristically brusque. "You've got to be at work tomorrow."

Dinah had turned away when she saw Netta reach out and lightly touch Martin's arm in thanks, and Dinah also saw David's face close down in anger. "I'll drive them, Dad," he said, his voice overloud and hollow. Dinah was stunned for a moment by sheer humiliation. Did her own children know of some alliance between their father and Netta? Dinah went upstairs, not waiting for Martin.

When Martin had come up to bed, she was awake and had no hope of sleeping. Sometimes it struck her as strange that, at a designated hour, she took off the clothes she wore in the daytime and put on clothes to wear at night, and then lay in bed staring at the ceiling or at the soft outlines of the windows until it was time to change into a new set of clothes and move through the daytime hours again. It seemed like such an arbitrary arrangement—and so much laundry.

That night, though, she had turned her head on the pillow to look at Martin as he settled down next to her. "Listen, Martin . . ." she began at the exact moment that he said, "Dinah, did you. . . ?"

They both stopped. "What?" she said.

"Did you notice the bruises on Netta's arms?" he asked her. "When she was leaning across the table? And on her neck?"

"I didn't. No," Dinah said, pushing the bedspread away and swinging her legs over the side of the bed. "I'm going to read for a while. I'm not sleepy."

"Okay," Martin said, rolling over on his side into his pillow. "I hope you can get some sleep later. 'Night, love."

Dinah went down the stairs, cursing him silently, loathing him, mimicking him with the fury of the insomniac for the sound sleeper. "I hope you can get some sleep later," she said aloud, softly, with a singsong, high-pitched mockery, cocking her head back and forth with each word, drawing her lips back over her teeth in disdain, like a child in the schoolyard.

Dinah and Martin had been married long enough to have run the course of dealing with the other's seeming infatuations with someone else. Each one had suffered through long periods of jealousy and speculation. They had attended the requisite number of parties where Dinah had glimmered and glittered and tested the waters of her own attractiveness, and Martin had flirted quite seriously with someone else's wife. Years ago. All of that posturing seemed to have happened so long ago; it was so tedious in retrospect. Pointless, after all. And Dinah felt fairly certain that Martin was interested in too many other things to take the risk of being involved with anyone other than herself. Besides, they did love each other, and they had honor and affection and humor and tragedy between them, and the constant awareness of the fragility of family life. Why would Martin tempt fate? But when she returned to bed that night, she didn't sleep well, just in snatches during the hours toward dawn.

Dinah found herself, in the last week of August before school started, browsing through the rows of David's neglected garden, stooping here and there to pull up weeds, bending to stake the tomatoes firmly, shooing Duchess away so that she wouldn't trample the flowers and strawberries. The cats taunted the poor dog as they followed Dinah sinuously through the rows, stopping to shake off any bit of water that clung to an impeccably clean paw. Duchess paced the perimeter of the plot, sometimes shifting her front paws excitedly, wagging her tail unctuously, and crooning low in her throat to Dinah, begging to join her in the center of the garden.

"Oh, Duchess! Lie down! No! Stay! Lie down! That's a good girl." And Duchess settled restlessly with her head on her paws, eyeing the cats, who shot her narrow-eyed glances from among the foliage. Dinah looked at the woebegone dog and laughed, and began to sing to her from the row of tomatoes she was tying up:

> Lie down Duchess.
> Just leave me alone.
> If you stay right where you are,
> You'll get a bone.

Dinah was making up silly words to the tune of an old Eric Clapton song called "Lay Down Sally." The air was brilliant with its lack of humidity and haze, and the temperature was so moderate that it was one of those days that David had once characterized as having no weather at all. She was glad to remember his phrase. He was right. It was one of those rare days when one is not conscious of being a separate creature on the planet. She went ahead singing

to the dog, making up unclever lyrics, enjoying herself
wholeheartedly.

> Stay there Duchess.
> Stay just where you are.
> You're not missing anything.
> I won't go far.
>
> Don't move Duchess.
> Lie there in the yard.
> Pulling up this bishop's-weed
> Is really hard.

It was a good, sexy sort of tune, with a funny, offbeat,
Southern rhythm, and she liked the sound of it in the vivid
green yard. It reminded her of fraternity parties, of stepping into a room ahead of some boy, moving toward the
band, slightly shimmying her shoulders from side to side
with the beat and then turning to dance—not just with her
partner, but for the onlookers, the boys standing along the
wall with sweating paper cups of beer in their hands. She
had been a terrific dancer. She straightened among the tomato plants singing bits and pieces of the real song, empha-
sizing the funky beat, doing a dance that had been called
"The Jerk" when she was nineteen.

She undulated from side to side, while weaving her
arms back and forth with a flick and curl of her wrists. She
raised and crossed her hands above her head in a whiplash
motion, and sang on to the next verse. Then she changed
to a version of another dance, almost a bump and grind,
taking small steps that turned her slowly in a circle while
she swung her hips and shoulders in opposition to each
other and in double time to the beat.

She continued to dance among the staked vines and
hum the tune, with her lower lip caught between her front
teeth, while she looked down at her intricate footwork in

admiration until she heard something and dropped her arms and went still in embarrassed alarm.

David and Anna Tyson were standing at the edge of the garden plot clapping, and David was grinning at her while Anna Tyson looked on somberly. Dinah put her hands up to her face in surprise, and then she laughed.

"God, David! That's not fair."

"Hey, you're great. If you got it flaunt it. I can't dance at all. I always feel like a fool," he said, still grinning. "Netta had to go to the dentist, so Anna Tyson and I were going to work in the garden. Do you mind some company?"

"Sweetie, it's your garden. I'd love some company."

David dispatched Anna Tyson to get baskets and paper bags for zucchini and tomatoes, and he waded in among the rows, bending over and swinging back and forth to pull up the heavy-leafed and shallow-rooted weeds that were choking the zinnias. Anna Tyson helped for a while, and then wandered off to play on the old swing set. Dinah and David remarked to each other occasionally about the flowers or vegetables, and the whole atmosphere was easy and companionable. Eventually Anna Tyson grew tired and lagged after them in the garden. Her face was flushed with heat, and she had that glazed look of exhaustion that young children get. Dinah took pity on her.

"Why don't we take a break and go up to the house where it's a little cooler? I have some chocolate milk, Anna Tyson. And *Sesame Street* is on."

The three of them made their way up the slope of the yard, Dinah and David on the grass, and Anna Tyson determinedly jumping two-footed up one slate step to the next.

"Netta won't let me watch *Sesame Street*," she said, looking at Dinah to see if perhaps Dinah would.

"Well, I always watch *Sesame Street*," Dinah said, "so I'm sure your mother won't mind if you watch it with me."

"That's all right, Anna Tyson," David said. "I'll read you one of the books you brought."

Anna Tyson's face puckered in reproach. "I want to watch *Sesame Street*. Sometimes I watch it at Melissa's, and Netta doesn't care."

"David," Dinah said softly, "it won't hurt for her to watch this once. She's so tired I think she'll probably fall asleep if she lies down on the couch to watch television."

He looked worried. "The thing is, Netta thinks that all those images flashing on and off the screen so fast aren't a good way to teach. She thinks that the whole concept of that show undermines a child's own ability to figure out how to learn in his own way."

Dinah looked at David to see if he found this amusing, since he had loved the show himself when he was Anna Tyson's age, but clearly he didn't. "Umm. Well . . . It won't make any difference if she watches it for one hour. And I promise you she'll be asleep in about fifteen minutes."

Dinah settled Anna Tyson on the couch in front of the television with a glass of chocolate milk and a straw before rejoining David in the kitchen. He had poured tall glasses of iced tea for both of them and was sitting at the table. Dinah was delighted with the afternoon, with David's company, with the plethora of vegetables in piles on the counter and filling a brown paper grocery bag sitting on the floor.

"I haven't talked to Dad about this yet, Mom, because I really just decided it," David said across the oak table, "but I think I'm going to request a deferment from Harvard for next year." He glanced up at her. Dinah's face was immobile while she tried to absorb what he had said, and so his voice became explanatory, persuasive. "I mean, what's the point of going so soon? I don't have any idea what I want to do. And at Harvard you have to choose your major by the end of your freshman year, and I don't think I can know by then what I want to do."

"Oh, David. Requesting a deferment's a major decision to make. Have you really thought about it? All your friends will be gone. Well, Christie will be here, but you don't have any job. . . ."

"They already said I could stay on at the café. And I could get some reading done. Reading on my own. I think it's the right thing for me. I mean, I'm not going to Harvard for any *reason* except because they admitted me."

"Well, David, your decision is what counts, but I don't think you've thought it out entirely. You don't have any other real plans, like a year in Europe or anything. I think working at the café during the winter could get real stale real fast." Her voice was gentle, though, not at all reproachful, and David looked up and smiled at her.

"I know. I've thought of all that. I'll see what Dad thinks. I could make some money toward tuition, too." He pushed back from the table and took his glass to the sink. "I'd better get Anna Tyson home. I won't be back for dinner. I'll probably be home late."

When they had gone, Dinah stood at the sink washing the dirt off the tomatoes and zucchini and yellow squash, and putting some in a basket for Martin to give to Helen LaPlante. Dinah looked out the window and studied the garden as, row by row, it was lost in the dusk, and she forgot that David had fairly well abandoned it. She imagined the seasons ahead through which it would pass under his tutelage. He would plow it under as it died back, mulch it against the winter, gaze out at it from his bedroom window upstairs in January and February when it would be protected under a blanket of snow. She imagined the life he would be leading, books they would discuss, dinners she would fix when Christie came over and when Sam and Ethan were home for holidays. And then in the spring, he would till the plot, start the seedlings, and ready the garden once again for the growing season.

In her contentment she let herself drift cautiously into thoughts of Martin and Netta. She wondered if the odd flash-ins she had experienced—the image of Martin and

Netta together in the car, for instance—had been some sort of subliminal early-warning system. But she thought not. Her every instinct was baffled by Ellen's information, because now that she considered the possibility from every possible angle, she was certain that Martin was not involved in any sort of real intimacy with Netta. Dinah loved Martin, and she knew she could never, ever be attracted to a man who was sexually—or even emotionally—interested in a woman as wretchedly and earnestly literal as Netta Breckenridge.

CHAPTER ELEVEN

LOSING WEIGHT

IN THE COURSE OF their marriage, Dinah and Martin Howells had slowly evolved an unspoken code of behavior that was peculiar only to themselves. Over the years the landscape of their domestic life had been delineated in greater and more intricate detail; it had become its own country with its requisite legends and myths, heroes and villains, victors and victims, customs and religion. Toby, of course, during his lifetime, and Sarah and David had absorbed and become part of the family lore, its mystique, and all its etiquette, even in its quirkiness. They adhered to it without a thought, although not one of the four of them realized they shared fairly rigid ideas of the right and the wrong way to live one's life.

When David, for instance, was called into the principal's office several weeks before his graduation from West Bradford High School and told that he would possibly be the recipient of three prizes during the ceremony, but that he and Ted McWayne, who had not distinguished himself otherwise, had come within one vote of each other by an outside panel in a competition for the Harold J. DeLong Book Prize, David had, without a moment's hesitation, suggested it go to the other boy. That night at dinner he told Dinah and Martin and Sarah about the fact that he had won, but the notion of spreading this news beyond the family never once crossed any of their minds. They all operated more or less on a principle of *oblige* without the *noblesse*.

Martin's father, who had been a captain in the army in World War II, had steadfastly refused to accept the Veterans' Housing Benefit, even when the family was hard-pressed, because he had never left Staten Island, had never been engaged in real warfare. It made no difference to him that, had he ever mentioned this subtlety of patriotism to friends or colleagues of his in Sheridan, Mississippi, they would not have admired him for it, would probably have thought him a fool.

Dinah's parents had honed through the years an equally individualized integrity. When she arrived home from her first year at Ohio State with her sorority letters on the rear windshield of her Volkswagen, both parents expressed disapproval, even disdain. And her father had been beside himself when the festivities of her brother's wedding to the daughter of good friends had been covered lavishly by the local press. "By God, the two of them have their pictures all over the newspapers! It's all a bunch of who-shot-John!"

Dinah's brother Buddy had said to her in the aftermath of one of these outbursts, "What do you think? One of the Briggses was once on a 'Wanted' poster, or something?" She had laughed, but they had both understood that their father abhorred any sort of public display of one's private life.

Over time, Dinah and Martin unconsciously combined their separate legacies and established the mores of their own marriage, and now each of them was amused or dismayed at those customs and prejudices of his or her own parents that Dinah and Martin had discarded.

So, although the Howellses were indifferent about having their pictures in the paper, it would never have occurred to Martin, for example, to wear or carry his Phi Beta Kappa key, and he would have been hard-pressed to admire anyone who did. Neither he nor Dinah would have considered displaying any degrees or honors or personal photographs from their own academic careers, graduations, or wedding on the walls of any of the public rooms of their house, although snapshots of the children in small frames placed on end tables or on a bookcase were perfectly all right.

They both took a dim view of vanity license plates. Whenever Dinah was parking at the grocery or on Carriage Street, and caught sight of an acquaintance's sporty Mercedes convertible with the license plate "ALL MYN," she was offended. And the only decals that would ever grace any windshield of the Howellses' cars were the ones that allowed them to get rid of recyclable waste in the West Bradford landfill and certified that they were entitled to use the town park.

It was fine—when it was necessary—to buy a comfortable, safe car, but, even had they been able to afford one, they would have thought it tasteless to own an expensive car designed purely for pleasure. These facets of deportment and taste were symptomatic of a wider-ranging attitude: comfort was desirable, but excess or ostentation was very nearly immoral and just plain tacky. If other people were immoderate, however, no criticism was ever to be made of them; and above all, one honored one's word, one's promises, and adhered, in spite of any difficulty, to a tradition of honesty tempered by compassion.

Therefore, when David began to think that he would be staying on in West Bradford through the following school year, he could no longer avoid considering his long-standing relationship with Christie Douglas and how inexcusably unkind he had been to her over the last part of the summer. He had managed to rationalize his behavior thus far by persuading himself that he would be leaving her anyway, that he would be meeting people from all over the country—all over the world. Now he had to come to terms with the fact that he had been avoiding explaining this to her; he had been cowardly in putting off a possible confrontation.

David arrived at Christie's house ashamed of himself and quite miserable, but determined to apologize, to try not to hurt her feelings any more than he probably already had. He hadn't phoned ahead, but when he pulled into the drive, he could see Christie and Meg Cramer lying on towels beside the pool in Christie's backyard.

Since neither of her parents' cars was in the driveway, he made his way through the gate and around the side of the house, approaching the girls from across the pool. Christie glanced up at him and then lay her face back down on her arms, but Meg drew herself up into a sitting position and began gathering things into her backpack: suntan lotion, a hairbrush, an extra towel. She greeted David with a quick, polite smile, but was on her feet before David had come all the way around the pool. "I've got to get home," she said. "I have to be at work at five."

Christie didn't move or respond, and David was nervous. He sat down on the end of a chaise longue next to Christie's towel, but he still hadn't said anything by the time Meg's car pulled out of the driveway, and neither had Christie.

When he finally did speak, his voice was too loud in the echoing acoustics of the terrace and pool. "I hope it's okay that I came by," he said. The immediacy of his own voice almost made him jump. Christie didn't reply; her face was turned away from him, her eyes closed. "I mean,

I know I haven't called. I know I've been a real shit. I feel awful about what's happened." He still hadn't got his voice modulated, and his words rose hollowly or fell to a mumble.

"I care about you a lot, Christie. We were together for a long time. But I guess it just isn't going to work out. . . ." She had opened her eyes and turned her head on her folded arms, and was regarding him with what seemed to him like curiosity. "I know it's my fault. I didn't realize," he went on, "that maybe I'm too much older than you." She had slowly raised her head and was lying on her side with her elbow bent and her head propped on her hand.

"Do you think that's it?" she asked, not at all angrily, but with interest, and David began to feel relieved. He bent toward her, his forearms resting across his knees.

"Oh, yeah, Christie," he said, with a kind of muted enthusiasm. "I can see that I might have put too much pressure on you, especially this year." He was soft-voiced. This was the first year they had had sex together; he thought it was more tactful not to be blatant about it. "We probably shouldn't have stayed together for so long. . . . It wasn't fair. . . ."

"Really?" Christie asked, with soft curiosity. "I don't know," she said, considering it. "I really liked fucking. I thought that was great." Her voice was uninflected as if she were only stating a fact, and her tone made David unexpectedly defensive and angry.

"Fucking. God! Give me a break, Christie. *I* never would have said that. And what do you mean, anyway? You were always totally freaked out for days! You were always afraid you'd be pregnant even though . . ." He had raised his voice, and Christie cast a disdainful look over him, interrupting him.

"I liked having sex with you, I said. I didn't want to have a *baby* with you." She didn't raise her voice, but she sat up slowly and looking at him appraisingly. "And, you know,

I don't feel great about what's happened either." Her tone was almost dismissive. "I don't think *two years* is really all that much difference in age. But mostly I just feel so embarrassed for you."

David stood up, and Christie got up, too, shaking out her towel and folding it with calm deliberation. David had meant to be repentant; he hadn't intended to be furious. "What the fuck are you talking about?"

"Oh, it's just that it's really terrible to see you ... I mean, I've cared about you for a long time. . . ." and for a moment Christie seemed about to lose her poise. She paused and bent to pick up her sunglasses, and then straightened and gazed kindly at David and continued what she was saying. "I can't help it. I feel *humiliated* for you that everyone knows about you and Netta Breckenridge. Now *that's* a pretty big difference in age. I mean, what is she? Thirty? God, David, she has a little girl!"

David was enraged, and at the same time he knew he had no right to be. He hadn't even known that Christie knew anything about him and Netta. He had no idea that Christie had driven through Netta's parking lot night after night, and gone home and wept after seeing his car there. David didn't even understand that he was suddenly humiliated for himself, but all at once Christie understood it as she watched his expression become beleaguered. She crossed the carefully matched blue slate of the terrace, and put her arms around David's waist and pressed her face against his chest, and he automatically put his hands on her shoulders.

She had hoped for and rehearsed her part in this confrontation for weeks, but now she gave up her guise of aloofness. "I mean more to you than you think," she said. Her voice lost any pretense of neutrality as David stood there gently grasping her shoulders. He was so young that he didn't even understand that in this conversation Christie had nothing to lose.

"You *are* going to miss me," she said. "It's going to be harder on you than you have any idea, and you're wasting all the time we have left this summer because you think Netta Breckenridge is really interested in you. That makes you feel great, doesn't it? Shit, you feel so *mature!*"

She was crying, but he just stood there, waiting to leave. He felt terrible, almost sick, and angry and horrified, but he didn't move. He was paralyzed by his inability to control the consequences of his actions that were let loose over the rippling water of the long, blue pool.

"David. Oh, David. Don't you even know that Owen Croft spends almost every night there? Don't you know he's practically living with Netta Breckenridge? Everybody knows that. So why are you interested in her? She's not even pretty. She's not even *nice!*"

David stood frozen in place for a moment. Then he put Christie aside, moving her away from him in the same way he would move a piece of furniture, and turned and left through the gate in the backyard.

If there were not many people around, Martin generally paused to let Duchess off her leash near the two mysterious and modest gravestones just beyond the parking lot of the Freund Museum before taking his usual route up Bell's Hill. Duchess would dash frantically after the squirrels who leaped ahead of her from tree to tree, and Martin could take the steep grade unencumbered until Duchess, realizing he had gone ahead, came after him at a desperate gallop. He waited for her now, though, and stood in the late August afternoon, regarding the small grave markers while Duchess made ecstatic forays into the underbrush, rustling and barking enthusiastically when she flushed a squirrel into the high treetops where it sat scolding her.

The inscriptions had nearly been worn away by tourists who made rubbings even though there was nothing unusual about the markers themselves, except their unexplained location. Martin had asked about them once at the museum, and had been directed to the public library, but he hadn't pursued it, so perhaps even their location and the discrepancy in the dates of their deaths were perfectly reasonable.

Lydia
dau. of
S. A. and N. A.
Williams
died June 22, 1878
aged
2 years and 6 months

Henry
son of
Garland and Emma Meeck
died July 2, 1815
aged 2 yr. 4 mo.
In life beloved
Though dead remembered

As always, he regarded the little graves with a degree of awe and a great deal of respect, but he was so familiar with them that they no longer filled him with melancholy. Had these children lived out their full life spans, they would not be alive today, so the white rounded stone of the child Lydia and the age-softened rectangular marker of the boy Henry were solemn monuments to lives long past. Their existence predated Martin's memory; and when Duchess caught up with him, he began the gradual climb up the rise of the hill and put the two children out of his mind.

Martin prided himself on his own good nature, unaware that he sometimes used his amiability as a way to keep casual friends at arm's length. He preferred to approach those loose-knit friendships at an angle to spare himself the discomfort of facing any conflict of taste or opinion with someone who was less than dear to him. But he had been forced into an uncomfortable state of intimacy with Netta, and he had no idea how to discourage it. He had been uneasy about her ever since the evening they had spent polishing the last bit of her article before *The Review* went to press. He was especially distressed, since he knew from Vic that David was involved with Netta one way or another.

As he descended Bell's Hill, he tried to put the incident out of his mind, but he was filled with distaste nonetheless. When Vic had told him that David was spending a lot of time with Netta, Martin had chosen not to consider the implications too closely. Martin himself had seen David and Anna Tyson coming out of Berkshire Video with a cassette, walking together down a little alley off Carriage Street. David had been bending slightly over the little girl, holding her hand, looking out for her, and in retrospect their alliance seemed alarming. It made Martin think that David could be involved in a dangerous encompassment. Netta's peculiar notions of benevolence—her methods of extending charity—might be perilous to David.

Duchess dragged Martin along once he had snapped her back on her leash, and when he let her loose at the corner of the yard, she headed straight for the garden in a delighted rush. He trotted after her, calling her back, hoping to stop her before she got into the flowers or crushed the strawberries, but she came to a stop on the grass at the bottom of the yard, wagging her tail tentatively. By the time Martin reached her, he saw that David was in the garden, although his back was to Martin. He was standing upright and still. Martin stepped over the border of marigolds before he realized that David must have heard him, but hadn't turned to greet him. Martin stood still, too, straddling the row of flowers.

"Hey, David," he said. "Can I talk to you a minute?"

David didn't answer and didn't turn around. "Sure," he said finally, still not facing his father but stooping down to the strawberries, ruffling his hand among their leaves to search out the berries.

"I just want to talk with you about Netta Brecken-ridge." Martin's voice was light in an attempt not to sound advisory. In an attempt not to be interfering in David's life. "She's a complicated sort of personality," he said genially, as though he were settling in for a discussion, perhaps, of her endearing idiosyncracies. "I mean, you may not know . . ."

David was crouched among the strawberries; but his hands were clenched on his knees, and Martin fell silent as David stood up slowly and turned around. Martin had never seen David look as bleak or as stricken as he did just then. His lower lip was tucked in at the corners and his eyebrows were raised in an expression of anguished surprise, as though he had had the breath knocked out of him. "I don't want to talk about it," he said, and it was clear at once that David already knew more than Martin could ever have told him. And it was surprising to Martin that he had forgotten that David could feel such anguish. He had grown used to accepting his son's contentment at face value; it had not occurred to Martin in years that David might need championing.

"I'm sorry, David." Martin looked away and extricated himself carefully from the bed of marigolds. "Okay, then." Martin paused on the grass at the verge of the garden, but David didn't look at him. "I'm going in to get a quick shower. Your mother's home . . ." and he turned away and climbed the stepping-stones up the steep yard. As he neared the back door, he decided that he didn't want to sort all this business out right now, he didn't want to explain it to Dinah, and he veered off around the side of the house and angled across the front lawn. When Duchess came scuffling after him, he looked down and realized that he was still holding her leash in his hand. He stopped just long enough to snap it onto her collar.

All day long Dinah had been feeling relaxed and at ease. She had been afloat in the image of David's continued presence in the town of West Bradford, buoyed by the idea of her family continuing on the way it always had, without the disruptive prospect of any more departures. In fact, she had been thinking how pleasant it would be when the four of them, in the fall, drove out to the orchard where they bought cider and apples and home-baked pies—David liked the Macouns, and Sarah preferred Northern Spies, so they made up a bushel of half of each. Dinah forgot that for the past two years only Sarah had gone with them, and they had simply brought apples back for David. She was also looking forward to fall because the humidity this August afternoon was oppressive, and she anticipated with pleasure the crisp days of late September and October. She had come upstairs to brush her hair and pin it up to get it off the back of her neck. When she looked away from the mirror, she caught sight through the window of David and Martin chatting in the garden. When Martin turned and left, Dinah sat back in her chair and continued watching her son in his garden.

The other day Ellen had brought by a new book translated from the Chinese that she wanted Dinah to read. One of the greatest pleasures of their friendship was sharing books, but Dinah had been so distracted these past few days that she had only picked it up one evening and begun to thumb through it from back to front, the way she usually read magazines. She had been struck by an italicized poem or song that had caught her eye on the last page:

A woman is the most lovable thing on earth,
But there is something that is more important.
Women will never possess the men they have created.

It had infuriated her when she had read it, although she had no idea in what context it existed. But as she watched David tending the strawberries, she realized that the poem—intentionally or not—was sad, a piteous lament, in fact, in its seeming bravado. It struck her just then how humiliating it might be to be male, forever indebted to a female because of the simple event of his own birth. How terrible it must feel to be powerless against that inescapable burden of gratitude which one could never incur oneself—a primal offense to one's dignity. She was appalled at the idea of her own son humbled in such a way.

The thought only flashed through her mind—one of those slippery ideas that she might examine more carefully someday. It did, however, disturb her mood of optimism, and she watched David carefully as he made his way along the row of strawberries, legs spraddled in his old jeans, and swinging laboriously from the waist to gather the fruit in an odd, disconsolate rhythm.

The humidity was so high that the condensation on the glass through which she watched him was like a sheen of sorrow over her idea of him in relation to his garden. She thought of the solitary quality of his toil there, the melancholy determination that wouldn't so much ground him in reality, as she had hypothesized, but would quite possibly quench him. She knew just then that it was time for him to leave.

She realized simultaneously that eventually his absence would seem a natural condition of the world to her. She could even anticipate that eventually his homecomings, although always longed for, might be disruptive, even intrusive in her life. He would return as a visitor, as company. What she couldn't imagine, looking out of the blurred, moisture-beaded window, was the way in which she and Martin would lead their lives after the departure of their children.

Franklin M. Mount
Dean of Freshmen
Harvard College
12 Truscott Street
Cambridge, Massachusetts 02138

Dear Mr. Mount,

My father had an interesting solution to what he perceived as the problem of deciding whom he did and did not love. If he felt sure that—in the path of an oncoming bus—he would leap to his death in order to heave some other person out of its way to his or her safety, well, then, that was a person he loved. Over the years the number of people for whom he would be willing to make this last sacrifice shrank rather alarmingly, and oddly enough, he kept me posted about this.

Struck off the list, eventually, were his mother and father, his siblings, and, I suspect, though he may have been too tactful to say so, he was willing to abandon my mother to her own devices in oncoming traffic. But my brother and I—there was never any question. We made his short list. And do you know that it never once occurred to me to wonder if I would risk my own life to put my father out of harm's way? And, of course, I wouldn't have. Not for a minute. And it would have been an unnatural instinct if I had felt otherwise.

I've been thinking about you and how you must feel about your daughter. I'm going to tell you something, Frank, that you won't believe until it's too late for you, but none of all this new earnestness in child care makes any difference at all. As long as you don't bear your daughter actual malice, she'll be just fine. Don't worry about whether she was breast- or bottle-fed! Put her in day care or don't put her in day care! Let her watch television all day, or read educational books to her and refuse to have a TV set in your house. Give her nothing but organically grown food, or let her exist on peanut butter and marshmallow fluff.

Not that I think you should *abandon* good habits. Of course not. But my point is that since you are always going to be willing to push her out of the way of that bus, all this other effort you're expending won't be met or remembered with any gratitude. I know that's not the point—I know that's not why you're making the choices you're making, but unless you're a saint you're going to resent it when you'll only be to her—trivial! No—you'll be one of those extraneous people your own parents are to you.

Oh, Frank, it will shock you so much that when she grows up and leaves home she will resent the fact that it took effort to keep her alive. She won't care about that; all your efforts will have seemed to her only reasonable. And the hardest thing about it all is that you'll know she's absolutely right. If she's fond of you, then you've been a good parent. But if you're too much on her mind, if she's indebted, if she's bound to you, then you will have failed. My husband and I have been as good parents as we knew how, but I'm finding that for the time being it's a bitter victory.

Slade Road wound flat through sweeping acreage that had once been farmed by the original Slades, the builders of the Howellses' house in the late 1700s or the early 1800s. Eventually the Slades had given up farming and established a grocery store on Carriage Street where they had brought their vegetables to sell. Two large estates had been built on the farmland in the 1880s by prosperous owners of the woolen mills that had sprung up in nearby Bradford. The main houses loomed large across the road from one another, and the estate that had been built on the land adjacent to the old Slade farmhouse had become a sort of neighborhood all its own, with the clever renovation and habitation over the years of the carriage house, the two barns, the stables, and several other outbuildings.

Slade Road had been paved long ago and sidewalks laid out along the verges, but it retained the unpopulated feeling of a country lane. The chestnut trees that had once canopied the length of the road had all died off, but there were still, here and there, a few towering, ancient spruce and hemlock from the forests that had flourished long before any of the land had been cleared and settled. There were also huge walnut trees, oaks, maples, grand embattled elms, and other relatively short-lived trees like birch and soft maple. And there were still stretches of virgin forest, a swath of which ran along the section of Slade Road that dwindled off into a gravel track not far beyond Martin's house. These lush stands of deep woods were unheralded because of the fear that once they were widely known they would inevitably be widely abused.

As Martin made his way in the damp, gentle air up the hill that led to the town green and toward the campus, he could not understand how it was that he had not even been able to ensure David's happiness in a place such as this. There was undoubtedly the same proportion of villains and fools in West Bradford as there was anywhere else, but, nevertheless, the image of David's face turned to him in pale, outraged misery struck him as an unreasonable occurrence in the benevolent air, the placid landscape.

Arlie Davidson approached from the other direction with his corgi, who was immediately alert with interest in Duchess. The two men stopped and spoke about the warm weather while their dogs inspected each other peaceably, and then they parted company, continuing on their separate ways. Martin crossed Route 7 and skirted the green, planted lushly with flowers, and waited for traffic to ebb so he could cross again at the intersection of Route 7 and Route 2. It was a dangerous intersection that needed a traffic light, but many of the townspeople believed that any traffic light in their small town would spoil the idea of village life. The obtuseness of this notion always astounded and enraged Martin. He had agonized over the terrible possibilities of an accident when, at age seven or eight, his children began to ride their bikes to Carriage Street or to friends' houses, having to thread their way through this very spot where too many cars came barreling through town on the state highway, which was known as State Street for the several miles where it bisected the town.

After managing to make his way across, he entered the campus. He didn't have any particular destination in mind, and he wasn't in a hurry. He and Duchess walked downhill, avoiding afternoon joggers and passing under the beautiful elm in front of the college president's house. Martin regarded the tree critically, but it seemed to be holding its own against disease. He turned into the cordoned-off drive next to the Congregational church. The West Bradford Theater had reserved the space for parking for whatever play they were doing this evening. He and Duchess climbed the Lapham Hall steps, known as Lapham Beach by the students because, with the first hint of spring, they lounged against the columns of the Roman Revival building, wearing shorts and sandals even if it was only fifty degrees. Now that the students were gone, however, there was no one about, and Martin sat down on the top step, bracing his back against a column, and Duchess settled down beside him.

He could not disengage himself from the image of David in the garden, so filled with pain. Martin knew that he was partly responsible for that pain. It occurred to him for the first time that his resolution not to interfere in his son's life was more a convenient way to avoid unpleasantness than an act of restraint or generosity. Advising him would have been an unpleasant task; David would have resented the intrusion, but Martin could have tried to warn him. After all, he was David's father. Why hadn't he attempted to protect his own son from any vulnerability he might have had to Netta?

Some tourists parked nearby and began unpacking baskets of food and bottles of wine, and a young woman approached Lapham Hall with several collapsed webbed lounge chairs clasped awkwardly in one hand. Clearly the group was planning to picnic on the steps before the play. They were joking and calling back and forth to each other, and Martin thought they were probably recent graduates come back for a visit. He was in no mood to chat with them if they happened to recognize him. He rose, leading Duchess along behind him, and headed off toward his office.

Vic's car was in the parking lot; and for a moment Martin was undecided about meeting him, but then he thought it might be a relief to talk to Vic. It was Vic who had tried to alert him to David's interest in Netta in the first place. When Martin made his way downstairs and caught a glimpse of Owen in the anteroom, he veered off to Vic's office, ignoring Owen altogether.

Before Martin even sat down, Vic got up and closed the door. "I just tried to phone you. I stopped by for a minute to get some stuff to take home for the weekend, and Owen was here. I think he's been here all afternoon." Vic was anxious, running his hand through his hair, and Martin was puzzled. "I don't know what we should do," he said to

Martin. "Owen is really fucked up on something. Or maybe he's drunk, but I don't think so. He's been talking a mile a minute. I swear to God, Martin, I don't want to deal with this anymore!"

Vic paced the length of his office and back. "He's driving me crazy. Maybe I should call his father. I don't have any idea what he might have taken. You think I should call Larry? I'll tell you the truth, I'm not going to deal with this shit anymore, Martin! You've made all of us put up with him. Helen checks with me now before she'll even mail the letters Owen leaves for her. He's gotten away with murder all summer!"

Martin felt the hair on his arms and the back of his neck prickle. He was suddenly so filled with adrenaline that, when he turned around to open Vic's door, he felt stiff-legged, as though all his movements were slowed down. He approached Owen, whose chair was tilted back. His legs rested on his desk across a welter of jumbled manuscripts and carefully lettered, self-addressed, return envelopes, which had been enclosed with each one but were now probably hopelessly separated.

"Hey, Martin. I've been wanting to talk to you." Owen's voice was drawn out, the vowels elongated, the consonants soft and blunted. "A great story, here." He gestured toward the papers and attempted to swing his legs off the desk and sit upright, but the flex chair rolled backward a fraction. "Whoa! Whoa!" he said, reaching for the edge of the desk to catch himself. Martin was around the side of the desk and upon him in an instant, slamming the chair as far back on its spring as it would go. Owen's arms flailed desperately in an attempt to keep his balance.

Martin hovered over him, one hand clamping Owen's shoulder and the other grasping the back of his chair. "I saw what you did to Netta. Do you have any idea . . . do you know what you've done to David? You pathetic son of a bitch!" His voice rose, and he was bending over, shouting directly into Owen's face. "Netta should have left you alone. You never would have done anything to hurt *yourself*. But oh, God! Oh, God! I would be *glad* if you were dead. I would be so glad if you were dead! I could kill you!" He slammed the back of Owen's chair against the wall. "God damn you! You stupid, fucking son of a bitch. I could kill you!"

Martin's expression was a grimace of pure fury, and Owen was wild-eyed. "Hey, hey! What . . ." Martin shook him by the front of his shirt. "You're not worth shit! You're fucking well not worth shit! And Toby is *dead*! He is absolutely *dead*!" Martin's face was inches from Owen's, whose mouth had gone slack, who was by now terrified. Vic had hold of Martin's shoulders and was yelling at him to stop, but Martin was wound as tight as a knot.

"You're left, you *pathetic* little shit. Only you . . ." and Martin, gasping for breath, released his hold on Owen's shirt and clasped his arm across his own midsection, bending forward in sudden pain so that the top of his head grazed Owen's chin, and Owen remained pinned backward in the office chair, with Martin leaning on him now, a dead weight.

Vic wrenched Martin backward away from Owen, whose chair snapped forward and who remained sitting there, stunned. Martin was bent over, his face red, pulling in great drafts of air.

"Christ, Martin! Are you all right? Martin?" Vic was horrified, and Martin made an odd keening sound in the back of his throat as he at last managed to exhale. He straightened a little and put his hands out to ward Vic off, and then he was sobbing, leaning against the wall, bracing himself against the spasm of sobs that overtook him.

Vic had one hand on Martin's shoulder. He felt Martin heave forward slightly and then arch back against the wall in convulsive weeping. Vic looked away from his friend long enough to say to Owen, "Get out! Get out!" And Owen fled, his feet ringing on the metal stairs.

"Martin? Are you okay?" Martin had grown calmer, but he was still crying, and Vic watched cautiously as Martin made his way around the desk and collapsed in Owen's chair.

Martin looked up and made a sort of grimace of apology. "I'm sorry, Vic. I'm so sorry."

Vic waved his hand in dismissal. "Are you all right?"

"Oh, yeah. Oh, yeah, I'm all right. I don't want to talk about this right now. I'm sorry, Vic. I don't know what happened. I can't believe . . ."

"It doesn't matter. It doesn't matter," Vic said, "as long as you're okay." And when Martin nodded, Vic turned the light off in his own office and left him alone.

Martin sat on in Owen's chair, and Duchess recovered enough of her courage to slink in and lie down next to him on the floor. The light that filtered in through the small line of basement windows deepened into a dusky gray and then faded altogether, until only the arched desk lamp illuminated the room, but Martin was too tired to get up and go home.

He did not believe an honorable man would have behaved as he had just behaved. It pained him to have abandoned all that he deeply believed was decent to the one person in the world whom he finally understood that he despised. *Not* hating Owen had been the only action left for him to exercise on Toby's behalf. The notion of only *remembering* his second child was horrible to Martin. It would be as painful to him as looking through old photographs, which only emphasized the loss of the tangible person each time he held before him a flat, brittle approximation of the image of the boy his son had been.

Martin had never let go of the idea of a continuing association with Toby, and oddly enough it was Owen's existence in the world that had granted Martin the sweet encumbrance of that connection. He recognized that he had at last relinquished it. Martin was forty-five years old, and he felt terrifyingly disburdened. His father was dead, and his mother was failing. His oldest son was an adult, his daughter was growing increasingly aloof, and he and Dinah would soon be all that the other had left. It was too much weight to lose, all that.

He was afraid to be stripped so lean, to be attenuated, thinned, and chilled in the encroaching solitude. Martin sagged back against the chair, exhausted, as the determined tension of holding on to Toby dissipated. There was nothing left at the moment but sorrow and ashy regret.

CHAPTER TWELVE

SLADE ROAD

THE FIRST FEW DAYS in September hung over the northern Berkshires warm and humid and slightly hazy in the valleys. It was stale weather by now, wearing to the spirit. In the Howells household all the windows were wide open day and night, but the atmosphere was so still that there scarcely seemed to be an exchange of air. It was eerily tropical, with the calls of birds harsh and jarring among the quiet leaves. Even with the window fans on through the night, the interior temperature scarcely dropped by morning. The communal mood was subdued.

The heat was a little less fierce than it had been in late August, but still, almost everyone in town had given up the effort of putting together cool summer meals of pretty salads or chilled soups. Grocery shoppers crowded the supermarket deli or stood chatting at Duke's Market while waiting in line to pick up his special "broasted" chicken—which was battered, deep-fried, and then baked, and was good at room temperature. Fancies, a catering business and upscale takeout, sold over seven pounds of mousse de canard, a silky pâté, at $3.49 a quarter pound in only two days, while across the street at Minuteman Pizza business was almost at a standstill. No one wanted hot food.

The third evening in one week that Arlie Davidson, down the road from the Howellses', brought home a box of broasted chicken and containers of cole slaw and potato salad, he put the cardboard boxes directly down on the dining room table. His wife, Miriam, began to take serving platters out of the cupboard, but Arlie discouraged her. "Don't bother," he said. "It won't taste any different on a china plate." She hesitated, but then she agreed and sat down across from him, taking up a drumstick and nibbling at it listlessly. Similarly, Dinah brought home Chinese takeout and put the wire-handled paper cartons on the kitchen counter. Sarah and David and Martin drifted in and out of the kitchen, serving themselves room-temperature sesame noodles, or beef with broccoli, and taking it out to the table on the porch or to his or her own room. Martin rolled a pancake of mushu pork and bent over the sink to eat it in order to save himself the effort of any cleanup.

It was not hot enough to cause tempers to flare or to precipitate passionate arguments within families or among the boys who lounged in front of Minuteman Pizza in the evenings. The pervasive atmosphere that enclosed the town merely bred a sort of frazzled indifference.

At last, a cold front that had stalled over the Great Lakes edged its way slowly eastward, bringing unusually heavy rain and thunderstorms to the Berkshires for almost three days. The skies began to clear on the evening of the third day; and by the time the sun set, it illuminated the scudding, gray-bottomed clouds that were moving toward the coast. The day before David was to leave for college, the weather turned to autumn, with a high of sixty degrees and an expected low in the forties.

Martin had reluctantly folded down the back seat of the Volvo station wagon to allow as much space as possible to pack everything David needed for school, but leaving room enough for only the driver and one passenger. "We had all planned to drive you to Cambridge tomorrow, David. I guess I'll take you in so I can help you unload. Are you sure you need all this stuff?"

"Mom made out the list." David held up a sheet of notepaper, and Dinah glanced across the top of the car and recognized her careful list from five months back. But she knew she hadn't suggested that David take his skis. She thought about the fact that there wouldn't be any room for her to go with them, to see David's room, to get a picture of where he would be living, to tell him good-bye. She was queasy with apprehension. She wouldn't get a chance to see him until Parents' Weekend in early October. She went back into the house, where a mound of David's possessions sat right inside the front door waiting to be taken to the car; and she carried a gooseneck lamp and a long cardboard tube containing posters, she guessed, out to the driveway and set them down on the gravel.

Martin was wrestling with the skis, trying to fit them in over the footlocker, while David reached into the car to adjust them himself.

"David, you can't put them in at that angle. If I have to stop suddenly, they'll take my head off. You're much more likely to come home to ski." When David didn't respond, Martin continued to try to find a way to wedge the skis in.

"Maybe I can borrow Sam's ski rack. We ought to have one, anyway," David said. Martin scowled at him, and David didn't make any more suggestions, although he assumed an expression of pained tolerance, which Martin was too busy to notice.

Dinah was standing by just looking on, with her arms wrapped around herself, and when she realized there was nothing more for her to do that would be helpful, she decided to leave them alone. "It's too chilly out here for me. I'm going inside unless you need me."

Martin emerged from the rear of the station wagon and stood running his eye over the items on the lawn that were yet to be packed. He didn't seem to have heard her.

"What is this with the damned stereo?" he asked her. "My God, his room would have to be the size of an auditorium to do the thing justice." David had gone back to the house and was emerging with a large box that housed one of his stereo speakers in its Styrofoam womb. He had saved the original packaging. Dinah simply shrugged, but Martin was aggrieved. "You know, his roommate will probably bring his own stereo, too. It's the new macho thing, I guess. The same way we were about our cars. A *sound* system. Christ."

"Well, at least no one can get pregnant in the back seat of it," Dinah said, turning and making for the house, but by that time Martin had already directed his attention to some other item that needed to be fit into the back of the car.

Dinah went inside and made reservations to have dinner that evening at their favorite restaurant. She wanted to be sure to disperse the heightened climate of exasperation that David and Martin's packing had generated. And besides, as she watched the car slowly fill up with David's belongings, she had decided that it was important to attempt a modest celebration to mark the beginning of his college career.

When she announced that she had made reservations for seven o'clock that evening, however, David's face registered slight irritation, and Martin said that they were both tired, but Dinah was adamant.

"I need to see Christie tonight, Mom," David said. "It's my last night at home."

"I'd love to have Christie come, sweetie. Vic and Ellen are going to meet us there, too. And, you know, we'd like to see a little of you your last night at home," she said lightly. "And we never did really celebrate Sarah's birthday, anyway. This is an occasion. It needs to be observed. But we won't be that long over dinner. You and Christie will have the rest of the evening. I know you'll want to see some of your other friends, too." She looked directly at him with an expression of huge good humor that brooked no disagreement.

The Candlelight Inn was the first civilized restaurant to which they had ever taken David and Toby. At the time, Dinah had been heavily pregnant with Sarah. Vic and Ellen had invited the four of them to meet there to celebrate Ellen's birthday, and Dinah had insisted the boys wear blazers and slacks, which she had still been hemming fifteen minutes before they left the house. On the drive over to Lenox, Martin and Dinah had instructed the two little boys in a tone of deadly seriousness about *not* behaving as though they were at McDonald's.

"Absolutely no diving under the table if you drop your napkin," Martin said. "Or for any other reason," he added, remembering how David and Toby could become giddy and silly at the Formica tables of McDonald's while they waited for their parents to finish a quick cup of coffee. The boys' voices would become loud and excited, they would kneel at their places or slide under the table to change seats, and Dinah and Martin would pretend to be surprised to find a different child sitting beside them on the vinyl banquettes.

Dinah had remembered to explain on the drive over to the inn that if either one of them dropped a knife or a fork, they were to let it lie. At home Toby so often forgot to keep his hands still, accidentally sweeping things off the table, and being lectured for it, that, once seated inside the restaurant, he had nervously clasped his hands together in his lap.

They had been in the East Room at a table in front of the fireplace. Toby and David were stiff and overdressed in their blazers, and were amazingly subdued as they drank Cokes and listened to the four adults discuss the menu over their drinks. David had opened his own menu and studied it solemnly, and when their waiter had come and taken Ellen's and Dinah's orders and then had turned to David, he had looked up at the man and inquired, "How is the lamb tonight?" And without a blink of his eye, the waiter had replied, "It's very good, sir."

Dinah's and Martin's eyes had met in amazement in one of those moments of revelation when one must acknowledge the individuality—the utter separateness—of one's children from oneself. And because of the absolute lack of hesitation on the part of that waiter, The Candlelight Inn had been Dinah's favorite restaurant in the world ever since. But she loved it anyway, as did the whole family. The food was excellent and unpretentious, the service was discreet, the rooms were charming, and the Howellses had fallen into the habit of celebrating the significant events of their lives there.

This evening, though, when Dinah looked down the table, she realized that eating dinner in public affected people as if they were performing onstage, and she thought that in this case it was all to the good. Vic and Ellen hadn't yet arrived, and conversation flagged. Sarah launched into a long tale illustrating the unfairness of her field hockey coach, and Christie helped her out, chiming in with remembered incidents from her past. If there had not been waiters coming and going, however, and diners at other tables who glanced their way occasionally, the five of them would have sat silent in an atmosphere permeated with the tension of David's imminent departure.

Dinah opened her menu, and said down the table to Martin that they might as well go on and order a first course. David and Christie studied a menu between the two of them. Christie thought she might only want to split a first course of the house smoked salmon. "They have the best desserts here," she explained, "but I always eat too much of everything else to have any."

But before the waiter approached the table, Ellen swept in on a wave of dramatic euphoria, with Vic just behind her. Dinah could see Ellen's mood wash over everyone who glanced her way as she unwrapped a scarf from her luxurious hair, swept off her cape and gave it to the young woman who greeted them, and shook out her hair, ruffling it with her fingers to bring back its volume. Sometimes Dinah was put off by Ellen's theatricality, but this evening she rejoiced as her friend blithely wove her way among the tables, already initiating conversation, her voice swooping over the tables around them.

"We saw you, David. We weren't that far behind you. I don't know how you got here so much ahead of us. We saw you turn off on Route Forty-three and then you simply disappeared!" She was seating herself with much fussing about, slinging the strap of her purse over the back of her chair but removing it when it swung to and fro, nudging her hip. The hostess materialized at her side, and Ellen beamed at her with approval. "Oh, yes, yes. Please put this with my cape! That will be wonderful. Just wonderful." And then she looked back to David. "You ought to lighten your foot on the accelerator, my dear."

Dinah and Martin and Sarah had arrived together in Martin's car, since there was only room for two in the fully packed Volvo. David had picked up Christie and driven over on his own. Now David relaxed in his chair for the first time that evening, grinning at Ellen, crossing his arms, and rocking gently against the chair back. He and Ellen had been good friends all his life. "Oh, yeah. I really have to watch it. A car like that Volvo wagon. I wouldn't want it to get away from me. Four cylinders of Swedish lightning!" They all laughed, and Dinah was glad to see that the meal would be a comfortable affair after all. David went on to explain. "There's a shortcut through Richmond. It saves about twenty minutes. That's how we always go to Tanglewood."

"It's a terrible road, though, David," Vic said, and the conversation became easy while they all began to look at their menus and a waiter brought drinks to Vic and Ellen.

Sarah leaned around Christie to speak to David. "Do you remember when we tried to convince Mom that the next time we buy a car it should be something besides another Volvo?" She glanced around the rest of the table, signaling amusement, but David shook his head that he didn't remember.

"Oh, David. You do. Don't you remember? Mom was saying how safe they were, that we didn't need to be able to go any faster. That the 'point of having a car at all is just to be able to get from one place to another.'" Sarah made her tone didactic.

David smiled. "Oh, yeah. We were at the mall?"

Sarah laughed and nodded, and Dinah smiled, too, knowing now where they were headed. "Yeah. At Crossgates." She paused, to ensure the attention of these closest of her family's friends. "And my mom pulled up at a stoplight and looked over at this car next to us and she said, 'Now, I can see that a car like that might be handy just for doing errands around town.' And David and I looked over at it, and it was this incredible white Porsche!"

Dinah shrugged and joined the general laughter, raising her hands in a gesture of resignation, of culpability, shaking her head in a show of wry wonder at her own naïveté. She was glad to have Sarah and David reminiscing; she was pleased to be in good company. She could hear the fondness in her children's voices, the affection in which they held her. But it was also as if the lovely, sharp, first chill of fall had crept into her own spirit, because she came up hard against the fact that she no longer had any power to protect the children from anything at all. She couldn't, in fact, be sure they traveled only in safe cars—a phobia with her since Toby's death. She could no longer be sure that they wore their seat belts, put on life jackets if they went sailing. She was virtually powerless; she could not keep them from harm. And all her efforts at having done so— "Be home before dark! Don't talk on the phone during a thunderstorm! Those plastic bags from the cleaners are *not* toys!"—would be relegated to the nostalgia of their youth. She and Martin had become anecdotes in the lives of their own children.

Martin slept soundly, as usual, but Dinah heard David come in about two o'clock in the morning and move around the house, opening the refrigerator door, running water. She stayed where she was, turning from one side to another in an attempt to get comfortable. She was too hot under the down comforter and too cold without it, and she would have liked to go downstairs and read, but she knew she should give David the solitary run of the nighttime rooms. When she did wake up early in the morning, she had thrown the comforter off and was cold. She was surprised to see that Martin wasn't asleep beside her. His side of the bed was empty.

In the kitchen she discovered she was the last one to come downstairs, even though it was only six-thirty. Martin had made coffee, and Sarah was having a glass of orange juice at the table. Dinah had planned on preparing a grand meal to see David off. She had bought beautiful cured bacon from a little store in Vermont that smoked its own meat, and blueberries at The Whole Grain Elevator for pancakes, but everyone had eaten.

Martin and David were huddled over an enormous schefflera in a terra-cotta pot that Christie had given David for his dorm room.

"There's no way in the world we can fit that thing into the car, David. We'll bring it on Parents' Weekend."

"I know I can fit it in. Scheffleras are probably the best plants to clean toxic substances out of the air. They work almost like a scrubber."

"Well, you'll have to hold your breath until October, then. There's not one inch of space left in that car."

"Dad, don't worry about it. I'll get it in," David said stonily, and went out the back door and around to the driveway, where the car was parked, to survey the possibilities.

Dinah moved around the kitchen helplessly, collecting cereal bowls, putting things back in cabinets. "Doesn't anyone want some bacon and pancakes? I have beautiful huge blueberries that I bought yesterday."

Martin finished his coffee and poured another cup. He was already dressed in khakis and an old plaid shirt, while Dinah had only taken the time to search for and slip on her pink flannel winter robe. "I'd like to get going as soon as we can," Martin said. "If it takes us about three and a half hours, we'll probably be earlier than most, and it won't be so hard to unload all this stuff. I don't imagine I'll get home before about four o'clock."

"Don't you think we all ought to sit down and go over this list one more time to be sure he's got everything?" Dinah asked. This was flying past her, this moment before David would be gone.

"God, no, Dinah. If he's forgotten anything he'll have to buy it in Cambridge. Or we can mail it to him, if it's that important."

Dinah was scanning the list when David came back into the room. "I can fit it in, Dad. There's no problem."

Martin was uneasy this morning, too, with a kind of

regret and tension that he hadn't expected to feel. He wanted to get this over with. "Okay, then? Are you ready to hit the road?"

"What did you do about the standing lamp, David?" Dinah asked. "Did you get it packed?" And David nodded in her direction, but he avoided holding her glance.

"Yeah," he said to his father, "I'm all set."

Martin rinsed his coffee cup and headed out the door, and David and Sarah followed him, while Dinah still stood in the center of the kitchen, running her eye down the carefully printed and now smudged list, each item having been crossed out, she presumed, as it had been put in the car. She looked around at the empty room in bewilderment, and her eyes filled with tears that she could not stop. She wiped them away quickly with her sleeve before she trailed after the rest of her family.

Martin was sitting in the driver's seat with the door open, unsuccessfully trying to slide the seat back against the immovable mass of David's possessions. "I'll have to sit closer in than I like until we unload," he said to David, who was leaning against the open door while Sarah stood by, holding the schefflera.

David straightened away from the driver's side and made his way around the car. Then he stopped and turned to his mother, who was standing in backless summer slippers on the cold, damp grass along the drive, fiddling with the sash of her robe. He stopped just there in front of her, and when she met his eyes she saw that he, too, was near tears. She simply moved toward him, and he embraced her fiercely, raising her up on tiptoe, wrapping his arms up around her shoulders, and putting his face down against the top of her head.

"Oh, sweetie," she said, overcoming the break in her voice, "oh, sweetie! I hope everything is just perfect. I hope you have a wonderful time and . . . I hope . . . well, I'm so excited for you! Harvard's lucky to get you."

David held on to her tightly. "I love you, Mom," he said, almost brusquely, and then turned and climbed into the passenger seat of the car. She followed him into the drive and stood beside the car while Sarah gave him the schefflera to balance in his lap. Dinah bent down into the car and kissed him on the cheek. "I love you, too, sweetie. We'll miss you." She backed away a bit so David could close the door. Then she bent forward again to say to Martin to be careful, and the car began to back slowly into the U of the driveway to turn around. Martin put the gear in neutral while he twisted to shift several items to one side so that he could see clearly from the rearview mirror, and then the car began to move slowly toward the end of the drive.

"Wait, Martin," Dinah called. "Wait a minute!" She waved the list at him frantically, and the car stopped and then slid back toward her in reverse. She was standing on the passenger's side, and David rolled down the window, looking more businesslike now, more harried.

"David, look at this," Dinah said, holding up the list to him and indicating an item that hadn't been crossed out. "You didn't get this in! You forgot to pack a trash can for your room."

"I don't need a trash can. I can get one there."

Dinah felt almost frantic at this omission, and David saw it on her face.

"All right, Mom. I'll get the one from my room." He was not a bit rude, not even impatient, but all the sentiment of a moment ago was gone. He handed the schefflera to Sarah and dashed for the house, appearing again in moments with the blue metal wastebasket in his hand. He opened the rear station wagon door and squeezed it in and then, with Sarah's help, he quickly resettled himself and the schefflera in the front seat.

"Have a safe trip," Dinah said as the car moved slowly down the drive again, and David waved his hand up over the roof at her and Sarah as the car passed by them.

Dinah watched as the car paused before turning onto Slade Road. The last thing she noticed before it disappeared from view was David's trash can, wedged against the tip of his skis and the rear window, mouth outward, still full to the brim with trash.

473 Slade Road
West Bradford, MA
September 7, 1991

Franklin M. Mount
Dean of Freshmen
Harvard College
12 Truscott Street
Cambridge, Massachusetts 02138

Dear Mr. Mount,

We appreciate the effort Harvard College makes to know its students, and we welcome the opportunity to offer you our own insights and reflections concerning our son David, who will enter the freshman class this September. It seems to us that David will have very little trouble becoming acclimated to his new academic environment, and we don't expect he will have a great deal of difficulty establishing a comfortable social life for himself in fairly short order. He has always been a good student, a person of integrity, and he has dealt successfully with the tragedy of the loss of his younger brother when the two of them were twelve and thirteen years old. We think, quite frankly, that he would be happy in any challenging situation and that Harvard is lucky to have him.

David has no medical problems that require

special attention and has never suffered an allergic reaction to any medication. We think he has a wonderful year ahead of him, as we hope all the Harvard community will enjoy.

Thank you for your attention and your interest. We look forward to visiting Cambridge and seeing David during Parents' Weekend in October.

Sincerely,

Dinah & Martin Howells

Mr. and Mrs. Martin Howells

Dinah decided to accompany Martin when he took Duchess for her afternoon walks. For the first few weeks after David's departure, she had been reluctant to leave the house in case her son might phone. In fact, he had called only once, and nothing he had said had appeased the longing that his brisk, busy voice evoked. He had needed to ask her advice about setting up a bank account, and then he had said he was fine. His classes were fine. He liked his roommate, and his room was fine. She hung up the phone, assuring herself that she was delighted he was content, but she had been momentarily shattered with yearning.

As she and Martin cut across the front yard to reach the sidewalk, Duchess kept circling back on her leash, tangling herself around their legs, wagging her tail, and bobbing in a little prance of her front feet in her excitement and delight at having Dinah with them. "This will be a good thing," Dinah said. "I mean, to take a walk in the afternoons. I never get any exercise."

"Walking with Duchess isn't very invigorating," Martin said.

"Maybe we can train her to heel," Dinah mused, but they both looked doubtfully at the shambling dog, and

Dinah realized Duchess's muzzle was almost completely gray.

Once they reached the museum grounds, Duchess calmed down, taking Dinah's presence for granted and on the alert for squirrels. The tourist season was over. Although the students were back, they never minded if there were dogs loose on campus, and Martin stopped at the foot of Bell's Hill and let Duchess off her lead. Dinah had paused by the small markers at the edge of the parking lot and was bending over to make out the words, rubbing her fingers over the engravings to feel the letters. Martin went a little distance up the trail to be sure that Duchess hadn't strayed too far, and then he stopped and waited for Dinah to reach him. They made their way along the path fairly briskly, Martin leading the way and Duchess crashing through the brush behind them.

When they reached a natural summit, Dinah's face was flushed and she was out of breath. She sank down to sit on the ground, bracing herself against the trunk of an enormous spruce, and looked out on the valley. She hadn't climbed this hill, she realized, in five or six years. "This seems pretty invigorating to me," she said to Martin, who hadn't sat down, and she looked up at him. "Can we stop for a little while?" she asked. "Or you can go ahead. This is a wonderful view, and I'm out of shape. I need to catch my breath." She was apologetic, because Martin seemed to be impatient to go on. He probably had work to do.

He lowered himself to the ground beside her, his back against the tree, and the powerful scent of evergreens enveloped them. Dinah was always amazed, whenever she paid attention to this landscape, at the notion of the violent ages of geological activity that had resulted in the sanguine rolling hills and modest-sized but ancient mountains. It astounded her to remember that these gentle hills had been thrust violently from five miles beneath the earth's surface twenty thousand years ago, their spires and peaks sculpted and softened by glaciers and fifteen thousand years of erosion and weather. Now they undulated in benign waves of hills and valleys under a furze of brilliant green grass where black-and-white-spotted Holsteins grazed over the landscape like little wooden child's toys spread out on green felt.

"You were thinking about Toby, weren't you?" Martin asked her. "In the parking lot?"

She looked at him in surprise. "No, not really." She didn't want to talk about Toby's death. She thought that with David's recent departure they were both susceptible to opportunistic sorrow, as if a flu had been going around and their white counts were low.

"Well, you were." Martin was insistent.

"Not only Toby . . . Those two children . . . the dates on the gravestones. I'd never read them before. They were both about two and a half years old. I was wondering if it was any easier—if it was a different kind of grief, somehow—to lose such a young child."

Martin was silent. They both kept their eyes on the landscape, and Duchess came loping down the slope and sank down next to Martin, panting even in the cool weather.

Dinah said, "I don't think it would make any difference. It would be just as terrible."

Martin nodded. He thought so, too. "You know," he said, "I still keep wondering if there wasn't some way I could have avoided that wreck. I've gone over it and over it. I was so distracted. . . ."

"If you could have avoided it?" Dinah's voice rose a little in consternation. "Don't even think about that, Martin. Of course you couldn't have avoided it. That's not fair to yourself—it's not even fair to me—for you to try to . . . oh . . . take on the responsibility." Dinah knew that the wreck that killed Toby was nobody's fault, but in spite of herself she held *herself* accountable. She constantly fought off this absurd idea, but nevertheless she had been his mother.

"I know. I know. But I can't help it. If I had checked my rearview mirror . . ."

"What could you have done?" Dinah stood up and brushed the spruce needles off her slacks. "There was a car in *front* of you. You were caught. It was just bad luck. That's all."

Martin stood up, too, but Duchess lay there looking at them imploringly. "God, luck," and he bent to pick up a stick, waving it at Duchess to tempt her along. When he tossed it far ahead of them, Duchess rose and went lumbering after it. "But I *was* distracted, Dinah. Toby was so excited. He kept leaning forward, grabbing the back of my seat. It made me . . . *cross*. You remember how he sometimes would get so carried away? How he just didn't pick up on when to stop." They were walking side by side on the level ground, and Martin put his hand to his forehead and brought it down across his face, as though it were unbearable to have vision, as though he were pulling a shade. "He was so excited about scoring that goal in the scrimmage."

"What?" Dinah said, suddenly alert.

"In the soccer game. He was so excited. You know how Toby always talked with his hands? He was distracting me. I'd told him to calm down, but he wasn't paying attention."

"Martin. You never told me that Toby scored a goal in that soccer game."

"I must have. I'm sure I did . . . he was really good at soccer."

"You never even told me that he was good at soccer. He used to get so nervous about going to practice. You never told me he scored a goal that day. He hadn't scored a goal before that, had he?" They had reached the narrow path that they would have to descend single file, and Dinah reached out and detained Martin by holding on to the crook of his elbow.

"No. Well, not in Group Three soccer. He'd just been moved up that year." Martin was distracted from his brooding by this curiosity on Dinah's part. "He was pretty young for that group, but he was one of their best players. He was the youngest kid on the team. He was a good athlete."

Dinah was still for a moment. Then she pulled Martin closer to her and reached her head up to kiss him lightly on the cheek. "We'd better go ahead. I don't hear Duchess anywhere."

"She won't leave the path," Martin said, turning and preceding Dinah down the hill.

She followed him slowly, tantalized by this new way to understand Toby's death. She had always thought that the tragedy of the death of children is that they haven't had a chance to complete any of the natural cycles of their lives, and therefore it strikes a universal chord of injustice. Their lives seem incomplete to the survivors. But now she thought about the whole of Toby's life. Maybe it had been happily complete in that very instant before his death. There he had been: a hero in his own mind. He had been gesticulating and excited and pleased, and then his life had ended. Of course, she couldn't let go that easily; she would forever grieve for all that Toby hadn't had a chance to accomplish, or attempt to accomplish. But at least she could feel a certain relief at knowing that the greatest sorrow of Toby's death was for her and Martin to bear, that it had never, for an instant, weighed heavily on Toby himself. And she and Martin would be all right, the two of them. When they reached the bottom of the hill, she linked her arm through Martin's. This new bit of knowledge about the mystery of Toby's life—and his death—was something she would bring forth and examine again and again, for the rest of her life.

She turned her mind to the problem of what she should fix for dinner. Ever since she had discovered the wonderful bakery on Carriage Street when they first arrived in West Bradford, she had stopped doing any baking herself. "I never bake," she would say, "because the house slants." She intended to be slightly amusing, but she also meant it as an explanation. They had moved to West Bradford at the height of a wave of domestic zeal.

"I'd like to get some bread at The Whole Grain Elevator," Dinah said as they made their way down the path and circled back through the museum parking lot. "Why don't we walk down to Carriage Street? You can hold Duchess while I run in and see if they have any of their oatmeal bread left. We can have tomato sandwiches for dinner." They continued on, with Duchess bobbing between them, and occasionally they had to pause and unwrap her from around their legs. They made their way haltingly along the shortcut down Marchand's Drive.

Dinah bought two loaves of oatmeal bread, a half dozen blueberry muffins, and eight apricot squares. When she came out of the shop, laden with two bakery boxes and a large bag to hold the bread, she found Martin chatting with Nat Kaplan. "I always like to see the students back in town," Nat was saying. "After three months of tourists they never fail to cheer me up, especially now that I'm retired and don't have to *teach* them." They all laughed, and Nat stepped around her, courteously taking her elbow so as not to jostle her as he passed by to enter the bakery himself.

Dinah smiled in acknowledgment when she saw Martin glance at all her parcels. "I shouldn't ever be allowed in there alone. Everything they have is wonderful. I think it's the real reason Bradford and Welbern is so popular." She handed the bread to Martin. "I'll have to freeze some of this stuff. I've gotten used to having so much food on hand for David's friends. Sarah likes these apricot squares, but she won't even be home for dinner tonight. She and her boyfriend are cooking spaghetti at his house."

She and Martin were in no hurry, and they strolled the length of Carriage Street and turned onto the sidewalk along Route 2. "Do they have boyfriends, still?" Martin asked. "Is it anything like it was when we were in the eighth grade? I always think of Christie as David's girlfriend, but I don't know how he thinks of her."

"I'm not sure," Dinah said. "I don't think they 'date' exactly. It's more like they socialize in herds. God, don't ever let Sarah know that I called Scott her boyfriend. . . . I can't tell what kind of relationship they have. Sarah told me last week that she was going out with Scott. I felt like a fool. I said, 'Where are you going?' and she gave me that sort of look. You know that new kind of ironic expression she gets? Sort of cynical? It means that they're going together, I guess. Going steady? I didn't press it. It's exhausting to have to explain your ignorance all the time to your own children."

They had reached the intersection of Routes 2 and 7 at the very worst time of day. With Martin holding the bread and Duchess's leash, and Dinah balancing the two boxes, they made several false starts across the road, leaping back each time a car came racing around the curve. Dinah had a memory, just then, of being in the third grade and playing jump rope at recess with the girls while the boys played softball out in the far schoolyard.

Two girls turned the long rope, and a line of jump-ropers formed, one at a time, gauging the rhythm of the rope hitting the dust and then arching up into the sunlight. You had to judge it exactly right in order to "run in," and Dinah felt that way all of a sudden, trying to cross the road. It was as if she were standing before the sweeping rope, rocking her body back and forth to match it to the rhythm of the slap, swish, of the circling rope, her hands held out slightly for balance and in anticipation before taking those few running steps and being caught up in the rhymes and turns and acrobatics of jump-roping.

Each time she had "run in" she had experienced that little pulse of adrenaline, not at all unlike the slight exhilaration she felt as she and Martin made a run for it when a large black car paused to give them the right-of-way, its huge engine thrumming. They dashed across the street and reached the sidewalk with Duchess at their side, their bags and boxes intact. She was pleased and pleasantly energized as she and Martin and Duchess strolled slowly along their own street, past the sweeping estate across the way and the various homes fashioned from a carriage house and outbuildings, past the Davidsons' renovated barn, and on to their own house at the end of Slade Road.